Tell Me No Lies

Instead of driving to the apartment, Sean found himself pulling into a parking space at East Beach. He got out, walked to the end of the weathered fishing platform and leaned his arms on the railing. Under the pale moonlight, he could make out the outline of pelicans and sea gulls resting on a spit of land created by the outgoing tide.

Short-range, his plan had worked well tonight. Long-range, he still needed to determine if Hannah was a good mother, especially now that she was a single parent. To accomplish that, he'd have to continue pushing himself into their lives, wheedle his way into their daily routine. In fact, he'd already formed several impressions. To Hannah's credit, the house had been neat and tidy, except for her work area. It would have been a stretch to call it her office. But her neatness didn't cover the cracked plaster walls or worn vinyl flooring. Moreover, it irritated him that Tory didn't even have a desk to study at. And although Tory seemed well-adjusted, he knew the friction he'd detected between mother and daughter hadn't been his imagination.

Hannah may have turned down his dinner invitation, but she was warming to him, Sean could tell. Worming his way into her good graces would be easy. However, he admitted, resisting his attraction to her wouldn't be.

Wings

Tell Me No Lies

by

Pat Worley

A Wings ePress, Inc.

Long Contemporary Romance Novel

Wings ePress, Inc.

Edited by: Cindy Davis
Copy Edited by: Sara Reinke
Senior Editor: Anita York
Executive Editor: Lorraine Stephens
Cover Artist: Christine Poe

Wings ePress Books
http://www.wings-press.com

Copyright © 2005 by Pat Worley
ISBN 1-59088-660-7

Published In the United States Of America

January 2005

Wings ePress Inc.
403 Wallace Court
Richmond, KY 40475

Prologue

Angela is dead.

Sean Patrick Murphy slammed down the telephone, and stared at it for ten long seconds. Then he grabbed his coat and bolted out of his office, his broad shoulders narrowly missing the doorframe. "I'll be back later," he bit out, rushing past his assistant.

"What about the board meeting?"

"Cancel it."

"What? But it's in ten minutes!"

Sean heard none of her remark, the words lost behind the closing doors of The Murphy Group. Sean ran from the John Hancock Building and hailed the nearest cab. As it whizzed through the rain-soaked streets of Boston, he stared out the window, the water cutting squiggly pathways down the glass.

She can't be dead.

Sean's mind drifted back thirteen years, to a bright October afternoon on Boston Common where a group of friends played touch football. A younger Sean Murphy faded back for a long pass. Angie ran backwards, arms wide, the wind whipping her chestnut hair across her face. Sean saw her throw her arms up to catch the ball, then watched as it slipped right through her hands. He'd laughed, too, when she'd collapsed in shrieks of uncontrollable laughter.

Angie, I loved you so much.

Just saying her name caused an aching emptiness in Sean's heart. How long had it taken to finally shove all thoughts of her into the dark recesses of his mind? No matter now. The early morning phone call had dredged up the long-buried memories, and with the memories came the pain.

Growing up poor had given Sean the impetus to get out of his South Boston neighborhood. He'd realized his flair for taking a dollar and making it two in no time. Over the years, that knack helped make his investment firm one of the largest in the northeast. Every step along the way had been well thought out and executed. How then, he wondered, could one phone call alter his well-ordered life? The answer, he knew, lay in her mother's words: "Angela is dead, Mr. Murphy."

"Hey, mister, wake up. I said that'll be six fifty."

The cabby's annoyed voice jerked Sean from the past. He fumbled in his pocket for the fare, then walked into the virtually empty coffee shop of the Holiday Inn.

He spotted her immediately. Elizabeth Jenkins sat alone and even from a distance, he saw the resemblance between the middle-aged woman and the chestnut-haired girl he remembered. The similarity was there in the straight line of the nose and delicate cheekbones. Standing next to the booth, Sean turned down the wet collar of his trench coat and brushed the water from his thick black hair.

Angie's mother looked up at him, her faded blue eyes set in a face creased with age. "Thank you for coming. Won't you sit down?"

Her expression was a mask of cool reserve, but Sean saw the sadness in her eyes. He couldn't offer a sympathetic word or a comforting shoulder. Not until he heard an explanation, not until he could deal with his own anguish.

Without so much as a greeting, Sean slid into the cold vinyl seat across from her, and as if sensing his questions, she began the story he had come to hear. "Several months ago, Angela took her third grade class ice skating on Smith's Pond in Manchester."

Mrs. Jenkins looked down at her folded hands. "We'd had a brief warm spell, but living in Vermont, no one thought much about it. One of the children fell through a weak spot in the ice. Naturally, Angela crawled out to help."

Tears formed in the pale blue eyes, her voice cracked with emotion. "She fell through. She managed to push the child out, but by the time help arrived, she was gone. My baby was gone." The words came out in a hoarse whisper. Mrs. Jenkins looked away, her eyes glassy with tears, her fist raised to her lips to silence the sobs.

Sean swallowed hard. Angie had loved children, loved her job as an elementary school teacher. He'd always smiled at the light in her eyes when she'd talked about 'her kids.' It didn't surprise him that she'd given her life to save one of them.

Sean wasn't one to speak personal thoughts, but restraint eluded him, and he heard the words come out, dull and monotone. "The day she left, I'd gone to her apartment to pick her up. It was a Friday. We'd always had a standing date on Friday nights. When I got there, I found a note on the door." He dug out the memories, still crystal clear. "She said our relationship wouldn't work, that my feelings for her were stronger then hers for me. She didn't like Boston and she was going home." He laced his fingers and his vision blurred as he stared at the table. "I was going to ask her to marry me."

Panic had spread through him that night, so raw and jagged, it had slashed his heart with a vengeance.

"She wouldn't return my phone calls," he continued. "All my letters came back. I finally gave up." Softly, he added, "I loved her very much." The familiar ache spread through him like an old war wound that never let him forget.

Hesitating a moment, Angie's mother drew a deep breath and straightened her spine. "Mr. Murphy... Sean, two months after Angela came home, she told me she was pregnant."

His jaw dropped. "What?"

The impact hit him like an emotional right to the chin and his world careened out of control. An invisible hand closed around Sean's throat as he choked out, "She never told me. Why?" His eyes narrowed. "She had no right to keep that from me."

"Maybe not," Elizabeth Jenkins answered gently. "I know she cared for you, Sean, maybe more than she let on to me, but she told me you were obsessed with building an empire. She always felt second best."

The woman must be lying. Angie would never say that. She couldn't. But he hadn't thought she would leave him without a word, either.

Then it dawned on him. "What about the baby? Are you raising... Is he here?" Instantly, Sean assumed he had a son. And just as quickly, he looked around, his heart lodged in his throat, expecting to see his baby. No, he realized, not a baby, but a—teenager?

Mrs. Jenkins sighed deeply, as if to postpone the next bombshell. "Angela firmly believed in a strong family life. As a teacher, she'd seen too many children from broken homes, and she didn't want her child to have to experience that."

A dull sense of apprehension gripped Sean. *Abortion? No, she wouldn't have.* "And?"

"Angela went away to have the baby. She gave it up for adoption."

Sean glared at the woman, a blast of emotions hitting him from all sides. He turned his head, trying to assimilate the words, process the shock, define his feelings. How was he supposed to react? What should he feel first?

"Sean," she hurried on, "I know this comes as a shock, but that's not the reason I asked you here. You have a daughter and I have a granddaughter who's already thirteen years old. When my husband died, Angela became my entire life. Now she's gone, and I want to know her child. That's why I've come to you. I want you to find her. You have the money and resources that I don't." She leaned forward, her eyes desperately searching his.

Rage snapped at Sean's self-control, pain and betrayal searing his gut. *Go to hell* was on the tip of his tongue, but the fact remained he had a daughter. Did she look like him? Like Angie? Was she happy? Who had adopted her? *My God, I'm a father.* "I'll think about it."

"She's your child. How could you not want to know about her?" Elizabeth Jenkins' voice was strained with panic. "You can't just sit back and do nothing. Look," she said, hurriedly reaching into her purse, "I can give you a lead. I came across this old credit card slip among Angela's things. It's a receipt from a hotel in Atlanta, Georgia, dated during the time she went away to have the baby. Angela thought it best if I didn't know a lot of the details, but I do know she had the baby in a hospital in Atlanta."

Sean looked from her pleading eyes to the slip of paper in her hand. "Why didn't *you* tell me she was pregnant? Why didn't *you* pick up the telephone and tell me I was a father?"

"I realize now I should have," she said, a heavy sadness in her voice. "But Manchester is a small town ruled by unwritten mores of behavior. Even now, unwed mothers are treated as pariahs. Angela knew that. That's why she left town." Mrs. Jenkins leaned forward as if entreating him to understand. "She wanted her child to have a normal family with a mother *and* a father."

When Sean didn't respond, she leaned back and took a deep breath. "I didn't want to be looked down upon by my friends. I'm sorry to say that I bowed to social pressure with the excuse that I was respecting my daughter's wishes."

"Did it occur to you there might have been something equally as important as your daughter's wishes? Like my rights as a father? You denied me those rights, and now you want me to find this child." Sean shook his head in disgust. "You've got a hell of a nerve." Blame sought its target, and the guilt on her face satisfied him for a brief moment.

He slid out of the booth. "I'll let you know," was all he conceded.

Her voice trailed after him. "Be as angry as you want, Sean, but if you loved Angela as much as you claim, you'd want to find the child you created from that love."

He didn't look back, didn't want to hear her words. His mind reeled with anger, sadness and a profound sense of wonder. He needed some air. And time to decide what the hell he was going to do.

One

"I hate school!"

Hannah Stevens jolted at the slam of the front door that followed the angry words. Sighing deeply, she dropped the swatchboard onto the haphazard pile of fabrics she had placed on the floor and wondered, not for the first time in the past year, if life would ever be normal again.

She couldn't see her thirteen-year-old daughter from the tiny sun porch that doubled as her office. But she clearly heard Victoria's heavy footsteps across the worn floor, each one, she knew, a reluctant cry for Mom.

Following her daughter down the short hallway of the small, five-room bungalow, Hannah called softly at the closed bedroom door. "Tory? May I come in?"

She took the muffled response as a "yes" and opened the door, immediately recognizing Tory's sullen, hostile stance. The raging hormones of adolescence were difficult enough to handle on a good day. Since Paul's death twelve months earlier, matters had become steadily worse with few good days to be had.

Hannah wanted to reach out and pull her close, but Tory's body language stopped her. "What happened at school today?"

"Nothing."

Hannah let the word hang. Many of their conversations of late started this way, to the point where coaxing had become an art form. "You'd feel better if you talked about it."

She moved the pile of CDs, sat on the bed and patted the space next to her. After a long moment, Tory accepted the invitation. "Besides, didn't we agree to be honest with each other?"

Tory hung her head, her long, dark hair obscuring her profile. "The Y Club is having a father/daughter dinner next month."

"Oh, honey, I'm sorry." Quickly, Hannah pulled the slender child to her, wishing she could turn back the clock to happier times. For Tory's sake, if not for her own. Her heart broke at the sight of her daughter's trembling lip.

"Why did Daddy have to die? Why did he have to leave us?" Tory broke from her mother's grasp and turned her back. "My real dad never would have done that. He never would have left me!"

The knife twisted in Hannah's heart. "Tory, Daddy *was* your real father. You know that. He was the one who kissed you goodnight and helped you with your homework." Hannah's calm voice belied the turmoil building inside her. "He didn't want to leave us," she continued, trying to work through Tory's anger. "Dying is a part of living, honey. It's hard and it hurts, but in time, most people get past it. You will, too."

Tory slid back into her mother's arms, tears falling down her cheeks. "Oh, Mom, I just miss him so much."

"I know you do." As Hannah rocked Tory back and forth, she wondered if Tory expected her to say the same thing. Hannah couldn't. She didn't miss him. Not now. Not after what she'd found out.

"Everything's changed. Nothing's the way it used to be."

The confusion in her light hazel eyes tore at Hannah's heart.

"I want to live in our old house with our big yard. I want my old bedroom back. And I hate this horrible little house!"

Damn you, Paul, for leaving us in this mess! Hannah had learned the hard way that trust had its drawbacks.

"Let's look on the bright side," she said. "We have a roof over our heads and my decorating business is picking up. Before you know it, we'll be able to have a nicer home." She ignored Tory's skeptical expression. "Besides, we didn't have to move from St. Simons and you still have your friends and you can still go to the beach. We need to be thankful for that."

Tory nodded, but Hannah could tell her heart wasn't in it. "I guess I won't be going to the father/daughter dinner."

"We'll work it out somehow, honey. Tell you what. Why don't you get your homework done, we'll have an early dinner, and then we'll ride our bikes down to the pier."

"We do that all the time."

"I know, but tonight we'll get some yogurt." Money was tight, but she would gladly make this small concession if it meant helping Tory get through the emotional roadblock.

A small smile lit Tory's face. "Okay."

Hannah gave her daughter one more squeeze. "I love you, sweetheart."

"Same here, Mom."

Another crisis averted, thought Hannah as she got up to leave. But she worried that Tory was still having a difficult time dealing with Paul's death. Of course, the two of them had been close, but she'd hoped that after a year, time would begin to lessen the grief and anger.

She had reached the door when Tory called out, "Mom, do you know who my... other parents were?"

Hannah stopped, the doorknob turning cold in her hand. She turned, then swallowed past the lump in her throat. "Why do you ask?"

Tory shrugged. "I was just wondering."

"No, I don't." *Didn't we agree to be honest with each other?*

An awkward silence followed. "Could I find out who they are?"

"No, you can't."

The sharp retort made Tory look at her in confusion.

Hannah struggled to soften her tone. "The records are sealed and no one can see them."

"But yesterday on Oprah Winfrey, she had these people on her show that were adopted and they found their real parents."

"It's not all that easy," Hannah said. Her self-control slipped a notch, allowing a slight quiver into her voice. "Do you want to find these people?"

Tory lifted her shoulders again and quickly looked away.

"Dinner will be ready in an hour. Why don't you start your homework?" Hannah closed the door and leaned against the wall in the small, narrow hallway. *Lord, please don't throw anything else at me. I don't think I can take much more.*

As she walked into the tiny kitchen, memories came flooding back. She and Paul had wanted a closed, private adoption. She hadn't wanted to know the mother's name or her circumstances. She'd reasoned that should Tory ever question her or Paul, they could honestly tell Tory they didn't know the identity of the people who had given her up for adoption. Hannah didn't want to have to lie. But when they'd signed the final adoption papers, the name had stared up at them in black and white, a name she would never forget. Angela Jenkins. Revealing the mother's name had been an error, an oversight. However, the damage had been done. Especially now. Hannah had already lost a husband. She wasn't about to take even the slightest chance of losing Tory to anyone. The thought of someone else possibly taking her place in Tory's life made Hannah's heart pound with fear.

~ * ~

What the hell am I doing here?

"Welcome to the King and Prince, Mr. Murphy. Is this your first visit with us?" The pretty desk clerk, young, bubbly and the tanned embodiment of beach life, gave Sean a bright smile. He was oblivious.

"Yes, it is," he answered, handing her his credit card. *Maybe this isn't such a good idea.*

"We have a lot of things to do here," she continued, swiping the credit card through the machine before checking him in. "Swimming, tennis, golf, water sports."

Sean hadn't come to enjoy himself.

"And I'm sure you'll want to tour the Island. St. Simons has a number of historic sites." She handed him a stack of local brochures. "We also have a wonderful restaurant on the premises. Or you might want to try one of the many fine restaurants in the Village. Most of the tourists have gone by now, so you won't have to fight the crowds. After the season, a lot of the locals gather there."

"Thank you," Sean said, not really hearing the travelogue. "Would you have a bellman deliver my bags to my room?" He shoved a five-dollar tip across the counter, then walked through the lobby past the small indoor pool and continued to the bar. Choosing a table that looked out over the water, he loosened his tie, ordered a Jack Daniels and water, and glanced at his watch.

The day had been hectic, and he'd almost succeeded in putting this trip to the back of his mind. He'd had to run to catch his flight, leaving a critical meeting with a group of investors.

I should be at the office.

His courage had started to fail the minute the plane left the runway, and he'd almost backed out.

Coward.

Had it only been four weeks since Elizabeth's news had earthquaked his life? Four weeks of curiosity, confusion, and soul-searching. When he'd received the private detective's report, his responsibility had seemed clear, and he'd arranged for this trip without another thought.

Now all his good intentions and determination seemed irrelevant. Why should he even get involved?

Irritated at feeling so unsettled, Sean yanked his cell phone out of his pocket. The private number reached his executive vice president within seconds. "Brian, it's me. How did the meeting go?"

"Fine. I handled it. No problem."

Brian Cassidy had been at Sean's side since they were ten years old. A brother couldn't be closer.

Sean rubbed his tired eyes. "Thanks. Did you remember to tell them about the interest rate we can secure for them? And about—"

"Hey, this is me you're talking to. Stop worrying. I've taken care of everything."

"Sorry, I knew you would. You always do."

"Are you there yet?"

"Yeah, got in a little while ago. Nice place."

"Hmm," Brian said. "I still don't know if what you're doing is a good idea. Maybe you should have let the private detective do some more checking into this. But, hey, if this is what you feel you need to do, then go for it. I'll take care of things here."

"I appreciate it, man. I'll keep in touch." Sean hung up, thanking his lucky stars he had Brian to depend on. After Brian's initial shock at the news, it had taken him a little time to support Sean's decision to fly to St. Simons. Probably, Sean thought, because Brian knew how much he'd loved Angie, and how her leaving had devastated him. They'd been a threesome back then, the Massachusetts Musketeers, but he and Angie had never thought of Brian as the third wheel. No matter what, Brian would always be there for him.

Sean sipped his bourbon, letting the liquid warm a pathway to his stomach. Then, for the umpteenth time, he re-evaluated his purpose for coming here. It wasn't like him to be indecisive and he hated the feeling.

Scared. That was it. Bottom line. He swore under his breath, disgusted with himself. Deep down, he wanted to see the child he'd never known, if only once. He wondered if his fear stemmed from the unknown. Would seeing her strike some kind of parental chord, or would he abandon her just as Angie had done? Like Angie had abandoned him?

Only one way to find out. He emptied his glass in one gulp. He'd come here to battle the past and confront the future head on. And by God, that's what he would do.

Sean placed his glass on the mahogany table and followed it with a bill from his pocket. Tomorrow was soon enough to begin his search, and right now he needed to unwind. A walk on the beach, maybe. Then he'd have dinner. Maybe he'd take the clerk's advice and try out one of the local hangouts.

~ * ~

Under a slowly setting sun, Hannah and Tory drove down to the Village and parked in front of the yogurt shop. Hannah had lived in Georgia all her life and she loved St. Simons Island. Being able to stay here was one of the few things she hadn't had to sacrifice after Paul had died. She looked up at the centuries-old lighthouse, tall and white, standing guard over the Sound, a silent sentinel still guiding cargo ships into the port of Brunswick. In the nearby park, toddlers dipped and soared on the seesaws or slid down the miniature slide while watchful parents hovered over them.

Most of the tourists had left the Island for the summer. With school underway, the Village was quiet, with only a few vacation stragglers left behind to browse the quaint shops or sit on weather-beaten benches and gaze out over the placid water of St. Simons Sound.

She and Tory bought two waffle cones, then walked out to the pier. A group of senior citizens, the regulars who came every night to gossip and socialize, occupied the wooden seats that lined the concrete walkway, and Hannah greeted several of them by name. Mother and daughter strolled slowly past amateur fishermen and crabbers and peered into dirty white buckets for a view of the night's catch.

"You're awfully quiet," Hannah said between bites of her Alpine Strawberry frozen yogurt.

Tory gave her usual shoulder hiccup, the one Hannah recognized when her thirteen-year-old had something on her mind and had to be coaxed to talk about it.

"Is there something else bothering you?"

"No."

"Sure?"

Tory rolled her eyes. "Yes, Mom, I'm sure. Stop bugging me. Please."

"Okay, okay." Hannah backed off. It was like playing Russian roulette, knowing when to push an adolescent and when not to. Push too hard and you could lose them. Lie to them and... Hannah shook off the thought.

In a silent attempt to change the subject, Hannah made a show of devouring her waffle cone. As they continued down the middle of the pier, Tory said, "Mom?"

"Hmm?"

Tory lowered her spoon and looked at her mother through long, dark lashes. "I didn't mean to make you mad this afternoon. I was just curious about my other parents."

A mouthful of Alpine Strawberry caught in Hannah's throat. She stiffened, not wanting to discuss the subject again. "You didn't make me mad, honey." *Petrified. But not mad.*

"You sounded like it."

Frustration mingled with guilt. "I just don't want you to think finding these people would make you miss Daddy less."

"That's not it, Mom, honest."

A wave of confusing emotions washed over Tory's freckled face and Hannah's heart tightened.

"Sometimes I feel like—Oh!"

A fisherman standing near Tory jerked a fish out of the water, the momentum sent him crashing into her. She stumbled forward and the cone flew out of her hand.

To Hannah's horror, the missile landed dead center on someone's back. The tall, broad-shouldered man stood at the opposite railing, and when the scoop of yogurt hit him, he arched his back in surprise. Tory and Hannah watched, wide-eyed, as the cone fell away, leaving a blob of chocolate to slide slowly down the man's navy blue T-shirt.

"What the...?" He twisted, trying to look over his shoulder to identify the projectile that had hit him.

"Oh... oh dear." The lump headed for the man's belt. Hannah ran over and tried to catch the sticky mess with her crumpled napkin. "I'm so sorry." She felt the muscles in his back contract as she wiped away the coldness. Catching most of the yogurt, she threw it in the water. "It was an accident. Someone ran into my daughter and her cone flew out of her hand."

Tory stood back in the small crowd that had started to form, scarlet circles staining her cheeks.

"It's all right, honey," Hannah called to her, then wiped off the rest of the yogurt as best she could. "Thank goodness your shirt is dark." A few people in the crowd started to laugh. Hannah chuckled, too. "At least you won't look like someone painted a bull's eye on your back."

The more she thought about it, the funnier the situation became. Since she couldn't hold back the laughter, she covered her mouth trying to smother it.

"I don't mean to laugh," she said as the man turned around. "It really isn't funny." Having said that, she giggled even more. "If it's any consolation, this couldn't happen again in a million years."

The laughter was contagious and more people joined in. *Stop it,* she commanded herself. *The poor man will be so embarrassed.*

"You're probably right," he said, not the least bit red-faced. "That's the first time I've ever been hit by an airborne ice cream cone."

At least he has a sense of humor, she said to herself. An oncoming laugh stalled in her throat as she looked up into eyes too blue to be real. "It was yogurt," she choked out.

"Oh."

Her heart skipped a beat at the devastating grin that overtook his features. *Good Lord, this man is gorgeous.*

"Well," Hannah said clearing her throat. "I think I got most of it." Rich blue eyes were set in a handsomely reserved face, the frame completed by jet black hair the same color as Tory's.

"Thank you for your understanding. I hope we haven't ruined your evening."

His smile was blinding. "Not at all."

"Well, goodbye." She turned and called to her daughter. "Come on, Tory. We'd better go before we create more havoc."

Tory stepped out of the dwindling crowd and joined her mother. She passed the tall stranger and said, "I'm really sorry, mister."

Sean didn't respond. He didn't move. Couldn't breathe. He may have gazed down at a thirteen-year-old, but Angie's eyes looked back at him from a face he'd seen only once before in a photograph.

~ * ~

"I feel so bad," Tory wailed.

Hannah patted her shoulder. "Well, don't. It was an accident."

Who was he? Hannah wasn't one to ogle men, yet while she'd walked on past the pier, his face had remained vivid in her mind. He hadn't offered his name, but then, neither had she. Actually, she ought

15

to thank him for diverting Tory's attention away from a touchy subject.

"Oh, look, Mom, there's April," Tory said, pointing to her best friend. "Can I go talk to her for a while?"

Hannah nodded and looked at her watch. "I'll be at Marsha's. Meet me there no later than eight thirty."

"Okay."

Hannah watched her daughter run to a frizzy-haired girl seated under the sprawling live oak tree that spread over the playground. She wished she could pry open Tory's mind and help her deal with all the feelings she hid inside. Something still bothered her, but Hannah would have to press another time.

Trying to think of ways to draw Tory out of her uncommunicative shell, Hannah walked down Mallory Street and into a small shop edged between a bookstore and a sometimes-open café. Named 'The Dreamcatcher,' the boutique sported a colorful feathered one over the door.

"Marsha?" Hannah made her way around carousels of brightly colored Indian wear, from long, flowing skirts and beaded shirts to handmade moccasins. As she admired the turquoise and silver jewelry, Marsha Phelps stepped from behind an Indian blanket that covered the doorway to the back of the shop.

"Hey, there. It's about time you came to see me." Dressed in a long skirt of muted earth tones, a gauzy tunic top, and feather earrings, the woman was an advertisement for the merchandise she sold. Just this side of fifty, her long brown hair showed more than a few strands of gray, and the round, wire-rimmed glasses were a testimonial to her days of trinket selling in Haight-Ashbury. She gave Hannah a warm hug.

"I'm sorry I haven't been around. Been kinda busy."

Marsha set her at arms' length. "You look a little washed out. How about some tea?"

Hannah ran a hand through her short-cropped, blond hair. "No, thanks. Tory and I just had some yogurt." When Marsha looked to the front of the store, Hannah added, "She met a friend up by the playground."

"Well, come on in and tell me everything."

Hannah followed Marsha into a sitting room and plopped down on a worn sofa covered with an Indian blanket. In one corner was a curtained cubicle with a gurney-like table covered in sheets. The sight made Hannah moan. "What I'd do for a massage. Your hands are magic."

A licensed massage therapist, Marsha supplemented her income with a small but steady clientele. "Come in anytime, honey."

Hannah grunted. "Right. When I can afford it."

"Don't be silly. I wouldn't charge you," Marsha said, sitting next to Hannah. "How's the decorating business?"

"Slow, but it's coming along. There's a lot of competition here on the Island." She almost bit her tongue. That sounded like a pitiful apology for failure. Marsha nodded, but Hannah felt her scrutiny. "What?"

"You tell me," Marsha replied.

Hannah opened her mouth ready to come back with an 'I'm just tired' excuse. Unfortunately, her thoughts weighed her down like rock-filled saddlebags, and truth be told, she needed to unload. She leaned forward and hunched her shoulders.

"It's Tory. I really thought she was beginning to come to terms with Paul's death."

"And she hasn't?"

Hannah shook her head. "Today, she came home all upset because there's going to be a father/daughter dinner at school."

"I don't think there's a time limit on grief."

"I know, I know." Hannah stood and paced the floor.

"What about your grief?" Marsha asked.

A rueful laugh escaped Hannah's lips. "I don't have time for any. I'm too busy trying to keep food on the table. Besides, any grief I felt went right out the door the day after Paul's funeral, when his attorney called and told me Paul had lost every dime we had." This time she let the bitterness settle over her. "I was such a fool."

"You know that wasn't your fault, Hannah."

She sighed. "Maybe not totally," she said, "but I never took an active interest in the finances. I should have noticed some warning signs. Something—anything—that would have told me he had a gambling problem." She stopped pacing. "Maybe I didn't want to see it."

Marsha didn't speak for a long minute. "Are you wallowing?"

Hannah's head snapped up at the taunt. "No," she said with conviction. "I can make a good living for Tory and myself. It'll just take some time." She returned to her place on the couch and changed the subject. "So. How about you? What have you been doing lately?"

Marsha began a litany of her recent activities, and Hannah tried her best to look interested. She smiled and nodded, but Marsha's words didn't register. *What would Tory do if I told her the truth?*

"...then I stripped and danced naked on the tables."

"That's nice."

Marsha raised a brow. She leaned over and rapped Hannah on the head. "Hel... lo. Earth to Hannah. Would you like to tell me what's *really* on your mind?"

Chagrined, Hannah chuckled. "Sorry." She let out a long breath and intently studied the floor before answering. "I lied to Tory today."

With eyebrows raised, Marsha waited quietly for more of an explanation.

"She asked me if I knew her biological parents. I said no."

"Which means you do know them."

Hannah nodded. "Her mother. That is, I know her mother's name. It was on the adoption papers when Paul and I signed them. It was a mistake, but you can bet I'll never forget that woman's name."

"What about the father?"

"Listed as unknown."

"Why did you lie to her?"

"Because I'm afraid." Hannah went back to pacing. "Since Paul's death, Tory's been asking more and more questions about her adoption. And I've always been truthful in answering them." She hesitated. "Until now."

"Surely you expected her to ask about her real parents at some point."

Marsha's choice of words grated. "Of course I did. But I didn't think it would happen until she was older. And I thought I'd have a husband to help me deal with it."

"And now you're afraid Tory will want to find this woman?"

"Yeah." She hated the insecurity that constantly plagued her. Wasn't she a good mother? Could she make a success of her interior decorating business and provide a better life for herself and Tory? What if Tory found this Angela Jenkins and the woman turned out to be Cindy Crawford, Martha Stewart and Hillary Clinton all rolled into one?

"You really can't believe Tory would choose another woman over you."

Hannah laughed humorlessly. "My logical side says no. But deep down inside..." Hannah felt the spark of fear, a spark that was becoming more and more difficult to extinguish with each passing year. "I'd die if I lost her." She felt goosebumps, a prickly premonition, and rubbed her arms. "Anyway, now I've lied to her and I don't know how to get out of it."

"Mom?"

Hannah spun around, the floor of her stomach giving way. "Tory... honey. Is it eight thirty already?" She looked nervously at her watch. "We didn't hear you come in."

"Hi, Tory," Marsha said, with a smile.

"Hey, Miss Marsha."

Hannah took Tory's arm and moved to the door. "We'd better be going, Marsha. Tory still has some homework to do."

Her heart continued to pound as they said their good-byes.

How long had Tory been standing there? How much had she heard?

Two

"Is there a problem, officer?" Sean yanked off his Ray-Bans and squinted into the early morning sun.

"License and registration, please."

Sean reached for his wallet, annoyed at the terse command. He opened the glove compartment of the Explorer and took out the rental papers.

"Stay in the vehicle, sir," the brown-uniformed patrolman ordered when Sean opened the door.

Great. A cop with an attitude. Maybe the guy was ticked off because Sean didn't pull over right away. He'd been too busy driving past school bus stops trying to get a glimpse of his daughter to notice the flashing light behind him. He'd pulled over as soon as he'd heard the siren.

"What brings you to Georgia, Mr. Murphy?"

"I'm on vacation," he lied. Sean Murphy wouldn't know what to do with a vacation.

"Where are you staying?"

"At the King and Prince. Would you mind telling me what this is all about? Did I run a stop sign or something?" Sean did his best to hide the irritation behind his forced smile.

"Just sit tight, sir. I'll be with you in a minute."

Sean watched through the rearview mirror as the man got on the radio, then drummed his fingers on the wheel to ease his annoyance. After a few minutes, he let his thoughts wander.

The shock of seeing Tory had stayed with him long into the night. *Tory.* Probably short for Victoria. He liked the nickname. How had she come by it? *I would have called her Vickie.*

The picture provided by the private investigator he'd hired to find his daughter hadn't done her justice. The eyes, more green than hazel, and the delicate oval face were the mirror image of Angie, but the dark hair and the stubborn chin were his.

There was no doubt as to Tory's paternity.

As for the mother, Hannah Stevens certainly piqued Sean's interest. She was far from the middle-aged hausfrau he'd expected. When he'd turned and saw her dabbing at his sticky shirt, he'd wanted to smile. Cute had been his first impression. Short and petite, but well-built, not skinny. He preferred long hair, but her blond, pixie haircut suited her.

Though she must be close to his own age, her youthful appearance made him wonder if she was old enough to be a mother, or at least a good one. Did mothers wear short shorts and tank tops and walk around barefoot?

The investigator's four-page findings had given him a quick, just-the-facts report, leaving Sean to draw his own conclusions about a lot of things.

He'd been given a pleasant surprise when he'd driven over the causeway to St. Simons Island. Huge, live oak trees laden with gauzy-gray Spanish moss guarded the roadways, and through the open window of the car, the damp, salty smell of marshland tantalized his nose. The shimmering water had been so peaceful, he'd almost wished he really was on vacation. A strange tranquility had threatened to settle over him, but he'd managed to shrug it off. He wouldn't be here long enough to enjoy it.

Armed with a map from the local Chamber of Commerce, Sean had found his way to 817 Oglethorpe Street, the home of Victoria Stevens. The house was old, small and needed work. Gray-shingle siding covered the square structure and the white trim begged for another coat of paint. A mildewed, aluminum awning hung precariously over the front door and a small Toyota Corolla sat in the shell-covered driveway. The grass needed cutting.

Suddenly, he was back in South Boston. He'd never experienced the closeness of his blue-collar Irish neighbors or the pride in being a "Southie." He remembered his mother, a small, frail woman who'd always known where to find her husband six out of seven nights a week. His father, longshoreman Jack Murphy, had been a well-known patron of the pubs of South Boston. There'd barely been enough money for food or clothes or a roof over their heads, but there had always been money for Irish whiskey. The memories of his father's drunken rages were vivid. He could still hear his mother's screams and the sound of flesh hitting flesh. At the vivid recollection, bile burned Sean's throat.

After his mother had died, Sean had crawled out of that life and never looked back. And he wouldn't stand for a child of his having to experience any kind of hardship.

Looking again at the houses around him, Sean saw that not all were in bad shape. But where one was neat and tidy, the next was unkempt and trashy. He could give his child so much more.

The officer's voice brought him back to the present. "Mr. Murphy, we've had several reports this morning of a suspicious vehicle cruising the area, and this Explorer fits the description."

Sean didn't expect that. He wondered whether or not to tell the man the truth, but decided the whole story sounded too farfetched. He wasn't quite sure he believed it himself.

"I've been looking for my daughter."

The patrolman raised his eyebrows.

"Her mother and I are divorced and although we have joint custody, she left without a word. I've followed them here." A small lie, but probably more believable than the truth.

After a moment, the other man nodded slowly, his expression softening. "I know what you're going through. My ex makes it hard for me to see my kids, too. But you're going to have to find some other way to locate your daughter. The parents around here notice anything out of the ordinary, and I don't blame them. They just want to protect their kids."

Sean thanked the man for his understanding and drove off, deep in thought. Sean came from a different world, one of mergers and deals and making more money when some wasn't enough. He thought of all the headlines he'd breezed over on his way to the financial page. Teen violence, guns in schools, runaways, kidnappings, teen pregnancy. Sean didn't have a clue as to the problems that faced families today. How *did* parents protect their kids?

He had a lot to learn.

~ * ~

At 2:30 p.m., Sean heard the afternoon bell ring at Glynn Middle School. The doors swung open and a wave of children half ran toward waiting buses and cars driven by parents craning their necks to look for their children. Sean glanced around and decided he looked just like one of those parents as he sat in the Explorer that blended inconspicuously with the vans and four-door sedans lined up on the street. He watched each child eagerly, wondering what he'd do if he missed her.

Frustration mounted as the minutes passed. *Maybe she didn't go today. Maybe she stayed after school.* Then, he spotted her, surrounded by several other girls. His heart leaped at the sight of her, and a smile curled at his mouth. Slightly taller than her friends, Victoria wore blue jean overalls, a white top and sneakers. Her long black hair was pulled back in a ponytail and like all the others, she carried a backpack. Sean's hand tightened on the steering wheel. His insides twisted. He had a sudden urge to call to her, wanted her to climb in, give him a kiss and say, "Hi Dad!"

His gaze followed her onto the school bus and ten minutes later, he started the Explorer and trailed at a discreet distance. The bus left the coastal town of Brunswick and headed back to the Island, making frequent stops once it crossed the causeway. Sean frowned when Tory didn't get off at Oglethorpe Street, and then he started to worry as the bus drove on toward the north end of the Island. When it stopped, seemingly in the middle of nowhere, he pulled off to the side and watched Tory and two other girls walk down a dirt road. He waited until the threesome disappeared, then eased up and read a washed-out sign nailed to a tree: *Marshland Stables.*

Very slowly, so as not to be noticed, he continued down the road behind them. Half expecting a chomping alligator to jump out of the surrounding swamp, Sean finally emerged into a grassy area outlined in weathered fences, a lunge ring and barn. He shut off the Explorer's engine and looked around. An old man forked hay into a wheelbarrow while two barn dogs sprawled out in the nearby shade. A cool breeze drifted through Sean's window, carrying with it the soft nickering of horses and the distinctly familiar odor of horse manure.

He felt it again. The atmosphere. It softly enveloped him and beckoned to him like the lonely, searching cry of the seagulls that flew overhead. Before his mind began to drift, a movement from the barn made him sit up straighter. Tory led a saddled Appaloosa to a paddock where she mounted with practiced ease and cantered around the ring. She was good. His heart burst with pride.

It took less than five minutes for a plan to take shape in his brain.

~ * ~

"Did you see NSYNC on MTV last night?" Dust swirled around April Roberts and her two friends as they walked their horses back to the barn. "They were so cool. Justin Timberlake is so cute, don't you think, Tory?"

"I didn't even know they were on," Sara Higgins wailed. "Why didn't you call me? I could have taped it. I just love Justin. Tory, which one do you like the best?"

Tory led her horse into the barn ahead of the other two girls and attached the lead rope to the halter. Tory liked NSYNC, too, but her thoughts weren't on rock groups.

"Tory? Did you hear me?" April asked. "What's the matter with you?"

"I heard you. I just don't feel like talking about NSYNC." For three days straight she hadn't stopped thinking about the words she'd overheard at Miss Marsha's. Who had her mother lied to? *Me?*

As she untacked the Appaloosa, she wished she didn't feel so angry and confused all the time. Sometimes, the least little thing triggered a rage that bubbled up from nowhere and took control. That usually launched a full-scale battle with Mom, which was becoming more and more frequent since Daddy had died.

"Wouldn't it be terrific if, like, you found out you were related to Justin?" As April brushed her bay mare, she rolled her eyes and smiled. "That would be way cool."

Tory looked up as April giggled at the fantasy. "How would you find out?"

"Find out what?" April asked.

"That you were related to Justin of NSYNC?"

"I'm not, silly."

"I *know* that, you dork. But if you were, how would you find out?"

"How should I know? I'm pretending."

"Maybe," Sara interjected slowly, "you were with Justin's family on a camping trip out in the woods and they lost you. And you were found and raised by a crazy couple who had lost their only daughter in a plane crash."

Tory made a long face at her friend's dramatics. "I'm serious."

"Oh." Sara shrugged. "I don't know. Why is it so important?"

Tory hesitated. She couldn't decide whether or not to confide in her friends, especially Sara, notoriously known for not being able to keep a secret. But Tory knew what she had to do, and she wouldn't change her mind. First, she needed to find out where to start.

"Because..." Tory's voice started out with strong conviction, then softened with a touch of uncertainty. "Because I'm going to find my real parents. And I don't know how to do it." She looked at both girls, trying to gauge their reactions.

"What do you mean, your real parents?" Sara asked.

Tory didn't answer.

"Does your Mom know?" asked April.

Tory shook her head.

Sara looked from one to the other. "What are you talking about?"

"She won't like it," April continued.

"I'm not going to tell her." Tory paused when April's eyes widened. "I have to do this. I just have to."

"Would you two *pul-ease* tell me what's going on?"

Tory put down her currycomb and looked Sara straight in the eye. "You have to promise not to tell anyone, Sara Higgins. Not a soul. If I find out you've told, I'll kill you."

"I can keep a secret," Sara said, indignantly.

April rolled her eyes. "Yeah, right."

"I'm adopted," Tory said, "and I'm going to find my real parents." She refused to squirm under Sara's shocked expression. Why should she feel funny? There wasn't anything wrong with being adopted.

"You are? You never told me. April, did you know that?"

April nodded.

"Well, thanks a lot, Tory," Sara said. "You tell April, but you don't tell me." With hands on hips, Sara pouted for a moment, then asked, "What are you gonna do when you find them? Will you live with them?"

Tory shrugged. "No."

"Then what's the big deal?"

"The big deal is," April said, "her mother might not want Tory to find them. She might think Tory will go off and live with these people and then her mom will be all alone. God, sometimes you're so dumb."

"I am not! And how would you know anyway?"

"Because my mother is a lawyer and she works with adoptions all the time," April shot back, then stuck out her tongue.

"I wouldn't leave my mom," Tory said. "I love her. But I feel like a piece of me is missing. And I have to find it, you know?"

April shook her head. "For some reason, I don't think it's a good idea, Tory."

"I don't care. And you both have to swear to keep this a secret."

April reluctantly nodded while Sara bobbed her head with exuberance.

"April, if your mom knows about adoptions, how would I find my real parents?"

April was her best friend, but for a second, Tory was afraid she wouldn't help. Then April replied, "I know that when people adopt a kid, they have to sign some papers. Your mom and dad must have signed some papers, too."

"Yeah? So?"

"So your mom might have a copy of them."

Tory thought for a moment. "Would the names of my real parents be on the papers?"

"I don't know. Maybe."

It's a place to start, Tory thought. *The next time Mom's out for a while, I'll start looking.*

The blast of a horn interrupted the conversation. "Come on," Sara said, throwing the tack over the stall. My mom's here to pick us up."

"Mr. Haverty won't give you a lesson next week if you don't put your tack where it belongs," April yelled after her. Sara came to a halt, ran back and hung up the bridle on the nail next to her horse's stall, then raced to catch up with April.

Tory lagged behind as the two girls argued over what horse to ride at their next lesson. April's information should have strengthened her resolve. It didn't. Though Tory felt the same stab of guilt that had plagued her since making her decision, she knew she wouldn't change her mind. She looked to the sky and closed her eyes. *Oh Mom, this has nothing to do with you. I hope you understand.*

~ * ~

"Tory, keep your heels down and your back straight."

Hannah parked her car and walked through the barn, following the deep, resonant voice. Standing in the shadows, she looked out to the large ring and smiled as she watched Tory atop a tall, spotted Appaloosa. Tory looked so mature, sometimes it was difficult to believe her only child was just thirteen.

Still concealed in her hiding place, Hannah studied the man in the center of the ring. She wanted to observe him undetected. The new instructor turned out to be "the yogurt man" as Tory had described him, and Hannah had laughed at the coincidence. But when Tory couldn't talk about anyone else except "Mr. Murphy," Hannah had raised an eyebrow. For all she knew, this guy could be a child molester. She scanned the barn area hoping to see old Sam Haverty who'd run the stables ever since she could remember. She couldn't imagine Sam hiring just anyone off the street. Surely this Mr. Murphy had some credible credentials.

The man stopped Tory, readjusted the reins in her hands, then pushed her knees slightly behind the girth. He seemed competent enough, even though Hannah had never been on a horse in her life. Stepping into the sunshine, she took her time as she made her way down to the ring. She climbed the weatherworn, wooden fence, hung crossed arms over the top rail, then waved when Tory looked her way.

Mr. Murphy stood with his hands on his hips, slowly turning as he watched his student. The tall form was clad in close-fitting jeans and boots that looked unaccustomed to the dirt of a horse farm. The white shirt he wore was collarless, the sleeves pushed up on muscular forearms to reveal the beginnings of a sunburn.

"Very nice," he called out to his pupil. "Remember to keep your eyes up. Take her around one more time, and we'll call it a day."

Pride swelled within Hannah as Tory rode the horse around the ring. Her daughter's fondness for horses helped to ground the unpredictable emotions of adolescence, and because of that, Hannah squirreled away every extra penny to pay for riding lessons.

As Tory trotted along the rail, Mr. Murphy continued to observe his young student with a seemingly critical eye. The late afternoon light glimmered over a strong, confident profile, and Hannah realized she hadn't noticed that when they'd met at the pier. When he acknowledged her presence with a casual smile, she took a quick breath, and although at least thirty feet away, Hannah could detect an almost arrogant stance as if he prided himself on his good looks.

Thick black hair grew back from a prominent widow's peak to stop an inch above the neckline of his shirt, the style a little too corporate, too boardroom perfect. The straight, almost haughty lines of cheekbones and nose showed an inherent strength and power that looked out of place on the face of a stablehand. She could more easily picture him in a tux on the front page of the society section of the *Atlanta Journal*.

Suddenly, an unfamiliar tingling grew quickly in the pit of her stomach. The sensation caught her by surprise, and she slid her hand to her mid-section to quell the tickle.

Tory brought her horse to the gate, then dismounted with the man's help. He patted her on the back and said something that brought their two heads together. The tingling inside Hannah's stomach turned into a prick of puzzling uneasiness.

"Hi, Mom." Tory appeared more lighthearted than she had in weeks.

"Hi, sweetheart." Hannah jumped down from her perch, put a possessive arm around her daughter and gave her an overly excessive hug. Tory protested in typical teenage form.

"Hello, Mrs. Stevens." Sean peered behind her back, the gesture exaggerated. "Not carrying any yogurt, are you?"

"No, I'm not armed today." Smiling, she took his offered hand. Masculine, but definitely not the hand of someone who worked outside for a living. The clear blue eyes that had stunned Hannah several weeks ago now held a charming twinkle. The effect was awesome.

"Nice to see you, too," she responded, "if not a bit of a surprise."

He ignored the opening she'd given him to explain his presence.

"Tory has a lot of natural ability with horses," he said. "You must be very proud of her."

"Yes, I am."

His gaze held Hannah's until she began to feel uncomfortable.

"Tory," he said, "why don't you take Bonnie back to the barn while your mom and I get acquainted."

Get acquainted? Odd way to phrase it. He made it sound as though they were on the brink of bonding. Hannah put his handsome face aside, determined to satisfy her curiosity about this man who belonged in an *Esquire* ad.

"Tory has spoken so highly of you, Mr. Murphy, I was beginning to think you were Justin Timberlake incarnate."

His brows drew together. "Who?"

"Justin Timberlake. You know, NSYNC?" Feeling foolish, she shook her head and changed the subject. "I don't see old Mr. Haverty today. Has he hired you to give lessons?"

Sean chuckled, the sound tickling Hannah's spine. "Actually, I hired on to help out around here and take care of the horses. A week later, Sam had a bout with his arthritis, so I offered to give a lesson for him. He promoted me on the spot."

She looked at him, unconvinced. "Is that right?"

He nodded.

"You have a lot of experience with horses?"

"Well, I've been riding since I was a kid."

"Really?" Hannah kept the smile on her face while her intuition told her something wasn't quite right here. Boots that were too shiny, a sunburn and hands with fresh blisters reinforced her suspicion.

"Are you new to the area, Mr. Murphy?"

He nodded. "I moved here about a month ago."

She nodded thoughtfully. "And how did you find your way to St. Simons from New England?"

Laughing, he said, "My accent, right?" He shook his head. "Sometimes I feel like a cranberry in a pot of grits."

Hannah chuckled, but waited for an answer to her question.

"An acquaintance of mine introduced me to the Island. I fell in love with it."

"That's not hard to do." She looked around her. "Is Sam here today?"

"No. He went to visit his sister in Ft. Lauderdale. Said he'd be back in a few weeks. I told him I'd keep the place running until he got back."

It would have been easy to accept his story, especially with his gorgeous, smiling face staring at hers. He radiated a sensuousness that attracted her like a magnet, yet her instincts warned her to resist the potent magnetism. She continued to look at him, pondering his explanation, not noticing the silence that stretched out between them.

"I hope Tory will continue to take lessons," he said. "Sam told me about some upcoming competitions. I thought Tory might want to enter."

"Competitions? Er, how much do they cost?" How she wished for the day she wouldn't have to worry about money.

"Well, there's an entry fee of course, and she'd have to wear riding pants, boots, coat. You know, the usual."

Hannah let out a breath. "Mr. Murphy..."

"Sean."

She hesitated. "Sean. I can barely afford riding lessons. Competitions are out of the question."

"Oh, well, maybe we can work something out."

She shook her head. "I appreciate your considering Tory, but I'd rather she stay with her weekly group lesson with April and Sara." Hannah's budget was already maxed out. There was absolutely no money left for anything else.

"If it's a problem," he said, "I'd be happy to talk to Sam about giving Tory lessons for free until your finances are in better shape."

His surprisingly generous offer caught Hannah off guard. Would the other students rate such a gesture? "That's out of the question," she stated flatly. "I pay my way, Mr. Murphy. I won't put myself in a position of owing anyone."

His brows pulled together in a frown. "I'm not offering charity, if that's what you think. You could pay it back a little at a time later." He looked at her intently as if waiting for her to say more.

"No, thank you." Hannah glanced at her watch. "It's getting to be dinnertime, and I'm sure Tory has homework. I'd better see what's keeping her."

She walked ahead of him to the barn under the shade of ponderosa pines and live oaks. It probably wasn't any of Hannah's business why he'd come to the Island or why he worked as a stablehand. However, his gorgeous eyes not withstanding, he was a stranger who'd showed up out of the blue, and she wouldn't allow Tory to be alone with him. She'd make sure either she or one of the other mothers was present whenever the girls took lessons.

Besides, having the girls chaperoned would be to his advantage as well. In today's society, it wasn't wise for a man to be alone with a young girl in any situation.

"What type of business are you in, Hannah?" Her name fell warmly from his lips, luring her from her thoughts until the realization jolted her.

"How did you know my name?"

For an instant, something flashed in his eyes, as though he cursed himself for some sort of blunder. Then, smooth as silk, he said, "I had the girls fill out a card with their addresses, telephone numbers, and parents' names." He paused. "May I call you Hannah?"

No. But not wanting to be rude, she nodded ever so slightly. "I'm an interior decorator," she said in answer to his earlier question.

"Really? Maybe you could give me a few pointers for my apartment. I'm afraid my taste runs toward New England cold rather than South Georgia warm."

Hannah smiled. Her decorating advice didn't come cheap, and she doubted that his salary would cover even fifteen minutes of her time. Although she might need all the clients she could get, her intuition told her to steer clear of this man.

When she didn't respond to his suggestion, he changed the subject. "Tory seems to be a good kid."

"Yes, she is."

"She told me her dad died last year."

That brought Hannah up short. It was difficult for Tory to talk to anyone about Paul's death. Yet, she had confided in a complete stranger. What else had Tory told him?

"I lost my mother when I was just a few years older than Tory," Sean said. "I know what she's going through."

Really? What a presumptuous statement. The entire conversation was getting much too personal, and his prying manner irked her.

"Tory's doing just fine."

"And you?"

Tolerance quickly gave way to annoyance. "Mr. Murphy, we're both doing very well." Deliberately, she turned her back to him and called out, "Tory, are you ready?"

"In a minute," came the reply.

Over her shoulder she offered a curt "Goodbye, Mr. Murphy."

"You were going to call me Sean."

She didn't know how to take the flicker of amusement in his eyes and decided to ignore his comment. "Remember, we'll continue with only the weekly lesson with the other girls."

"If that's what you'd prefer."

Hannah nodded, then retreated to the car, the closest protection from his extraordinary eyes.

Tory climbed into the front seat. "Bye, Mr. Murphy. See you next week."

"Bye, Tory."

Hannah saw him flash a smile that could easily cause butterflies to dance a jig in the stomach of a thirteen-year-old. And a thirty-three-year-old wasn't immune either.

She drove out to the main road only half listening to Tory's uncharacteristic chatter. Somehow, she felt he'd learned more about her than she had of him. And for some reason, the feeling was disquieting.

~ * ~

Sean watched the car disappear through the woods. A small piece of his heart went with it. He stood watching for several minutes, left alone to sort out his impressions of Hannah Stevens. Unhurriedly, he went about spreading wood shavings and forking hay into stalls. Despite the blisters and aching muscles, he was surprised at how much he enjoyed the routine he'd learned years ago.

He'd tried his best to charm Hannah, but the vibes didn't guarantee she'd fallen for his friendliness or the lies that had fallen smoothly from his lips. She would though, given a little time. She hadn't offered a lot of personal information, but it was obvious they were hard up for cash. And he wanted to know more about her dead husband.

The past two weeks with Tory had opened up Sean's world and his heart. His daughter was bright, beautiful and thoughtful, and every time he looked into her face, it brought bittersweet memories of Angie.

When Tory had mentioned her Dad, Sean had seen her pain and remembered how he'd felt when his mother had died. The urge to hug her had been so great, he'd had to grab the nearest stall to stop himself. The feeling had triggered an overwhelming sense of fatherhood.

Grudgingly, Sean admitted Hannah had been very protective of her daughter, but why had Tory shied away from her embrace? Was there some kind of friction between the two? What if this interior decorating business didn't fly? How would this woman support his child?

He tried to imagine Tory as a baby and felt the sharp loss of each of her thirteen years. Although he'd already decided to learn everything about Hannah and Tory, one thing was certain. He wouldn't be leaving St. Simons Island any time soon.

Three

"They have to be here somewhere." Tory flipped through the mounds of fabric scattered on the floor of the sunroom/office. Her mom had left a half an hour ago to meet with a client. Tory glanced at her watch and figured she had another thirty minutes to search for her adoption papers.

Deciding she'd given the room a thorough going over, she went next to the small foyer closet. She pushed aside coats and jackets, then stood on a stool and rifled through little-used winter hats and gloves.

Nothing.

Maybe her mom kept the papers in that small metal box at the bank. Tory remembered that her mom had once explained important things were kept there.

On the other hand, maybe there were no papers at all. Tory, hoping her best friend knew what she was talking about, reasoned that if some people signed papers when they adopted a kid, then everyone would have to. Right?

After her conversation with April several weeks ago, Tory had put off starting her hunt. Not because she'd changed her mind. Far from it. Finding her other parents had become a mission, a quest, and she knew, something that would make a big change in her life. Her hesitation stemmed from the unknown.

What would she do if she found these people? Would they want to know her? No answer came to mind. She'd think about it later.

Where could the papers be? Chewing on a thumbnail, she walked back into the kitchen, where she pulled open cabinets and drawers. Nothing. *This house isn't that big.* With a hand on her hip, she gazed out the window, spotted the aluminum shed in the corner of the backyard, then ran out and yanked open the rusty doors. It was stacked to the ceiling with boxes from their move. Her shoulders slumped with frustration; there wouldn't be enough time to go through each one.

The sound of a car door sent her heart leaping into her throat. She spun around, the breath she held coming out a second later. Just old Mrs. Thompson. Her bridge game must have let out early. Quickly, Tory shut the doors and went back to the house.

There was only one place left to look, and she decided it was now or never. Standing in the doorway of Hannah's bedroom, Tory felt it. Creeping guilt. *I shouldn't do this.* But how else could she be sure her adoption papers weren't here?

Swallowing her uneasiness, Tory started with the closet. She went through all the shoe boxes in case they contained other things besides shoes. Nothing there. No luck in the bottom of the closet either.

With guilt pressing harder, she hurried through the dresser, patting disarrayed T-shirts, shorts and lingerie, hoping for the rustle of paper.

Half relieved, half disappointed, Tory closed up all the drawers and shut the closet door, but before leaving, she scanned the room to make sure nothing was out of place to leave a telltale sign. An overlooked tennis shoe lay on its side by the bed. Not seeing the other one, she lifted the dust ruffle of the bed for a quick peek and noticed a dark box below the headboard up against the wall. She reached in and pulled out a green metal container the size of a large CD holder. It was locked.

Immediately, she ran to the kitchen and grabbed a bunch of miscellaneous keys that hung on the bulletin board. Not much time, she thought.

The fifth key did the trick. Inside the box lay folded papers, some in envelopes, some in vinyl holders. Her heart beat faster as she pulled them out. Life insurance. Medical insurance. Birth certificates. She found hers and learned she'd been born at Piedmont Hospital. Hannah had told Tory she'd been born in Atlanta, Georgia but Tory hadn't known what hospital. The parents were listed as Hannah and Paul Stevens.

She flipped through more papers. Last Will and Testament of Hannah Stevens. Some kind of certificates with 'EE' on them. Friends of Children. State Farm—. She stopped. What was Friends of Children? Her teeth scraped her bottom lip as she took out the slightly yellowed envelope and unfolded the long paper. Her heart pounded. *In the Matter of the Adoption of a Child To Be Named Victoria Louise Stevens.*

This is it, she thought, her hands shaking slightly. The words didn't make sense and most of them she couldn't pronounce. Each sheet looked the same except the last one. It was a form of some kind with her mom's and dad's signatures at the bottom. Above those was a name she didn't recognize. Angela Jenkins. Tory's stomach tightened. Underneath the name was printed 'Birth Mother.' *That's her. That's my real mother.* She looked in the next column. Over 'Birth Father' was typed 'Unknown.' What did that mean?

She stared at the pages in her hands, questions bombarding her from every direction, but she didn't have time to dwell on them. The slamming of the front door gave her a jolt. Frantically, she crammed the papers back into the box and pushed it under the bed.

"Tory?"

"Coming!" She ran out of the bedroom, then slowed her pace as she came down the hall to the kitchen.

"Hi, honey." Hannah set her briefcase on the floor and flipped through the mail on the table. "Anybody call?"

Tory shook her head, her heartbeat slowing to a near normal rate.

"Are you okay?" Hannah's brow creased as she reached out to feel Tory's forehead. "You look a little flushed."

"I'm fine." She pulled away and backed up several steps, suddenly wanting to be alone. "I'd better finish my homework." In her room, she leaned against the closed door, folded her arms over her stomach. "Angela Jenkins. Angela Jenkins." Tory whispered the name, waiting for some kind of connection. "Victoria Jenkins." Only confusion and questions reached out to her.

Why did she give me up for adoption? Who was my real dad? Tory's heart broke miserably as another realization dawned on her. Her mom had known about Angela Jenkins all along.

Why did she lie to me?

~ * ~

"X plus five divided by four equals nine divided by x minus seven." Hannah mulled over the problem, rubbing a small ache in her temple. "I can't believe you're studying algebra in the eighth grade."

"It's *pre*-algebra, Mom." Tory rolled her eyes.

They sat together at the kitchen table, Hannah wishing she'd paid more attention in Mrs. Prescott's tenth grade math class. "I'm sorry, honey. I just can't help you. Why don't you call someone in your class?"

Tory dragged her chin from the palm of her hand and slammed the book closed. "You won't help me with anything."

Praying for patience, Hannah took a deep breath and checked her temper. "You've been in a sour mood for the past several days, and I'm really sorry about that. But please don't take it out on me."

At this point, Tory would usually mutter an apology. None came tonight. Tightlipped and silent, she gathered her books and went to her bedroom, the door closing just short of a slam.

Almost at the end of her rope, Hannah shook her head. *What is wrong with that child?*

As she pushed back her chair, the front door buzzer rang. Maybe it was time to get professional help. *Right.* Where would the money come from to pay a psychologist a hundred dollars an hour? Perhaps Family and Children Services offered counseling services.

Stress ate away at her, a constant unwanted companion, and she was sick of it. Right now, she'd give anything for a strong shoulder to lean on.

Hannah opened the door and stared. Her wish stood with a large pizza box in his hands, a riding hat sitting on top. She couldn't help but grin.

"You moonlight?"

Sean's smile matched hers. "Only on special occasions."

"What's the special occasion?"

"Tory left her riding hat at the stable. I didn't want her to think she'd lost it."

His thoughtfulness struck a chord within her and she smiled her thanks. "Pepperoni?"

"And extra cheese."

"My favorite."

"Good. Then I guessed right."

They stood looking at each other for an awkward minute.

"Uh... the directions on the box say eat while it's hot." He leaned closer to her. "Nothing worse than cold pizza."

The amusement that flickered in his blue eyes made her heart skip a beat. Ordinarily, she would've debated about inviting a strange man into her home.

But he'd brought dinner and she wouldn't have to cook. Besides, she was hungry.

"Come on in." She grabbed Tory's hat from the top of the box. As he brushed by her, the smell of woodsy cologne mingled with Italian spices. His presence filled the tiny living room, black hair slightly damp, dark green T-shirt hugging a well-muscled chest. And the khaki cargo shorts he wore presented her with a nice view from the back. It dawned on her there hadn't been a man in her house in over a year.

Taking the box, Hannah said, "Let's put it on the table." He followed her toward the kitchen.

"This is really a peace offering."

She glanced over her shoulder and noticed him eyeing the rest of the house. Thank God she'd picked up when she'd come home.

Raising an eyebrow, she looked at him in surprise. "Are we at war?"

He leaned against the refrigerator and crossed his arms over his chest. "I thought I might have come on a little too strong when we met the last time."

Hannah knew exactly what he meant, but she decided not to be too easily won over. "You did." She focused on setting the table with paper plates and yellow-and-blue napkins.

"I apologize."

His simple words held a sincerity that zapped her. Her hand stilled and she cocked her head to meet oddly compelling blue eyes fringed with dark lashes. Something inside her gave way.

"Accepted."

"Mom? Who's here?" Tory entered the kitchen, her face lighting up like a sunrise. "Hi, Sean."

Hannah's eyes flew open. "Excuse me? Since when do you call adults by their first name?"

"Sorry," she said with an eye roll, then spied the Pizza Hut box. "Did you bring a pizza? Cool."

"He also brought the riding hat you left at the stables."

"Gee, thanks. But I knew where it was," she added quickly, heading off her mother's skeptical look.

"Tory, honey, you get the drinks." She turned to her guest. "I'm afraid I don't have anything stronger than ice tea or cola, Mr. Murphy."

"Cola's fine, but you'll have to drop the 'Mr. Murphy.'"

She capitulated. "Sean."

Dinner was a chatty affair with Tory doing most of the chattering. Her bad mood disappeared under Sean's attention, and his gentle camaraderie seemed to bring out a personality Hannah hadn't seen in quite a while. Even though she worried Tory might develop a crush on "the yogurt man," Sean didn't overly indulge Tory or patronize her. In fact, he seemed genuinely interested in cafeteria antics, girlfriends, and NSYNC.

"I love pizza," Tory said, stuffing the last piece into her mouth. "This is great."

"Yes, thank you, Sean. It was very thoughtful."

"My pleasure, ladies."

Hannah's gaze quickly danced over him as Sean took a long pull on the last of his Coke. He looked like he belonged here, sitting at her table, listening, laughing. When was the last time an evening had been so pleasant? Or could it be a man's company that caused this warm, sense of security?

A feeling of betrayal worked its way into the edges of her mind. Not because a man was in her home or even because she found him attractive. Paul was dead and nothing would bring him back. Still, she deeply regretted not having tried harder to make their marriage work while he had been alive. Indifference and complacency had become a hurdle neither she nor her husband had been able to cross.

"Tory," Hannah said, her voice catching, making her clear her throat, "did you finish your homework?"

"Not yet."

"You'd better get going."

"I will, I will," Tory moaned, then an idea spread over her face. "Mr. Murphy, do you know anything about algebra?"

"Uh, Tory," Hannah interrupted, instinctively knowing the direction of the question.

Sean nodded. "It was my best subject."

"Mom doesn't know how to do it. Could you help me?"

"I'm sure Mr. Murphy has other things to do."

"As a matter of fact, I don't. I'd be happy to help you." He looked to Hannah for permission. "That is, if you don't mind."

Hannah hesitated. First dinner, now homework. He was crowding her again. Ingratiating himself.

Sean must have seen her indecision and held his palms up in the air. "I promise I won't stay long."

She'd better learn how to protect herself against the easy smile that played at the corners of his mouth. If she didn't, she'd be in big trouble.

"All right," she said.

"Yes!" Tory exclaimed, and ran off to get her book.

Sean helped Hannah clear the table. With three glasses in his hand, he asked, "Where's the dishwasher?"

"You're looking at her," Hannah replied with a smile, throwing paper plates into the trashcan. "Just rinse them and leave them next to the sink. I'll take care of them later." For a second, she thought he was going to offer to wash and was relieved when he didn't. Doing dishes together seemed a little too... close.

Tory came back with her backpack and sat down at the table next to Sean.

"Well, I have some work to finish," Hannah stated. "I'll be in the office if you need me." Obviously, they didn't expect to need her; the dark-haired man had already begun to explain the laws of algebra to the dark-haired child.

Hannah turned at the office door, and as she studied the two, a stab of something hit her. Jealousy? Foreboding? Apprehension? Silly, she thought, and went to pick out wallpaper for Mrs. Shoemaker's powder room.

~ * ~

An hour later, Hannah sat cross-legged on the floor of the converted sunroom, engrossed in sketching a floor plan. She had talked the developer of a new subdivision into giving her the opportunity to decorate the model home. This could be the break she needed.

Lost in concentration, focused on the white trim that would set off the dark-mauve walls and give the den just the right amount of dramatic flair, she didn't hear anyone enter the small office.

"Nice colors."

Scuffed leather moccasins filled her vision, and she followed the well-formed legs up the trim body to stop at an amused grin and clear blue eyes. Her heart did that 'little thing' again.

"Oh. Sean." She pulled a hand through her hair. "I didn't hear you come in."

He held out a hand and helped her up. "I was complimenting you on your choice of colors. What are you working on?"

"A model home." She crossed her fingers. "Hope the builder likes it."

"I can't imagine he wouldn't."

"Thanks. Did you and Tory slay the algebra dragon?"

He chuckled. "I think she understands it. She's in her room going over vocabulary."

"I appreciate your help. Math was never my strong suit." Hannah began walking toward the front door, deciding he'd spent enough time in her home for one night. "And I appreciate your bringing dinner."

He followed behind her, his presence making her glance nervously over her shoulder. She opened the door. "Thanks again."

Halfway out the door, he stopped. "There was something I wanted to talk to you about."

She raised her eyebrows.

"You know, Tory has the makings of a fine rider."

"Well, I don't know much about riding," Hannah admitted, "but she does look good on a horse."

"There's a competition coming up I'd like Tory to enter." He held up a hand when Hannah started to object. "I know money's tight, but hear me out."

He was doing it again. Pushing.

"Since you won't accept help with the entry fee, how about letting Tory work for it?"

"Doing what?"

"She could help out at the stables, groom the horses, muck out the stalls. I'll talk to Sam, but I'm sure he wouldn't mind, and I could use the help." When Hannah didn't say anything, he added, "It would be good for her. Give her some responsibility and she'll get paid for it."

Tory would be alone with him. Not a good idea.

"She'd be there only when I give lessons," he said, apparently reading her mind. "And Sam will be hiring another instructor. Female." In a final attempt to win her over, he added, "I know Tory would really like to compete."

It took a long minute for Hannah to agree. "You'd have to pay her at least minimum wage." That way it wouldn't take Tory long to earn the entry fee.

"Agreed."

"And her schoolwork comes first. If her grades slip, that's the end of it."

"Understood."

As he walked down the front stairs, she said, "I guess you've already discussed this with her?"

The left side of his mouth curled up and he shrugged.

"Hmm."

"Oh, Hannah," he called as she closed the door. "How about dinner Saturday night?"

A quick flutter hit her stomach. She hoped she wasn't coming down with the flu. "You're doing it again."

"What?"

"Coming on too strong."

"Oh." He looked at the ground as if giving her comment some thought. "Is it working?"

"No." With a satisfied smile, she shut the door.

~ * ~

Sean drove back to his apartment, whistling all the way. The pizza had worked like a charm, allowing him entry into her home as easily as a burglar with a credit card.

Tory was a great kid. Sean would've liked to puff on his fingernails and polish them on his shirt and say genes had a lot to do with it. Her bubbly personality, so like Angie's, fascinated him, and she obviously loved school and enjoyed her friends. And she was quick, too. He'd only had to explain a math problem once, and he'd almost seen the light bulb go off in her head.

Angie, you would have been proud.

Amidst the joy in discovering his daughter, a small pain nicked Sean's heart, knowing Angie would never know the child they'd created. Never know the sound of Tory's laughter or her bright-eyed eagerness. He took most of the blame for that. In those days, he'd been far too hungry; for success, security, and power. Had he been too obsessive as well? Too single-minded? Probably. But that didn't explain why Angie hadn't come to him with her feelings and news of her pregnancy.

Tonight, Sean had felt so close to Tory, as if he was already a big part of her life. And why shouldn't he? He *was* her father, and damn it, after thirteen years, she should know the truth. But he wondered if that would ever happen.

Instead of driving to the apartment, Sean found himself pulling into a parking space at East Beach. He got out, walked to the end of the weathered fishing platform and leaned his arms on the railing. Under the pale moonlight, he could make out the outline of pelicans and sea gulls resting on a spit of land created by the outgoing tide.

Short-range, his plan had worked well tonight. Long-range, he still needed to determine if Hannah was a good mother, especially now that she was a single parent. To accomplish that, he'd have to continue pushing himself into their lives, wheedle his way into their daily routine. In fact, he'd already formed several impressions. To Hannah's credit, the house had been neat and tidy, except for her work area. It would have been a stretch to call it her office. But her neatness didn't cover the cracked plaster walls or worn vinyl flooring. Moreover, it irritated him that Tory didn't even have a desk to study at. And although Tory seemed well-adjusted, he knew the friction he'd previously detected between mother and daughter hadn't been his imagination.

Hannah may have turned down his dinner invitation, but she was warming to him, Sean could tell. Worming his way into her good graces would be easy. However, he admitted, resisting his attraction to her wouldn't be.

He shouldn't have wanted to push her glasses up on her exquisitely dainty nose or liked the feel of her hand in his when he'd helped her up off the floor. Disturbingly, he found her an extremely intriguing package. A short package maybe, but the T-shirt she'd worn hinted loudly at the rounded pleasures underneath.

Sean straightened up, inhaled the pungent combination of marsh and sea, and reminded himself why he was here in the first place. He could fantasize about Hannah all night long, but his questions remained. What if behind the caring façade, she was a negligent mother? What if her business failed?

What if he couldn't walk away from the daughter he'd just found?

Four

Henry Pipkin stood at the bus stop with his friends and, as he did every morning, pretended not to notice Victoria Stevens. He always called her Victoria because the most beautiful girl in the eighth grade deserved a more sophisticated name than Tory.

She stood with her own circle of friends, and the chasm between her group and his was insurmountable. As similar as the Montagues and Capulettes, he was a nerd and she was a prep, and ne'er the twain would meet. Besides, why would one of the most popular girls in school be interested in a tall, skinny computer geek with glasses and a cowlick when she could have any guy she wanted?

"It'll never happen." Alan Dworkin walked up behind Henry and followed his gaze. "Man, you're dreaming if you think someone like her is ever gonna notice someone like you."

"Shut up, jerk. What would you know?"

Alan grunted. "I know she's cheerleader material and you're dork material. The two don't mix. Who needs her anyway? She probably doesn't know bytes from rams. Probably's a snob, too."

Henry shook his head slowly. "Not Victoria." There wasn't a stuck up bone in her body. She always had a smile for him, and when she added a "hi," his heart answered with a back flip.

Ignoring Alan, Henry looked down the street, ostensibly for the bus, but wanting to keep Victoria in view. Usually laughing and outgoing, today she clutched her backpack closer to her chest and stared at the ground, her mouth pulled down into a frown. When she started to walk in his direction, Henry did a poor imitation of indifference, difficult to do with his pulse hammering in his ears.

"Hi, Henry."

"Huh? Oh, hi, Victoria." He made an awkward grab for the books that started to slip out of his arms.

"Could I talk to you for a minute?" She stood apart, as if not wanting to intrude on his world.

"Yeah." Henry felt the heat in his face. *Be cool. Be cool.*

"I wondered if you could help me with something."

"Sure."

"You know a lot about computers, don't you?"

"Yeah, I guess so."

"If I wanted to find someone, like, if I didn't know their address, could you find them through a computer somehow?"

"Why don't you just look them up in the telephone book?"

"Oh, she doesn't live here."

"Well, you could access the telephone directory for the city she lives in."

"I don't know what city, or even what state."

Henry shifted his stance. "I don't understand. You're looking for someone, but you don't know where they are. Who are you looking for?"

A brief flash of troubled hesitation crossed her face. "Just someone I need to find. Can you do it or not?"

Henry wasn't about to say he couldn't help her, not when he had her undivided attention, and he scrambled to think. "Maybe, if I had a Social Security number."

Victoria took a deep breath fringed with frustration. "I don't have one."

"I'd like to help you, Victoria, but I'll need more information."

She dragged her teeth over her bottom lip, and after a second she said, "I might have something else, but I don't have it with me. Could I bring it to your house?"

He lifted his eyebrows and started to sweat. *Victoria Stevens wants to come to my house!* "That'd be great... I mean, sure, if you want." He shrugged as nonchalantly as possible.

"How about tomorrow after school?"

When he nodded, she smiled. "Thanks, Henry." His stomach sank to the pavement.

The bus pulled up and Henry fell into line behind her. As she stepped up, she glanced back over her shoulder and said, "Oh, and you have to promise not to tell anyone about this. It's a secret."

He held up his hand. "Okay, sure, no," he stammered. "I won't tell anyone."

Before he took another step, Alan pulled Henry to the side, disbelief etched on his face. "What was that all about?"

Henry's smile started slow and ended in a satisfied smirk. "Wouldn't you like to know? Eat your heart out, dork."

~ * ~

"Oh, yes... please don't stop." Hannah moaned as she lay face-down on the massage table, her arms dangling toward the floor. "God, your hands are wonderful." With her cheek pressed flat, the words came out with the slur of a three-day hangover.

Marsha kneaded the tightness out of her friend's shoulders. Her long hair was tied back with a piece of rawhide and large loop earrings of silver and turquoise swung freely from her ears with each squeeze and press. "Some say it's better than sex."

Hannah took a deep breath and basked in the pull and push of Marsha's ministrations. "Really? I wouldn't know. Sex is only a vague memory. Ouch!"

"Breathe." Marsha dug her fingers into a particularly taut muscle. "In and out, that's right. You're as tight as a virgin, Hannah. You need to exercise more."

With a grunt, Hannah nodded. "I need a lot of things. Unfortunately, exercise isn't one of them."

Marsha made a clucking noise, her fingers massaging a bunched shoulder muscle. "There's more to life than working, you know."

"Hmm. I'll remember that when the rent's due."

"Well, your business must be doing better if you can take time out for a massage."

"It was either a massage or a permanent stay in the mental ward at Focus Health Systems. A massage is cheaper."

"Turn over."

Hannah grabbed the sheet and rolled to her other side. "I did get some new business, though. The builder of that new subdivision at the north end of the Island wants me to decorate his spec homes."

"That's great!"

"Yeah," Hannah agreed, but the words that should have come with enthusiasm sounded flat. She sighed and looked around the small cubicle-shaped room. A number of dreamcatchers in a variety of sizes and colors hung on the walls and absently, she wondered if they worked.

"Don't sound so excited," Marsha said, as she worked her way down to calf and ankle muscles.

Limp, languid, and lax, Hannah fell under the hypnotic spell of the massage, wanting nothing more than to lie here all day. Not think about the business or worry about the future or talk about Tory. Just for a while.

"I am," she mumbled. "Relieved, too. Guess I'm just tired."

"You ought to do something wild and crazy with your extra money."

"I already have."

"What?"

"Opened up a savings account."

Marsha made a face. "I'm serious."

"So am I. I need a little security, a little peace of mind."

"What you need is to lighten up. How's your social life?"

Hannah stifled the laugh that started out of her mouth. For the past year, the only thing social in her life had been the occasional Wednesday night church supper. However, the memory of Sean Murphy's telephone call the night before made her smile with guarded anticipation. The deep smoothness of his voice had given her chills and long-forgotten goosebumps of pure physical desire.

She reminisced only a second before a sharp dose of realism slapped her. *Oh, forget it.* There was no time in her life for anything but survival. That's why she'd stalled his dinner invitation again. *Right?*

"I met a man recently and he asked me out."

"Ooooo, lucky you. Does he have a friend? A brother? A distant cousin?"

"He's Tory's riding instructor."

Marsha's hands stilled, her brows drawn quizzically. "You have a date with old man Haverty?"

Hannah chuckled. "No, no. Haverty hired a new stablehand. His name is Sean Murphy."

"Sean," Marsha repeated on a dreamy sigh. "Aye, 'tis a romantic name. Does he have hair as black as a rogue's soul and eyes the color of a summer sky?"

Hannah raised her head off the table at her friend's exaggerated brogue. "You've met him?"

"Ha, I wish." Marsha dropped the accent like a hot potato. "Do tell."

Hannah could have declined or changed the subject and just enjoyed this rare, relaxing moment in silence while Marsha worked her magic. Instead, she found herself recounting Sean Murphy's entrance into her life. She didn't mention her initial reaction to him, though, the suspicions and doubts that had troubled her. In fact, none of that seemed important now that she knew him better. Or did she?

"And when did he ask you out?" Marsha asked, after Hannah went through her story.

"When he came over a few days ago with a pizza in one hand and Tory's riding hat in the other. I couldn't turn him away, so he had dinner with us and then helped Tory with her homework." She paused. "Actually, it was a very pleasant evening," she admitted, remembering how content she'd felt having a man in her home. "As he was leaving, he asked me to dinner."

"You accepted."

"No. I told him he was being too pushy. Then he called me again last night."

"What did you say?"

"That I'd let him know."

Marsha pursed her lips, nodded. "Raw, hot sex."

"I beg your pardon?"

"Raw, hot sex. *That's* what you need."

Hannah chortled. "I've never had any."

"What? Surely you and Paul..." Marsha stopped at the look on Hannah's face.

"Paul was never hot and sexy with me. Maybe with his other women, but not with me." Then she could have bit her tongue. *This massage must be getting to me,* she thought. She'd never admitted to anyone about Paul's affairs. Humiliation and guilt had been the great silencers.

The silence hung for a second. "I'd heard the rumors," Marsha told her. "Why didn't you leave that jerk?"

"I couldn't. Tory was so close to Paul, she never would have understood a divorce. And even though he may not have loved me, he loved his daughter very much." *Maybe if I had been more attractive, more experienced in bed.*

"God, men can be such shits sometimes. If you ask me, he deserved that heart attack. Well," Marsha continued, "surely one of your other lovers was good in bed."

Hannah smiled sweetly and shook her head. "I married Paul when I was nineteen. There's been no one else but him."

Slowly, Marsha straightened and shook her head. "My God, I didn't know women like you existed anymore."

Hannah tried not to squirm under the woman's incredulous stare.

"Well, honey, there's only one remedy for your condition. Just go out and do it."

"Oh, Marsha," Hannah admonished. "Maybe your life is that simple, but mine isn't. First of all, I couldn't have sex just for the sake of having sex." *Could I?* "And there's Tory to think about."

"Didn't you say she likes him?"

Hannah nodded. "Quite frankly, she's a different child around him."

"How so?"

"She's happy, not so moody. Yet when she's with me, she's been withdrawn and quiet."

"Is it Paul?"

Hannah shook her head. "I don't think so. She usually shows her grief through anger. Something else is bothering her, but I can't get her to talk about it."

"I wouldn't worry about her too much. She'll come around."

"Hmm." Hannah wasn't so sure. Maybe she should make that call to the family counselor.

"So what are you going to do about your date?"

Hannah shrugged. "What does one do on a date?"

"You talk, have fun, fool around."

Hannah raised a tolerant brow.

"Look, I think you ought to go out with this guy. If you're worried about it, why not bring Tory with you?"

"Oh, that should go over well."

"Why not? She likes him, he likes her and you won't feel like he's focusing totally on you."

Hannah thought for a moment and found herself smiling at the idea. "I just might do that. Of course, he may never ask me out again," she joked.

"Then, you don't have to worry about it, right?"

What the heck. She didn't have anything to lose. "Right."

~ * ~

As Tory knocked on the door of the two-story, stucco home, she glanced around her old neighborhood, glad she couldn't see the house she'd grown up in. It would hurt way too much. Although the familiar surroundings caused an ache deep in her heart, memories of her and her Dad riding bikes all over the Island brought the start of a smile that faded seconds later. Reminders of happy days gone forever.

Before Tory could dwell too deeply on the past, Henry Pipkin yanked open the door. "Hi, Victoria." His voice jumped an octave making him clear his throat.

"Hi, Henry." Walking past him into the high-ceilinged foyer, something caught her eye. Something different. Then she saw it. "Henry, you have an earring," she stated in disbelief, and watched his color shoot from natural beige to crimson in two seconds flat.

With his head down, Henry hunched his shoulders and shoved his hands in his pants. She hadn't meant to embarrass him but she'd known Henry since kindergarten, and, well, he looked funny. Nerds didn't wear earrings. They wore glasses and carried a collection of pens and pencils in a plastic holder in their shirt pocket.

"It looks cool," she fibbed with a smile. "So," she went on to change the subject, "where's your computer?" He took the lead and led her to a small room off the kitchen that housed his extensive computer system.

"Wow," Tory exclaimed, feeling like she'd stepped into another time dimension. Hard drives, monitors and printers dotted with colored lights sent out a dull drone that filled the room. "This is awesome! You know how to work all this stuff?"

"Yeah. It's really easy. I could teach you, if you want."

"Thanks, but I don't have time right now. I'm kind of in a hurry to find this person."

"Oh. Right." Henry sat, swiveled around in a cushioned gray chair and wheeled himself to one of the computer stations. She watched him with renewed respect as he flipped one button, pushed another and hit the enter key several times with the touch of an expert.

"Okay, who do you need to find?"

"Her name is Angela Jenkins."

"Uh huh. And where does she live?"

"Well," Tory responded with a trace of annoyance. "If I knew that, I wouldn't be here. Duh." She rolled her eyes. *He's still a nerd,* she thought.

"You have to give me something to start with, Victoria. What state does she live in?"

Why does he always call me Victoria? "I don't know what state. But maybe this will help." She flipped open the math book she'd brought with her and handed him a green-tinted piece of paper.

Now looking totally confused, Henry took the paper, glanced at it and waited for an explanation. When he didn't say anything, Tory knew she'd have to tell him.

"See," she began, with practiced aloofness. "I'm adopted. And I just found out Angela Jenkins is my real mother and I want to find her." She gestured to the birth certificate still in Henry's hand. "I thought maybe you could find her through the hospital where I was born." She sat in a nearby chair, her hands twisting nervously in her lap.

"I didn't know you were adopted." Henry leaned forward and for a moment, Tory thought he would reach for her hand.

"It's no big deal," she said, her nonchalance not quite masking her defensiveness.

Henry's voice softened. "If it wasn't a big deal, you wouldn't be here."

Taken aback by his words, Tory looked up into warm, brown eyes, suddenly seeing him in a different light. He didn't accuse or blame or ridicule, but made her feel like he understood.

"Guess your mom doesn't know why you're here."

Tory shook her head. "I told her you were helping me study math."

"She believed you?"

"Why shouldn't she?"

He laughed. "Well, it's not like you come over here all the time."

"She looked at me kinda funny," Tory answered with a lift of her shoulders, "but she didn't say anything. She doesn't know what I'm really doing."

"How did you find out this Angela Jenkins is your real mother? I thought you couldn't do that if you were adopted."

Tory hesitated. She decided he knew enough details. "It's a long story." She couldn't tell him Hannah had lied to her. She didn't want *anyone* to know that. "So, will you help me?"

He didn't hesitate. "Of course, I'll help you. It might take me some time to figure out how I'm going to do this, so I'll let you know when I've got something." He handed her the birth certificate. "You'd better keep this."

"Won't you need it?"

"No. I'll remember. Angela Jenkins, Piedmont Hospital and your birthday."

With a sigh of relief, Tory smiled. "Thanks, Henry. You're a good friend." *He ought to grow his hair a little longer,* she thought. *I never realized how tall he is.*

Henry wasn't part of her crowd, the popular crowd, but she'd known him all her life. It bugged her when her friends made fun of him and the geeks he hung out with. She'd never joined in, but guiltily, she hadn't done anything to stop the taunts.

"And don't forget," she said, standing up to leave.

"I know, it's a secret. You know I'd never tell anyone." He followed her through the kitchen, trailing behind as close as possible without tripping over her. "Can I help you with your math?"

"That's okay. I understand it now. Mr. Murphy explained it to me."

"Who's Mr. Murphy?"

"My new riding instructor. He was over at my house the other night and helped me. He's really good at it."

As they reached the front door, Henry didn't seem interested in knowing any more about Mr. Murphy. "You wanna stay for dinner?"

Tory smiled and shook her head. "I can't. I've got to get home." The disappointment etched on his face made her feel bad and prompted her to add, "But I'll see you at the bus stop tomorrow." She walked down the front stairs and turned back. "Thanks again for doing this for me, Henry. It means a lot."

Silently, he watched her go. "I'd do anything for you, Victoria," he whispered to himself. Even if it meant breaking the law.

Five

"Are you coming back anytime soon?"

Because there was no frustration in Brian Cassidy's tone, Sean figured The Murphy Group was running smoothly.

"Or are you going to leave the company to me?"

Sean laughed. Brian's sense of humor was still intact. Their camaraderie had always consisted of good-natured ribbing, some practical jokes and a soft undercurrent of competition. A Mutt and Jeff combination, Sean was the tall, lean, dark one while Brian was the short, stocky one with carrot red hair. Sean could see his friend now, feet propped up on his desk in his corner office, his Armani suit no doubt perfectly matched with a crisp cotton shirt and silk tie. Brian always liked the finer things in life.

"Yeah, you'd like that, wouldn't you? Sean joked, with a laugh, then waited for a response. "Brian? You there?"

"I'm here. Seriously, when do you think you'll be back?"

"It's only been a few weeks. Pretend I'm on vacation." Sean stood in the barn, the light wind carrying the pungent odor of hay and manure through the open breezeway. His cell phone was lodged between his ear and shoulder as he unbuckled the bridle and pulled it off Apollo, a huge palomino with a particularly gentle nature. He patted the horse's broad neck, closed the stall door and hung the bridle on a nearby hook.

"Right. You never take vacation. I've put together a very lucrative deal, but since you're not here, I'll go ahead and sign the contract."

Sean's brow furrowed. "Whoa, partner. You can fax the contract to me. I'm having a fax installed tomorrow and a computer system. We can keep in touch by phone or e-mail."

Brian's exhale rang of annoyance.

"What's bothering you?" Sean asked, then had to wait through a strained silence.

"What do you hope to accomplish down there?"

"I hope to get to know my daughter."

"Get to know her? I thought you were just going to see that she was all right and come back to Boston."

"It's a little more complicated."

"I was afraid of that. What happened?"

Before Sean could get into a lengthy explanation, Apollo stuck his head through the stall opening and nudged Sean's shoulder. A loud neigh came from behind curled lips and large yellowed teeth.

"What the hell was that?"

Sean reached into a nearby cooler, took out a carrot and offered it to the playful animal. "That's Apollo. He's a horse. See, I'm working at this stable—"

"You're doing what?"

"And I'm teaching my kid how to ride."

"Now I know you've lost your mind."

"You should see her. She's bright, pretty and can she sit a horse."

Brian paused and when he spoke again, his tone leveled off, as if realizing any objection was useless. "You haven't been on a horse since you shoveled out stalls for Boston PD's Mounted Division. Old Sergeant O'Malley would roll over in his grave if he knew you were teaching someone how to ride."

"What do you mean? I was a pretty good rider, and I could muck out a stall with the best of them."

Sean's joviality met with a long pause. "Brian? Can you hear me?"

"Sorry, something must be wrong with this line. So, tell me about the kid. "Does she…look like Angie?"

"Yes," Sean said, remember his reaction to seeing Tory in person for the first time on the pier.

"Then she must be beautiful."

The wistfulness in Brian's comment caught Sean off guard. But Brian had hurt, too, when Angie had left. After all, she'd been a good friend to him.

"I've found out," Sean continued, that her father... I mean her adoptive father, died and left them in a financial mess. The mother's trying to make ends meet." He snorted derisively. "You should see what they're living in. It's not much better than what we grew up in." Sean tightened his grip on the telephone. "I won't have my child living like we did."

"What about the mother?"

"I don't know about her yet. I sense some kind of tension between her and Tory."

"You know," Brian interrupted, "it's just a thought, but maybe you should leave it alone."

"I can't. Not now." Sean couldn't do that, not until he was sure about Hannah. And besides, Tory might need him.

"I think you're out of your league here. You don't know anything about being a parent. And who are you to judge this woman's credentials as a mother?"

Sean tried to keep the annoyance out of his voice. "First of all, *I'm* the father. And ever since I met Tory, my whole outlook has changed." He searched for the right words. "You begin to look at everything differently. You want to protect, encourage, teach..." Sean shook his head. "I don't know. I can't explain it."

"And what if this woman doesn't meet your requirements? As if you knew what those requirements would be. What are you going to do? Demand your fatherly rights? Drag it through the courts and have the kid end up hating you?"

"Wait a minute, dammit," Sean shot back, "you make it sound like I'm the bad guy here."

"Not at all," Brian said. "Just playing devil's advocate. It's not your fault. But it would be a shame if you had to go through any more crap because of Angie."

Always looking out for me, Sean thought as his temper died. Brian had been there to pick up the pieces when Angie had left, had been there the mornings after the nights before, there throughout all the hazy recollections of drunken numbness. How many had there been?

That week of oblivion had scared the hell out of Sean. Jack Murphy had visited him in his dreams, the jeering, wasted face taunting him to follow in his father's alcoholic footsteps.

Desperately, Sean had crawled his way out of that emotional wasteland and had never traveled the road to love again. There had been other women since then, but none had found their way through the convoluted maze to his heart.

"You're a good friend, Brian, and I appreciate your concern," Sean said sincerely, but with a dismissive tone. "Fax me those contracts and I'll look them over. You can handle things for a while longer. That's why you're my Executive V.P. Just don't move into my office, okay?"

"What if you can't leave her, Sean?" Brian tried again. "What if you just can't walk away?"

Brian voiced the question that had plagued Sean since the night he'd come face-to-face with his daughter. "I don't know."

The whispered words hung heavily in the air.

~ * ~

Boston's most eligible bachelor stood at Hannah's door with a bunch of flowers in his hand. Sean chuckled to himself. When was the last time he'd given a woman a bouquet, especially one bought in the floral department of the local grocery store?

The society editor of the *Boston Globe* would have a field day, Sean mused, as he imagined the caption under his picture standing in front of this dilapidated bungalow. *This Is The Bachelor of Beacon Hill??*

He rang the doorbell.

Hannah's telephone call three days earlier had come totally out of the blue. He'd had visions of having to woo her little by little, using every ounce of his practiced charm. Yet, she had changed her mind, and while he wasn't about to analyze her motives, his curiosity was definitely aroused.

The flowers had been a last minute thought even if it was a bit calculated. He'd almost bought a dozen roses, then decided no.

Something inexpensive for the first date. Women loved to get flowers, right?

Tory opened the door with a jerk and Sean smiled at his only child. A surge of love jolted his heart, a reaction fast becoming more and more common every time he saw her.

"Hi, Sean... oops." She looked over her shoulder. "I mean, Mr. Murphy." She giggled when he winked at her, then stood back, inviting him to come in. Her ebony hair was pulled back into a ponytail and she was dressed in the teenage uniform of shorts, tennis shoes and T-shirt. He'd never noticed kids before as they had never been a part of his world. Now he noticed them all the time, the way they dressed and spoke and acted. Their fresh outlook on life and naïve enthusiasm made him wonder if he'd ever, even once, been so young and carefree.

"Those are so pretty," she exclaimed. "Are they for me?"

Sean raised his brows and scrambled for an answer. He hadn't thought to bring Tory flowers, too. Thinking fast, he picked out the only rose.

"For you," he said, bowing as he handed it to her.

Tory sniffed the pale pink bud and he wished he had a camera to capture the image, a frame of youthful innocence. "Gee, thanks."

He stood watching her, the urge to hug so strong, he had to step away from her in defense. "You'd better put that in some water," he suggested.

"Okay." She headed to the kitchen and over her shoulder she added, "I'm ready to go, but Mom is still getting ready."

Frowning slightly, Sean wondered what she meant by that remark, then decided she was probably going to a friend's house for the evening.

As he waited, Sean looked around the small living room. The walls needed painting and there were several cracks in the wallboard, but even with only the few pieces of functional furniture and inexpensive accessories, he could see a definite flair for decorating. Everything was neat, clean and comfortable. Homey. Definitely homey. Was that baked beans he smelled?

Hearing Hannah's footsteps, he quickly hid the flowers behind his back.

"Hi, Sean," Hannah greeted him. She entered the room cocking her head to one side to fasten an earring, a gesture he found strangely provocative.

"I'm sorry I'm late. I got caught with a builder and..." She stopped in mid-sentence. "Flowers," she said as he pulled them from behind his back. "They're beautiful."

The warm surprise in her voice matched the look on her face. She buried her nose in the petals, closed her eyes and inhaled the perfumed scent. "No one has given me flowers in a long time," she admitted with a rueful chuckle. "It was very thoughtful of you. I'll get a vase."

You're good, Murphy. He mentally patted himself on the back. The last-minute idea had worked like a charm. A few more like that, and he'd have her eating out of his hand.

But her open look of appreciation also revealed a measure of vulnerability, a weak spot that for a second, he felt guilty exploiting.

When she returned with the vase in her hands, he took in her appearance with a critical eye. She wore a floor length shift in a green floral print that outlined her slim figure to perfection. He preferred long hair, but her short pixie style complimented the shape of her face and he decided not too many women could pull it off. If she wore makeup, he couldn't tell and the big loop earrings added just the right, sexy touch. Casual but elegant. An intriguing combination that brought about an unwanted tug in the pit of his stomach.

"I made reservations at Delaney's for dinner. Someone told me it's small and quiet and the food is excellent." But his hopes of impressing her died in seconds when he saw her hesitate and noticed a slight tinge of pink brush her cheeks.

"Oh. Well, I thought we might do something different tonight. Our church puts on a Wednesday night supper, and since you're new here on the Island, Tory and I thought it would be a good way for you to meet some people." Her brows rose in question and she waited, wringing her hands nervously.

With a suave smile, he hid his chagrin at being so unexpectedly out-maneuvered. So much for an intimate dinner for two.

"Now you're the thoughtful one," he said. "I appreciate that. And maybe afterward we could have a drink somewhere."

She let out a breath. "I'm sorry, I can't. Once we get back, Tory has homework to finish."

It dawned on him. "Tory's... coming... too."

"I hope you don't mind."

"Hey," he answered with a shrug, "no problem. It'll be fun." He tried to sound convincing.

"Great. Tory," she called, "we're ready to go." She grabbed her purse and went to open the door. "Oh, I almost forgot the baked beans."

"We wouldn't want to forget that," he mumbled, under his breath.

"I'm sorry?"

"Uh... I said we wouldn't want to be late."

"I'll just be a minute," she assured him.

Baked beans. Church supper. Not exactly what he had in mind.

Oh, what the hell, he thought. The beans smelled delicious.

~ * ~

Why am I doing this?

Hannah sat in the front seat of Sean's Explorer, her sweaty palms leaving damp marks on her dress where she placed them on her knees. She tried unsuccessfully to take control of the butterflies that marched through her stomach with all the precision of a Marine platoon.

Driving down Frederica Road, Tory kept Sean's attention with an abundance of teenage chatter, while Hannah wondered if she'd regret accepting his invitation.

He'd taken it well, she admitted, even though she could tell the change in plans from a dinner for two to a dinner for many hadn't been on his agenda.

And then to bring my daughter? What was I thinking?

You were thinking, a defensive voice inside her rebutted, *that you're tired of being alone and you wanted to have some fun. Anything wrong with that?*

Hannah gave an inward sigh. Even if he never asked her out again, she was determined to enjoy the evening. Besides, her Good Samaritan side reasoned, he needed to meet new people and this was as good a way to accomplish that as any. Hannah hoped she could hold on to that rationalization.

When they arrived at the church, Tory ran off with her friends while Sean helped Hannah from the car. He placed a guiding hand in the middle of her back, his touch sending a delicious ripple to the pit of her stomach. Had Paul ever shown such propriety? If he had, the memory was lost on her.

The church sat well off the road, its wooded steeple and tabby construction typical architectural traits of the Island. Huge live oak trees, the state tree of Georgia, surrounded the church, offering sanctuary under its wide spread limbs. Grown only in the coastal areas of the south and southeast, a live oak lived for hundreds of years, thus becoming the Southern symbol of strength.

The serenity made Hannah realize she'd been away too long. Sunday services had always given her a sense of peace and belonging. A sense of connection. It was the firm ground under her very unstable existence.

Many church members had already arrived. The women placed bowls and platters on tables covered in red-and-white checked tablecloths and the men grouped around the handmade barbecue pit, grilling the usual summer fare of hot dogs, hamburgers and chicken. The smaller children played on swings in the fenced playground while the older ones started a softball game in the adjacent empty lot.

Hannah left Sean for a minute to add her baked beans to the table and when she returned, it surprised her to see him already talking with the minister. A confident air surrounded Sean, not one of arrogance, but an attractive aura of power Hannah found intensely appealing. Dressed in navy slacks and striped tennis polo, his handsome form was definitely easy to look at. *This may well be my only date with him,* she thought, *but he's mine tonight.* And she felt oddly proud.

"Hannah, good to see you," said Reverend Ray Culberth, as she came up behind Sean. "We've missed you."

"I know," Hannah said, apologetically. "I've missed being here. I promise to do better." She turned. "I see you've met Sean Murphy." Sean moved closer to her side and again his hand moved to the small of her back. She noted how the Reverend Ray's brows raised slightly at the gesture, and she didn't know whether to languish in Sean's touch or step away in embarrassment.

"Sean's been telling me he's working for Sam Haverty."

Hannah nodded. "He's giving Tory riding lessons. I thought this would be an opportunity to meet some of his neighbors."

"Good idea. I hope you'll like it here, Sean."

"Oh, I already do, very much," Sean answered, giving Hannah a pointed look.

The preacher took Hannah's hand and said, "You and Tory been doin' all right, Hannah?"

She smiled slightly. "We have our ups and downs, but we're going to be fine."

"How's the business?"

"Getting better and better." She wished it was as good as she made it sound.

"Ann's lookin' to have new draperies in the living room. She'd sure appreciate your help."

"I'd be happy to. I'll call her tomorrow."

"Thanks. And Sean, get out there and meet some more folks. Have yourself a good time. And come to Sunday services. 10:30 a.m."

"Thanks, Reverend, I'll do that."

As they watched the preacher take his turn at the barbecue pit, Sean commented, "Nice guy. And you got a new client. You think you should give her a discount because she's the preacher's wife?"

"Oh, no," Hannah corrected. "I could never charge her or any of the others here if they wanted my help."

"Why not? I was under the impression you were trying to build a business."

She looked into his face, surprised at the touch of criticism in his tone. Nothing showed but curiosity. She must have been mistaken.

"When my husband died, these people gave me and Tory more support than you could imagine. I was never close to my own family and when I needed help with funeral arrangements, they were there. They brought food and even cleaned my house.

"When Tory and I had to move out, they never made us feel embarrassed or pitied. Their kindness was overwhelming."

Hannah glanced out over the group with a warm glow in her heart. "That little place we're living in was really a mess when we first rented it. Some of the men came over and fixed it up. I didn't have to ask, they just showed up.

"So I'm happy to return the favor any way I can." She paused. "You have to admit, people like that are hard to find." When she glanced at him for a response, Hannah found him studying her. His expression held more than mere interest. It was almost searching, as if he wanted to peer into her soul for a glimpse at what really made her tick.

A long second passed. "Sean?"

"You're right." He stood straighter as if to shake himself from an intense concentration. "You couldn't find better people."

Before Hannah could dwell on his strange behavior, she heard an authoritative voice.

"Hannah Stevens. I'm very disappointed in you."

Tall and erect with permed blue-gray hair, the elderly lady stood with hands laced together, shoulders squared.

"Oh, Edith," Hannah said, giving the woman a peck on the cheek. "It's so good to see you. I'd like you to meet..."

Edith gave Sean a quick glance. "I'll get to him in a minute. Where have you been? I haven't seen you in weeks."

Hannah knew the woman's verbal raking was more concern than criticism. "I've been so busy trying to get my decorating business off the ground, there doesn't seem to be much time for other things."

"You know what they say about all work and no play, young lady. Besides, we miss you in the choir." The matron turned her attention to Sean. "Now, who is this?"

"Sean, I'd like you to meet Mrs. Edith Hayes, one of the founding members of our church. Edith, this is Sean Murphy."

Sean bowed in a courtly fashion and brought her hand to his lips. Hannah smothered a chuckle as Edith, her eyes wide and big as silver dollars, gasped, sputtered and turned crimson. However, Hannah noticed the older woman didn't retrieve her hand.

"Well," she said primly, regaining a modicum of composure, "how very gallant. But I hope you're not wasting all this charm on old ladies. What are your intentions?"

It was Sean's turn to sputter. "My intentions?"

"Yes. Are you courting our Hannah?"

"Well, I..."

"Edith," Hannah interjected, coming to Sean's rescue, "Sean moved here recently. He's a friend of mine."

"I see." She nodded, pursed her lips. "I hope you're a *good* friend to Hannah, Mr. Murphy. She's very special to us."

Sean shifted his gaze to Hannah. "I'd like to be more than a friend, if she'd let me."

Hannah's smile faltered for a split second as her heart skipped a beat. What did he mean by that?

"If you're lucky, she'll let you." Edith turned to leave, and grinned as if pleased at the silent interchange between the couple. Bending down, she whispered into Hannah's ear. "I'd keep this one if I were you. He's *hot.*"

Hannah almost choked on a laugh. Yes, Sean Murphy was definitely hot. Maybe a little too hot. Another case of nerves hit her stomach.

As Edith walked away, Sean turned to stand in front of Hannah. He didn't touch her, at least not with his hand. His warm blue eyes, however, rooted her to the ground. "What do you think, Hannah? Could we be more than friends?"

A trickle of perspiration worked its way down her back. She opened her mouth, but nothing came out. Oh, how she wanted to say yes. But something held her back. At that moment, she saw the minister raise his hand for the blessing. "Time to eat," she said.

Sean's expression told her their discussion was far from over.

Within seconds, everyone attacked the mounds of potato salad, slaw and desserts. Tory came up and slipped between Hannah and Sean with an empty plate in her hand. When they reached the end of the buffet line, Sean, his plate piled high, looked at Tory's dinner and frowned.

"Is that all you're going to eat?"

Two deviled eggs, a roll, and jello salad sat on the Styrofoam plate like two eyes, a nose and a mouth.

Tory nodded.

"What about some vegetables?" He looked down the table. "Or something green?"

Tory glanced at her plate. "The jello's green."

Hannah saw him raise a brow.

"So it is," he said.

"I make sure she takes vitamins," Hannah told him, but he still looked dubious.

They watched Tory find a seat with her friends, then found two seats for themselves at one of the long tables.

Hannah made introductions but she didn't have to worry about a topic of conversation. Sean slipped into the flow, shaking hands, answering questions and laughing when teased about his Boston brogue. His pronunciation of "park the car in Harvard Yard" got a laugh more than once.

After dinner, while Hannah plastic-wrapped the leftovers, she found herself watching Sean as he helped dismantle tables and collect garbage. He fit in with ease, didn't stand apart as an outsider, and Hannah wondered why that pleased her so much.

"I don't blame you," said a mother of five who'd snuck up behind her. "I'd keep my eyes on him, too. He is *something else*." When Hannah explained Sean was just a friend, the woman's "uh huh, right" look was like all the others she had encountered that evening.

Ten minutes later, Hannah felt a hand on her elbow and a warm breath close to her ear. "Is there something I can do for you?" Sean asked, peering over her shoulder. A polite question, helpful, even innocuous. Yet, she shivered when a highly charged current danced over her skin as if he electrified the air around her.

I have to stop reacting to him like this.

"Thanks, but I think I have it under control." She took a deep breath. "So. Tell me who you've met."

"Well, let's see," Sean answered, steering her away from Tupperware and plastic spoons toward a wooded pathway that led to a garden sanctuary. Azaleas and camellia bushes spread under the protective arms of old, live oaks and in the center stood a monument to John and Charles Wesley, the founders of Methodism. They sat on a wrought iron bench, Hannah keeping her distance.

"First, there was Joe Summers. He filled me in on the local politics and gave me his stand on everything from the water treatment plant to beach erosion."

Hannah nodded and said, "He's up for re-election for County Commissioner."

"Then there was Alvis Jenkins. He asked me if I was interested in insects. Said he had a collection of over four hundred different types of bugs he'd be happy to show me."

She found it hard to contain a smile. "A little eccentric, but sweet."

"And I met a woman by the name of Lila Luvalotte." Sean made a face. "That's not her real name." His statement doubled as a question.

"It is," Hannah assured him, with a chuckle.

"She asked me how old I was, and what I did for a living, and what my favorite foods were. All the while checking out my left hand."

His brows did a cute little jumping thing she found adorable. "Uh oh, better be careful. Lila's a divorcee. Sounds to me like she's on the prowl." His feigned look of horror made her laugh outright.

"And all evening, I've had to side-step Mrs. Edith Hayes. Her eyes narrowed every time she looked at me. I couldn't decide if she was giving me the evil eye or trying to focus."

"Probably a little of both. She's being protective, that's all."

"I'm teasing," Sean said, his smile one of understanding. "They all seem to be very concerned about you."

Hannah saw that look again, as if he was trying to figure something out.

He leaned forward, his arm resting on the back of the bench, his fingers touching her shoulder. His gaze captured hers and like a hypnotic spell, she couldn't break away. *He's going to kiss me.*

"Mr. Murphy? Mr. Murphy, where are you?"

Sean kept his eyes locked on hers, then backed away slowly as Tory and two friends ran up.

"We're starting another softball game and we need a pitcher," Tory said, breathlessly. "Can you pitch?"

"Can I pitch? Why, you're looking at the best right-hander to ever come out of South Boston." He stood, turned to Hannah and pulled her off the seat. "Come on, you can be our cheerleader."

Sean was a good pitcher, she decided, as she watched him strike out parents and kids alike. He laughed, encouraged the not-so-good batters and argued good-naturedly on a close call at second base. She'd seen him listen with interest and join in conversations with church members and help when there was work to be done. He was charming, she thought, handsome, personable, and polite...

And he's interested in me.

That realization alternately thrilled and scared the daylights out of her. Yet, having fun with a man, being able to lean on him, trust him, were luxuries she wasn't sure she could afford. She'd done that once.

Admittedly, she'd gone through many a lonely night, lying in bed, wishing someone would hold her, love her. Sometimes she'd wake in the morning ashamed of her dreams, the ones that left her curled up like a snake, trembling, her insides exploding, heart pounding. That's when she wished there was a real man next to her, stroking her to fulfillment. Sometimes, the emptiness was unbearable.

Hannah whistled and clapped as the game ended victoriously for Tory and Sean's team. Sean put his arm around Tory and gave her a hug as the two of them walked toward her. It pleased her to see Tory smiling and having a good time. If Sean had something to do with that, then Hannah was grateful.

Yet, seeing them together, standing so close, bothered her in a small, indefinable way. Was she jealous, or was she afraid Tory would see him as a replacement for the father she'd lost?

"That was a great game," Hannah congratulated.

"Mr. Murphy's a great pitcher," Tory said excitedly. "That's why we won."

"Just the luck of the Irish tonight," Sean explained. "Did you see Tory hit that double? And catch that line drive?"

"I sure did." Hannah pushed a stray strand of hair behind Tory's ear. In that second she thought he sounded exactly like Paul, the proud father extolling the virtues of his child.

"Mom, April asked if I can spend the night. Can I?"

"No, honey. You've got homework to finish."

"I can finish it at her house."

Hannah shook her head. "Not tonight, honey."

"But she's invited a couple of other girls, too."

"On a school night?"

"So? Ple..ee..se?"

"Tory, you know you don't go out on school nights. That's always been the rule."

"Can't you make an exception? Just this once?"

"Tory," Hannah said, with a quiet warning, "no more discussion. The answer is no."

Tory's pleading face vanished in an instant. Her lips pressed into a thin line, eyes narrowed in anger. "You never let me do anything."

Hannah's eyes flew open at the vehemence in her daughter's voice. "Stop that," she said, sharply.

"No, I won't. You're mean and I hate you!"

Before Hannah could react, Tory stomped off, leaving Hannah stunned and mortified. She lowered her head and sighed. She was used to Tory's mood swings, but this was something else. What was bothering her?

Hannah mumbled an apology to Sean and went after Tory. Had she seen Sean's grim expression, it would have added to her list of worries.

Six

The uneven cadence of frogs and crickets filled the open windows as all three rode the several miles home in silence. Although Sean tried to draw Tory into a discussion of her upcoming riding competition, her answers were monosyllabic.

Hannah responded a little better to his attempts at conversation but he could tell her mind was elsewhere.

When he pulled into the crushed shell driveway, Tory wasted no time stomping into the house. Hannah followed with her eyes, then let out an audible sigh and shook her head. "I apologize for her behavior."

Sean didn't answer right away. He turned and leaned his back against the door, his left arm draped over the wheel. His first instinct was to defend Tory. He'd never seen her act so ugly, but then, he reasoned Hannah must have done something to bring about such a radical change in his daughter. Somehow, without causing suspicion, he had to find out.

"Does Tory do that often? I mean, I'm not an authority on kids, but why did she react that way?"

"I think part of it is being thirteen."

"You think? Aren't mothers supposed to know these things?" He hoped his chuckle covered the accusation that tipped his tongue.

"Contrary to popular belief, mothers aren't all-wise or all-knowing. I wish we were." She rubbed a spot above her eye. "Truth is, it's trial and error. You learn a little every day, but not quite enough for the next day."

She sounded sincere and he admitted, even troubled. But he didn't want a philosophical quip.

"Thank you for putting up with us, Sean," she said, as she started to open the door. "I know a church supper wasn't what you had in mind tonight. I hope it didn't ruin your evening."

He reached out and held her arm. "The only way you could ruin my evening is by saying goodnight." He couldn't let her go, not without learning more about her relationship with Tory. "May I come in for a cup of coffee?"

She took a moment to answer and then a slow smile formed on her face. "All right."

Coming around the Explorer, he helped her out and followed her inside. "Where did Tory go?" he asked, not seeing her, but spotting an empty backpack in a corner.

Hannah looked down the short hallway. "She's in her room, hopefully doing her homework. I'll check on her in a minute." She went to the kitchen and pulled out the coffeemaker.

"I'll do that," he offered, "while you look in on Tory."

"Oh, okay. Coffee's in the fridge and filters are in that cabinet."

He made the coffee and rummaged around, finding spoons and two stained, chipped mugs. Then he found the sugar and took out the milk jug from the refrigerator.

Ten minutes later, Tory appeared while Hannah hung back, arms crossed and brows raised in anticipation.

"I'm sorry I acted like that," Tory apologized to Sean, her eyes downcast.

His heart melted instantly and he had to stop his hand from tilting her chin up and looking into eyes so like Angie's.

"Apology accepted." He paused. "Hey, we really beat the pants off the other team tonight, didn't we?"

His attempt to lighten her mood worked easily. "Yeah, that was great. Thanks to you."

Sean winked at her. "You'd better finish your homework. Will I see you after school tomorrow?"

Tory nodded.

"Good," he said in a semi-serious tone. "The stables need to be mucked out."

She made a face, but added, "I've almost got enough money for my entry fee for the competition. I can't wait." With that she said good night and walked past Hannah without a word.

The smell of coffee filled the room and only the drip of the coffeemaker broke the silence.

Hannah exchanged the mugs for two cups and saucers and poured milk into a small pitcher, a feminine touch that wasn't lost on Sean.

"You seem to be good with kids," Hannah said, handing him his cup. "Do you have any of your own?"

Yes, I do. "I've never been married. Came close once, but it didn't work out." They sat on the chintz-covered sofa, Hannah at one end, Sean at the other. "But I like working with my students. It's a new experience for me."

"Oh? What did you do before?"

He shrugged. "A little of this, a little of that. I dabbled in finances." The understatement of the century. The Murphy Group was one of the biggest financial institutions in the northeast. "Is Tory still angry with you?" he asked, deftly steering Hannah's interest away from him.

"Probably. But she'll get over it." Sean thought he heard her mumble "I hope" but couldn't be sure.

"You don't allow her out on school nights?"

"No."

"Why not?" *So what if Tory wanted to spend the night with a friend,* he thought. *Was that such a big deal?*

Hannah gave him a strange look and he hoped he hadn't pushed to far.

"I've learned it's not a good practice to get into unless it's a school function. I wouldn't know what time she got to bed or if she finished her homework and finished it correctly."

"She's a good student, isn't she?" Her obvious strictness began to annoy him.

Hannah nodded. "For the most part. But the past year has been tough on her. She was very close to her father and his death has left her struggling."

I'm her father. It hit him then, an irrational combination of compassion for his daughter and jealousy of Hannah, and he suddenly realized how difficult it was going to be keeping his real identity to himself.

"And now that she's becoming a teenager, she has to deal with a lot of changes, both mentally and physically."

He frowned. "What do you mean?"

"Well," she said, as if stating a well-known precept, "all adolescents go through the raging hormone stage. I'm sure you remember that," she added, regarding him with amusement.

Sean grunted. The only thing he remembered was trying to avoid his father's fists.

"And because of all these changes, I've tried to keep our communication open." She placed her cup on the table. "It works... usually."

Sean saw the troubled line on her forehead again. There was something more here. Something she wasn't telling him. "And how does Mom handle all of this?"

A tired smile appeared on her face. "With as much patience and understanding as possible. Although I'll admit, sometimes it's not easy. Especially when I'm trying to make a living."

He sipped his coffee. "How's that going?"

"We're getting by. We have a roof over our heads and food on the table. It's just going to take some time to build up my clientele. Which reminds me," she said, glancing at her watch. "I have an early appointment tomorrow."

So keen was he on collecting every piece of information, it took him a minute to catch her meaning. "Oh, right." He gathered up their cups and set them in the sink. "I hope Tory doesn't stay angry with you for long," Sean said, as she walked him to the door.

"She'll be fine. I'll pick her up at the stables around five tomorrow."

"She's really looking forward to her first competition. Will you be there?"

"Of course. I wouldn't miss it." Unspoken love and pride glowed in her soft brown eyes, and Sean found himself envying her parental status.

"Thank you for tonight, Hannah. I enjoyed meeting your friends."

Her mouth curled up on one side in a sheepish grin. "Really?"

"Really." Folding his arms across his chest, Sean lounged lazily against the door jam and found it impossible not to return her disarming smile. "But next time, I'd like to take you some place where we won't have so much company." He saw a light of pleasant surprise cross her face. He *had* to be sure she'd see him again. There was much more he needed to find out.

"Next time?"

He nodded. "That is, if you'd like to." Purposely, he lowered his voice to a sexy level. He watched her swallow.

"Yes, I'd like that."

Her whispered words pulled him closer as she stared up at him, lips parted, inviting, expectant, tempting. In the next few silent seconds, he began to lose himself in the gentle glow of her eyes and the way her high cheekbones sat in a perfectly oval face. His gaze dropped to her mouth and he itched to trace the pink contour with his finger.

Something intense flared up inside him.

He imagined how soft her lips would feel on his. And it would be easy. Just one kiss to relieve himself of this sudden craving to put his hands all over her.

He fought through a haze of desire. This wasn't part of the plan.

Abruptly, he pulled back from an invisible brink and put some distance between them. "I'd better go."

He took a step back and almost fell down the front stairs. Feeling like a fool, he gave Hannah a lame wave and climbed into the Explorer. He turned on the airconditioner full blast—*damn, was it always this hot in September?*—and waved again as he backed out. The plastic smile on his face belied the pounding in his chest.

It took five miles and a cup of black 7-Eleven sludge for his vitals to return to normal.

She fell for it, he admitted, with only an ounce of satisfaction. In fact, after that episode at her door, the self-confidence he'd started this charade with gave way to uncertainty. How could he explain his reaction to her? Had his practiced come-on backfired? He shook his head, trying to rid the memory of her from the edges of his mind.

He grabbed for a reason, something to explain his behavior and quickly chalked it up to not having been with a woman in a long time. That was it. Had to be.

Straighten up, Murphy. If this is going to work, you'd better stop thinking with your glands, he chastised himself. *Tory's welfare is at stake.*

Seven

Hannah smelled dry grass and horse manure through the airconditioning vent the minute she pulled into the crowded fairgrounds. She glanced hurriedly at her watch, then took a deep breath. Fifteen minutes to spare. She'd pushed the speed limit all the way over the Brunswick River and down I-95 to the small town of Kingsland, hoping she wouldn't draw the attention of a state trooper. Hannah tried not to work on Saturdays, especially this particular Saturday, but it was unavoidable. Still, she'd made it without being late.

She mentally thanked old Mildred Peevy for making a quick decision on wallpaper for her bathroom, then turned off the car—and cringed. The engine knocked, shook and hissed before coming to a premonitory standstill. She dropped her head on the steering wheel. "Come on, car," she whined. "Don't die on me."

Tomorrow. She'd think about it tomorrow. As she opened the door, her attention was drawn to the car pulling in beside her and instantly her spirits rose.

"Hi, Marsha," Hannah called, stepping out into a swirl of red Georgia dust that sent dirt clouds exploding over her sandals. "I didn't think you'd be able to come. You didn't close the store, did you?"

Marsha shuddered. "No. I left that nitwit Shelley in charge. God help me, she'll probably put me out of business before noon." She gave Hannah a hug then added, "I did want to see Tory ride." She paused. "And I wanted to meet your new boyfriend."

"He's not my boyfriend," Hannah insisted as they walked toward the crowd gathered around the center ring.

"From what you've told me, he certainly sounds interested."

"Well, maybe, I guess."

"Did he ask you out again?"

"No."

"Well, get with it, young lady. He's going to think you're *not* interested."

Hannah rolled her eyes, yet Marsha's words started her thinking. What if she was right? Perhaps Hannah should show Sean she wanted to see him again. But how to do that was beyond her. Should she dress provocatively? Make suggestive comments? She almost laughed at that uncharacteristic picture. Just be yourself, her common sense dictated. Besides, she had too much on her mind and too little time in her life to worry about her lack of feminine wiles.

"So, do you like him?" Marsha prodded.

"What's not to like? He's gorgeous, charming, my daughter's crazy about him, and when he comes within two feet of me, my knees start to knock."

"Hmm. Is that a romantic response or a case of rickets?"

Hannah laughed. "Who knows? With my limited experience, I probably wouldn't recognize the difference." She thought a moment. "I do enjoy his company, but you know, I don't know much about him. Every time I ask him a personal question, he changes the subject so smoothly, I end up telling him something about myself."

"Ooh, a mystery man. Wouldn't you love to find out his secrets?"

"Oh, most likely there's nothing to it," Hannah remarked, trying to ignore the annoying itch at the back of her mind. "No doubt he's a very private person. Nothing wrong with that."

She hoped.

They walked carefully among horses and riders and spotted Tory standing in a circle with April, Sarah, and several of Sean's other riding students. In the middle was a young woman dressed in boots, jeans, and blue chambray shirt.

"Who's that?" Marsha asked.

"Her name is Jackie Driggers. Sean hired her to give lessons."

Marsha raised an eyebrow. "Jealous?"

"Don't be silly." Hannah did, however, feel considerably more comfortable with a female presence at the stable. And she had liked Jackie right off. A country girl complete with a drawl of lazy i's and homespun similes, she reminded Hannah of a way of life left behind long ago.

The closer they got to the group of girls, the bigger the lump grew in Hannah's throat. Tory looked so mature in her riding outfit, so close to bridging the gap between child and young lady. Wasn't it only yesterday she and Paul had brought her home from the adoption agency? Soon the boys would start calling, then high school and college. And Tory *would* go to college, Hannah vowed, if she had to work night and day to make it so.

A sweet ache enveloped her heart as she gazed at the center of her world. The years were passing too quickly and she wished she could slow down the clock.

"Hi, Mrs. Stevens," Jackie said, as the two women joined the group. "I was giving the girls some last minute pointers."

"Hi, Jackie." Hannah saw Tory's expression brighten but it wasn't directed at her.

"Hey, Miss Marsha," Tory greeted Hannah's friend. "I didn't know you were coming."

"What? And miss the chance to see you win that blue ribbon?" Marsha gave Tory a hug. "No way."

"Don't count on it," Tory grumbled.

"They're all about as nervous as a bunch of pigs at a barbecue," Jackie explained, making the girls giggle. "Y'all have enough time to get something to drink before things get started. Hurry back."

"Tory," Hannah called as the girls walked off, "come here a minute." She ignored the look of impatience. "I just wanted to wish you luck."

"You promised you wouldn't work today," Tory shot at her. "You said you'd ride here with us. April's mom did."

Hannah sighed. "I'm sorry, honey," she apologized, but the guilt pinched her conscience anyway. "It couldn't be helped."

"You always say that." She turned. "I've got to go."

"Wait a minute," Hannah ordered. "Marsha, would you excuse us?" Hannah took Tory's reluctant arm and drew her around the side of the concession stand.

"Listen to me. You know it's not easy for us. I have to work, sometimes a lot, so we can have a place to live. I hate having to work so much because it takes me away from you."

Tory looked at the ground, her lips tight.

"It was wrong of me to promise because I had to end up breaking it. And for that, I'm very sorry. Next time I'll say I'll do my best. But I *am* here," she said with a smile. Hannah's coaxing died in the face of Tory's pouting silence. She braced herself and tried once more.

"Tory, I know you're angry with me for something. I don't know what it is, but whatever I did, I'm sorry. Maybe you'll tell me when you feel the time is right, but I'd never, ever, do anything to intentionally hurt you."

Hannah's hands slid down to Tory's and she held Tory's fingers in her own. "I love you, honey. More than life itself. You're everything to me. I know things have been tough since Daddy died, but they *will* get better. And that I *can* promise you."

Hannah waited, the silence stretching to uncomfortable. When Tory raised her head with a tear sliding down her cheek, Hannah's heart broke.

"Oh, Mom," Tory cried, throwing her arms around Hannah's neck. "I love you, too. I'm sorry for being such a brat lately."

Hannah squeezed her eyes shut, feeling the prick of her own tears. "It's all right, honey."

"I didn't mean it. Honest. It's just that when I found out..."

She felt Tory tense and gently pushed her away. "Found out? Found out what?"

Tory hesitated, shook her head. "Nothing. I'm just sorry."

"It's okay." A wave of relief swept over Hannah. Finally, a breakthrough even if only a small one. She couldn't imagine what Tory had found out, but at the moment, it didn't matter. She had her daughter back. "Here, we'd better put your hair up."

"And you have to pin this number on the back of my shirt," Tory added, wiping her face with her sleeve. "I'm kinda nervous."

"You'll do fine."

"Mr. Murphy said I was his best student."

"He did, huh?"

Tory nodded. "He said I'm good enough to win a blue ribbon."

"Just do your best. That's the important thing." She paused. "Is he here? Mr. Murphy?" She finished the pinning, hoping she sounded sufficiently nonchalant.

"Yeah. He went to make sure we were all registered."

"Oh. Well, good. We'd better get a move on. It's almost time to start."

"Okay." Tory reached out and took Hannah's hand, but Hannah needed more than that. She squeezed an arm around Tory's shoulders, feeling happier than she had in weeks.

~ * ~

At Jackie's suggestion, Sean headed to the concession stand to find Hannah and Tory, but when he didn't see them, he bought a soft drink and surveyed the crowd, wondering if he'd missed them. By chance, he glanced around the corner and his world seemed to fall into place at the sight of them. He almost called out but instinctively, something stopped him. Frowning, he stepped back slowly, not wanting to catch their attention.

Hannah and Tory stood in the shadows of the building, their body language telling him a serious conversation was underway. Sean wasn't an eavesdropper, but the temptation was too compelling. He stood with his back to the wall and listened.

And what he heard left him with emotions so diverse his stomach clenched in confusion.

Any doubts he might have had of Hannah's love for Tory vanished as her heartfelt words reached his ears. Perhaps he'd known that all along, but refused to acknowledge it. A sad smile tugged at his mouth at Tory's "I love you, too" and he peered carefully around the corner in time to see her fling herself into Hannah's waiting arms.

The bittersweet image sent a bullet to his heart.

He turned back, stunned by their closeness, a closeness that made him a stranger, an intruder.

Suddenly, his mission here lacked purpose, his goal not so clearly defined, and for the first time, he looked more closely at his motives. Had he come here deliberately to find fault with Hannah? Was he really seeing to the welfare of his daughter? Or was he directing his misplaced anger at Hannah, anger at being kept in the dark all these years?

Sean lost himself in the crowd when he heard them approach, and unseen, he watched them. Even with telltale puffy eyes, Tory's smile glowed, and there was no mistaking Hannah's love. It shined in her eyes, weighed in her touch.

Although they had only each other, Hannah and Tory were a family, Sean admitted with envy, although not the kind of family he'd ever experienced. Despite their problems, the lack of money, the loss of a husband and father, their love held them together.

They must have resolved their quarrel, whatever it had been, and he was glad for them. On the other hand, that resolution prompted a hollow emptiness inside. Never had he felt so alone or excluded. It took every ounce of self-control to stay rooted to the ground because he desperately wanted to be on the receiving end of the love they shared.

Sean walked from out of the crowd and stared after them. The bond between mother and daughter was almost tangible, so strong that it hit him with all the force of a sledge hammer. An irrational sadness bubbled up in his chest at the thought of being on the outside of Tory's life, always looking in. He swallowed hard, and held the feeling at bay.

Damn stupid thought, he decided determinedly. He had his own bond with Tory. Maybe not like Hannah's, but blood bonds were strong, too, weren't they?

The harder he might have tried to ignore the truth about Tory, the more it now persisted. She was in his life to stay; he'd never leave her.

And what about Hannah? Rubbing a hand over his mouth, he wondered if she represented the one truth he wasn't ready to admit.

~ * ~

Puffy white clouds dotted the sky, looking like stepping stones of cotton in a sea of brilliant blue. The sun covered the two riding rings in a blanket of heat that not even the hint of a fall breeze could break.

Hannah sat in the stands, her sun hat and sunglasses providing barely enough protection from the elements. The dressage competition was about to get started in the front ring, and she positioned herself in a choice seat with a perfect view. Tory pulled number eighteen out of a group of twenty-five, with each competitor having to walk, trot and canter their horse. With a long day ahead, Hannah wished she'd changed into shorts.

Hannah hadn't seen Marsha since leaving her with Jackie, but as she read the program, her friend came up with two drinks and handed her one. "Listen," she said, as Hannah took a sip of the cool, sharp lemonade, "if you decide Mr. Sean Murphy isn't for you, let me know and I'll take him off your hands."

Hannah threw her a bland, skeptical smile. "A little young for you, isn't he?"

Marsha didn't take offense. "Honey, they're never too young," she zinged back with a wink. "He's a real looker. And *so* charming."

"Where did you see him?"

"He came up when I was talking to Jackie and asked where you and Tory were. I introduced myself and we chatted for a moment, but he seemed very anxious to find you."

Hannah had wanted to see him, too, but when she had, at ringside after wishing Tory luck, Sean had acknowledged her presence with a brief smile and an almost curt nod. His gesture surprised her. Expecting something a lot more cordial, she'd turned away, confused and more than a little irked.

"Did he?" Marsha asked.

"Did he what?"

"Find you."

Hannah nodded. "I ran into him at the ring, but he didn't seem too interested to see me."

Marsha raised her eyebrows, her mouth turning down. "Maybe he was preoccupied." She paused. "You know, with the competition and all."

Hannah shrugged. "It doesn't matter." She picked up the program and pretended to read, hoping Marsha didn't see how much it did matter.

His brush-off made her mad on the surface and dented her self-confidence underneath. She didn't know what to make of it and it only confirmed her earlier thoughts that dating wasn't for her.

Hannah tried to push Sean to the back of her mind as the announcer called the first rider into the ring. To Hannah's untrained eye, each girl looked no different from the next and she wondered how the judges scored each event.

Instructors took to the fence, calling out encouragement when their pupils rode past. Hannah noticed Sean was no different when April and Sarah took their turns. Maybe he had been preoccupied, Hannah thought, wanting to give him the benefit of the doubt.

By the time Tory's number was called, Hannah's motherly anticipation turned into a sour stomach and the beginnings of a headache. Then she swallowed a gasp as Tory came out on a golden horse, so huge it made Tory look like a midget on an elephant. Was Sean crazy? Tory wasn't experienced enough to handle such a huge animal. She grabbed Marsha's arm.

"Oh, my God, look at that horse!"

"Beautiful, isn't he?" Marsha responded, obviously misinterpreting Hannah's meaning.

"He's too big for Tory! She's only thirteen, Marsha. She can't handle such a big animal. What is the matter with Sean? Has he lost his mind?"

She started to stand but Marsha held her down. "What are you doing?"

"I'm going out there and get her off that horse before she gets killed!"

"Hannah, wait a minute. I'm sure Sean wouldn't let her on a horse she couldn't control. Do you really think he would? Or Jackie? Besides, if you make a scene, Tory will never forgive you. You know how much she's been looking forward to this."

Silently cursing Sean, Hannah sat down, her heart in her throat as Tory went through her routine. It took a while, but Hannah's pulse slowed as she watched the horse respond to Tory's commands and although her daughter seemed to be in control, Hannah made a mental note to speak to Sean about his judgment.

"I hope he's not making her nervous," Hannah heard Marsha remark. "He says something to her every time she goes by him." Hannah shifted her attention to Sean. He stood on the lowest fence rail and she could hear him remind Tory to keep her back straight, hands low, legs back, watch her diagonal. How was the child supposed to concentrate with him badgering her?

"Just leave her alone," Hannah murmured, irritation mounting. It struck her once again that Sean showed Tory an inordinate amount of attention, acting like a father at a little league game. He hadn't prompted April or Sarah so intently. Why not? Perhaps it had been his previous casual greeting that had spurred her uneasiness, but Hannah's original suspicions of him crept over her again. This time, Hannah decided, she wanted answers.

Fifteen minutes after the last rider finished her sequence, the judges began calling the six finalists. Hannah hoped Tory would win something, but if not, the exercise was a good life lesson.

When five finalists were called, Hannah's hopes dwindled to disappointment. She sighed and placed the program in her purse, preparing to console her daughter and boost her morale at the same time.

"Come on, Marsha, let's go—" Then she heard the judge's voice call out Tory's number. A cry of relief broke from her lips and she clapped wildly as Tory joined the others in the middle of the ring. Tory was the youngest of the six, Hannah noticed, and the only one of Sean's students. She glanced momentarily at Sean, who clapped and whistled, his enthusiasm surpassing her own.

The judge called out the sixth place winner and by the time the third place winner was announced, Tory still remained. Hannah's pulse quickened. She closed her eyes, crossed her fingers. The silence was intolerable. Then in the span of a second, the judge declared Tory the winner.

Marsha whooped and hollered and Hannah felt the sting of tears. Tory, smile beaming, urged her horse forward, accepted her blue ribbon and held it up for Hannah to see, then turned to show Sean. He whistled through his teeth and pumped a fist in the air. "Way to go, Tory!" he shouted.

For a second, Hannah's smile faltered as she looked at Sean more closely. There was something in his expression that caught her off guard. Pride. So intense, it seemed out of place, almost inappropriate.

Hannah hurried from the stands as if she intuitively detected some unseen danger. Her eyes narrowed when she got to the ring in time to see Sean lift Tory in a bear hug and twirl her around.

A momentary panic she couldn't explain nipped at her heels, propelling her forward in an effort to reach Tory, as if some unexplainable peril loomed nearby.

"Tory," she called out as she reached the gate with Marsha close behind her. Tory released herself from Sean's grasp, apparently not hearing the sharpness in her mother's voice.

"Look, Mom," she said excitedly, holding up the blue ribbon. "I can't believe I won!"

"You looked wonderful, honey. Congratulations." Hannah took her turn and hugged just a little longer than necessary.

Sean's smile made Hannah uneasy as she looked over Tory's shoulder and although she reveled in the euphoria, it was time for a confrontation.

"Are you hungry, honey?"

"Starving."

"Marsha, would you take her to get something to eat? I'd like to talk to Mr. Murphy."

The look of pride lingered in his eye as he watched Troy walk away. "She did great today, didn't she?"

Hannah nodded. "She does great every day."

Sean's brow furrowed slightly and he cocked his head.

"Don't you think that horse is a little big for her?" Hannah asked.

He shook his head. "No."

"Well, I do. Tory isn't an expert rider."

"I agree, but Apollo is an exceptionally gentle horse. I wouldn't let Tory ride an animal she couldn't control."

He sounded convincing, but the nagging at the back of her mind refused to be stifled. "You seem to be very proud of her."

"Of course I am," Sean replied.

Hannah folded her arms over her chest, nodded. "She's done very well since you've been giving her lessons. I couldn't help but notice how you encouraged her while she rode."

"That's because she's my best student."

"I hope April and Sarah don't feel slighted. They didn't seem to get the same encouragement."

His smile dropped a fraction, brows creasing. "I don't understand what you mean."

Hannah dragged her teeth across her bottom lip, trying to choose her words carefully but falling rapidly into bluntness.

"I just find it a little odd that you show so much attention to Tory and not to your other students."

Something flashed in Sean's blue eyes. "I told you. She's my best student."

Hannah saw his jaw tighten, his face grow hard, and for an instant, a small sadness stung her heart. But protecting her child was more important than her friendship with this man. "Why are you so interested in a thirteen-year-old girl, Sean?" There. She'd said it, the unspoken doubt that had gnawed at her ever since he'd come into their lives.

Hannah watched his eyes grow wide with understanding.

"Do you think I'd hurt her? Do you think I'm some kind of pedophile?"

Hannah didn't shrink from his revolted glare. However, the allegation did sounded crass and revolting, and with the verbalization came a sliver of guilt.

When she didn't answer, Sean said, "That's a pretty strong and pretty low accusation."

"I didn't accuse you of anything."

His laugh was short and harsh. "Oh, no, not in so many words."

"I just want an answer to my question."

"Do you have any evidence of impropriety? Have any of the girls or their parents complained of indiscretions?"

Hannah stood silent.

Sean pursed his lips and nodded. "Don't you think you need some solid proof before you set out to destroy a man's life? Or is the overactive imagination of a paranoid mother enough for you?"

"Sean," she said with a tinge of contriteness. "I'm not imagining the amount of attention you give her."

Sean crossed his arms over his chest, his face a mask of scalding anger. Hannah didn't like the way he seemed to analyze her like he was observing a germ in a Petrie dish.

"You know what I think?" he countered. "I think you're scared. You lost a husband and you're afraid you'll lose Tory, afraid she'll look to me to take his place."

"Well, thank you, Sigmund Freud," she responded, temper beginning to flare. "My, my. A riding instructor *and* a psychologist. What other talents do you have?"

Suddenly, his face took on a different expression. Hannah hadn't known what to expect from him, but disappointment was the last thing she would have anticipated.

"I'd never hurt Tory," he said in a low, powerful voice. "And if I show her more attention than the others, it's because she's a natural on a horse. Because she's a good kid who's lost a father."

His eyes bored into hers. "And because I care about her mother."

He started to walk past her, then stopped so that his shoulder touched hers. "I guess that was a mistake."

Eight

Damn, he was out of shape.

The sand crunched beneath his Nike-clad feet as Sean jogged down the beach at a pace that reminded him it had been much too long since he'd exercised. Really exercised. Mucking out stalls and spreading wood chips hadn't replaced his three times a week at Flanagan's gym.

The low tide offered a wide expanse of firm sand for those few who jogged the beach. Some early morning risers walked, and all made their way through a layer of gray mist that covered the gently lapping surf. The sun climbed slowly over the horizon with a promise to burn off the haze in short order.

Sweat stung Sean's eyes as he came to a stop and leaned over, hands braced on his knees. God, it felt wonderful. Leg muscles screamed, lungs burned. He couldn't remember the last time his heart had pounded so hard.

Well, not exactly, he thought.

It had pounded the night he'd almost kissed Hannah. Pounded like a damn jackhammer.

The strenuous workout purged his spirits as he breathed in a chestful of salty air. He didn't want to think of Hannah today, not today when he felt so good, but she invaded his mind now as she had since the competition. Her accusation still hit hard, still hurt and angered him.

Sean straightened, shook out his legs, then started down the beach again at a steady run, trying hard to stay focused. He should have brought a Walkman to drown her out of his thoughts.

Hannah didn't know he was Tory's father, of course. Yet, how could she even entertain the idea that he'd hurt her child? Or any child? Did he strike her as some kind of deviant? With a disgusted grunt, he slowed his pace to a walk and looked out over the Sound, his good mood slipping into troubled frustration.

She'd misinterpreted his interest in Tory. Misinterpreted love for some kind of sick predatory stalking.

He did love Tory, more than he'd expected possible and now, he'd let his feelings show way too much. However, it was becoming difficult not to.

He turned from the watery view and sat on the rocks that lined the beach at Fifth Street. He tried to resist another realization, tried to think of something else or nothing at all. But the fact was undeniable.

He cared what Hannah thought of him.

How ironic, he admitted with a humorless chuckle. All the years he'd clawed his way to the top, he'd never given a damn who he'd climbed over, or how. Now it mattered what this pixie-faced woman thought of him.

You came here to see if this woman was a good mother, remember?

And if she wasn't? Sean hadn't allowed himself to answer that question, at least not outloud. What would he do, sue for custody?

Suddenly, the idea appalled him. What was he? Some kind of modern day Simon Legree? Could he actually be so callous as to take a child away from its mother?

What he really wanted was to get back into Hannah's good graces. He wanted the warmth of her laugh to make him smile, and see the love that filled her eyes when she looked at Tory.

Sean hadn't seen Hannah since the competition. In deference to her concerns, he'd turned over Tory's lessons to Jackie and countered Tory's disappointment with the promise he'd always be around to monitor her progress and give her pointers. When Hannah had picked up Tory at the stables, Sean had been sure to make himself scarce. As much as he wanted to make amends, the ball was now in Hannah's court, and he'd just have to wait for... something.

He climbed the wooden stairs that led from the beach, stomping the sand from his feet before climbing into the Explorer. It was still early. Maybe he'd stop at the Huddle House for a cup of coffee. The usual group of locals would be there, the plumbers, shrimpers, electricians. Sean had struck up a friendship with them, and he enjoyed the early morning conversations that usually centered around politics and gossip.

Or maybe he should go back to his rented townhouse, go over the paperwork that Brian had faxed to him by the box load. Or he could go to the stables and finish fixing the hay shed. Or, he thought, feeling very sorry for himself, he could pack his bags and leave and forget the past weeks had ever happened.

He pounded the steering wheel. *Don't be stupid, Murphy.*

Traffic was light on Saturday morning as he drove toward the Village and turned right on Mallory Street. The hum of lawn mowers and smell of freshly cut grass drifted through his window on a cool breeze. Autumn would be well underway in Boston by now. He missed the bright colors of maples and birch trees, but St. Simons was a pleasant change from gridlock, pollution and crowds. The tranquility helped to soothe his troubled soul.

Sean slowed his vehicle when he came upon a line of cars parked on the side of the street. A group of people was framing a small house and as he started to drive around, he recognized Hannah's car. Several heads turned at the short screech of tires, and he saw Hannah do a double take when she spotted him. He pulled over, unsure of what to do next.

They looked at each other for a long moment, then Hannah said something to the woman next to her, dropped the hammer from her hand and walked over to him. His pulse rate picked up. She wore a tank top tucked into cut-off jeans, heavy socks and work boots. A handyman's tool bag hung around her waist with a screwdriver sticking out of one pocket. On any other woman he would have laughed. On her it looked sexy as hell.

"Hi." Her smile was tentative.

"Hi."

"You're up early."

"I took a run on the beach."

"Oh." She paused. "I didn't know you were into jogging."

There's a lot you don't about me, he thought. "It's good exercise."

Hannah nodded and looked off to the side, then at the ground as if to fill the awkward silence. He wasn't going to help her. It was her call now.

She crossed her arms over her chest and kicked at the pebbles on the road. "I, uh, haven't seen you this week."

"I didn't think you'd want to." Did he see a flicker of regret in her velvety brown eyes? She felt ill at ease, he could tell, and taking no pleasure at her obvious discomfort, he changed the subject.

"So, what are you doing here?" he asked, pointing to the framed structure.

"We're building a house for Habitat for Humanity."

"Really?" His voice held more than a trace of startled amazement.

She laughed, raising a brow. "You sound surprised."

"I am. With your business and being a single parent, I wouldn't think you'd be able to find the time."

Hannah put her hand on the door, turning to the group of volunteers busily driving nails and cutting two-by-fours. "Well, I'll be honest with you. After Tory's father died, I almost drowned in self-pity. We had to start all over again with almost nothing. Then one day my friend, Marsha—you met her last week, didn't you?—she dragged me out one Saturday to work on a house." She laughed as if remembering. "I felt like the proverbial fish out of water. I'd never hammered a nail or poured cement in my life.

"When I was done, it felt so good knowing I'd helped someone less fortunate. It also took my mind off my own problems and made me realize I should be thankful for what I have. I can't give a lot of time, but I try to help when I can."

She wiggled her brows. "And boy, you should see me with a nail gun."

Sean laughed more in wonder than at the expression on her face. Every time he turned around, she hit him with the unexpected. Her affinity for others, even faced with her own personal obstacles, overwhelmed him. Had he ever been that good a person? She radiated a true kindness that made him feel unworthy of her company.

In the face of all her virtue, Sean was tempted to tell her the truth of his identity. Or he could wait and see where this conversation led them. Not feeling particularly noble, he chose the latter.

"So," Hannah said, with an irresistible twinkle in her eye, "you wanna help?"

God, how he'd like to grab her neck, pull her to him and kiss that temptingly curved mouth. "Yeah. Yeah, I would."

He got out of the Explorer, gesturing for her to lead the way when he saw her hesitate.

"Sean," she said, haltingly, "about last week."

Slowly, he lost his smile and waited.

"I may have said some things that were out of line, so I did some checking."

His heart skipped a beat. What kind of checking? What had she found out? "On me?" Had she discovered who he really was? No. If she had, their conversation would be taking an entirely different direction. "What did you find out?" he asked, bracing himself.

"That all the parents of your students like you, respect you. In their opinion, you're honest and hardworking."

Inwardly, he breathed a huge sigh of relief. "I'm glad you've changed your mind about me. Apology accepted."

Her brows shot up in surprise. "Just a minute. I'm not apologizing for anything. I did what I had to do. You have to understand Tory is all I have. She's at a very vulnerable stage in her life, becoming a teenager and losing her father. I have to be very careful about things—or people—that could be a detrimental influence."

A sharp-edged laugh exploded from his throat, and he barely managed to check his temper. "Now I'm a 'detrimental influence.' Well, I guess that's a step up from being a child molester." His sarcasm rang.

Hannah let out a frustrated breath and held up her hands as if to ward off his anger. "Look, Sean, the fact of the matter is I don't know you. And no matter what anyone else thinks of you, I can't trust someone I don't know."

That stopped him cold. Her words sank in, smothering his indignation and for the first time, he saw a strength of character he hadn't seen in her before. He had to admire her tenacity to protect her child—his child. The look on her face told him she wouldn't budge, wouldn't compromise, and her resolve almost made him smile.

"You're absolutely right. You don't know me."

Her eyes softened a bit, whether from relief or surprise he didn't know.

"But I want to change that, Hannah. Will you let me show you I'm really not the bad guy?"

A long moment passed, and Sean raised his brows in worried anticipation. Then, one side of her mouth lifted slightly. "How do you propose to do that?"

"We could start by going to dinner. Just you and me this time." She accepted with a nod, and the immense satisfaction he felt triggered an undeniable attraction he began to experience each time he saw her.

"How about next week?"

"All right. Call me."

"Does this mean we're friends?"

"Let's say it's a start."

They stood smiling for several foolish seconds.

"Well, we'd better get started here," Sean said finally, taking her arm. "Why don't you show me how to use that nail gun?"

His day was looking better by the moment. So good in fact, he shoved his hidden agenda behind him. He'd deal with the truth later.

~ * ~

"I got it, Mom!"

Tory ran to the phone, picked it up on the third ring and rolled her eyes when she heard Hannah's "Don't stay on too long. You have homework."

"Victoria? It's Henry."

"Hi, Henry. What's—"

"I found her."

Henry's barely restrained excitement traveled like lightning through the line, and when it hit Tory's ear, her stomach dropped. "You did?"

"Yeah. Can you talk?"

Tory glanced over her shoulder to where Hannah worked in the nearby sunroom. "No," she whispered. "Can I come over in about ten minutes?"

"Yeah. Bye."

She replaced the handset slowly, scrambling for a believable excuse, then gladly realized she didn't have to lie. "Mom, that was Henry. We have an algebra test tomorrow, and I asked him if he'd help me with some problems. Can I go over to his house?"

"He can come over here," Hannah suggested.

"Um... no he can't. He's got a history project to finish for tomorrow." Just a little lie.

"Are his mom or dad home?"

Tory nodded. "I heard Mrs. Pipkin in the background." At least she thought she had heard his mother. Maybe it had been the television.

"Okay, but only for thirty minutes. It's getting dark. And be careful crossing Frederica Road."

"I will." She walked quickly to the front door before Hannah's voice stopped her. "Tory, don't you need your algebra book?"

"Oh, yeah." She laughed, embarrassed. "Right." She went quickly to her room, then left with book and notebook clearly visible and hoped she didn't appear too eager. She breathed a sigh of relief once outside, but wouldn't have had she seen Hannah's quizzical expression.

Ten minutes later, she rapped on Henry's door, the brass knocker cold to the touch. Knots began to coil in her stomach and she almost chickened out. And she would have if Henry's mother hadn't opened the door.

"Hello, dear," she greeted warmly. "Henry's in the computer room."

"Thanks, Mrs. Pipkin." Second thoughts got in the way as she walked to Henry's sanctuary. Books hugged tightly to her chest, she took a deep breath, wondering why she was so nervous. This is what she'd wanted it, wasn't it? To find her missing link?

But what would she do when she found it?

Through the doorway, Tory saw Henry slouched in a chair behind his computer, his right hand deftly maneuvering the mouse. He looked so in control, so at ease, that the sight of him was strangely comforting.

When she knocked on the doorframe, Henry jumped up, sending the chair flying backwards. "Oh, Victoria." He scrambled for the chair. "I didn't hear you come in."

She made sure her smile didn't turn into a laugh. "Sorry I scared you."

He made an awkward gesture toward the monitor. "I found her for you."

Tory stopped just short of reading distance.

"Don't you want to see?" Henry asked, when she hesitated. He started to explain how he'd logged onto the hospital's computer and got into patients' records, but Tory didn't listen. Deep inside, a war waged, one of uncertainty and fear, a fear of knowing and of not knowing. What should she do?

"I have her Social Security number and an Atlanta address, but I couldn't get a phone number. I was just about to search for one from her Social Security number." He sat behind the screen and started pecking at the keyboard.

"No, don't," Tory interrupted, sharply.

His fingers stopped in mid-air. "Huh? What's the matter? I thought you wanted to find her."

Bourne out of curiosity, finding Angela Jenkins had become an urgent quest, almost an obsession, especially in light of her mom's lie. Now, faced with a difficult decision, Tory wasn't sure her mission was so important.

"I did. I do." She dropped her books on the desk and paused with uncertainty. "I don't know if I'm doing the right thing. What if she doesn't want to know me?"

A soft look passed over Henry's face. "I can't believe she wouldn't want to know someone as nice as you."

"Mom would probably kill me if she found out," Tory muttered, not hearing his wistful comment. However, her thoughts were just the opposite. She could stand being punished, but hurting her mother was a devastating thought. "Oh, I don't know what to do," she wailed, plunking down in the nearest chair. Struggling with indecision, she stared at the floor, hands clenched tightly over her knees.

"Hey, it's okay. Chill out." Henry leaned toward her in an effort to ease her distress. "Look, you don't have to do anything right now. You can look her up any time."

The simple suggestion solved her mountain-sized problem in an instant, at least for the time being. She breathed easier, realizing her friend was right, there was no rush. Time would shore up the courage she needed to go forward.

She nodded her head slowly as relief spread through her. "You're right. I can wait. And when I'm ready, we can do this together. Thanks, Henry."

Tory started to gather her books, then remembered. "Oh, would you help me with this algebra? I've got a test tomorrow."

"Sure," Henry answered quickly, his voice cracking.

As they sat down together, Tory reached over and touched his arm. "You're a good friend, Henry." She thought he looked so cute when the blush hit his cheeks.

Nine

It's just a date.

Hannah yanked off the third pair of earrings with an exasperated tug. She'd already tried on two outfits and four pairs of shoes.

Like I go out on a date every night. She finally settled on green linen slacks, a tank top and matching jacket, then took a critical glance in the mirror. Was she overdressed or underdressed? The indecision made her stomach lurch. She grabbed another pair of earrings and mumbled, "Going on a date can't be this nerve wracking."

While securing the plain, gold loops, Hannah walked to Tory's room and peeked in the doorway. "Have you packed everything you'll need for your overnight at April's?"

"Uh-huh."

"Mr. Murphy and I will drop you off on our way to dinner." Hannah started down the short hallway but when Tory didn't respond, she turned back. Tory shoved one, then two sneakers into her black backpack, but her expression held no excitement of spending the night out.

"Are you okay, honey?"

Tory's signature shrug set off Hannah's internal alarm. She looked more closely at the set of Tory's shoulders, caught the tight line of her mouth. Hannah fastened her watch slowly, glancing at it and deciding Sean would have to wait until she got to the bottom of this.

As Tory closed the bag with an accentuated zip, Hannah came up and gently turned her around. "Talk to me."

Tory started to pull away, then hesitated. She sat on the bed, looking as if she couldn't find the right words.

"Are you okay with my going out with Mr. Murphy?" Hannah prompted, sitting down beside her.

"I guess so. It just seems... funny. You going out on a date."

"You like him, don't you?"

"Oh, yeah," Tory responded, enthusiastically. "But..."

Hannah waited. "But what?"

Tory picked at a cuticle then blurted out, "Mom, did you love Dad?"

Hannah's eyes flew open in surprise. "What?" It was the last question she would have expected, and she would have been insulted if a sliver of guilt hadn't crept up on her. She leaned close and took Tory's hands in hers. "Of course I loved him, honey." *In the beginning, before the other women.* "Why do you ask?"

When Tory didn't answer, Hannah offered, "Do you think I'm betraying your Dad by going on a date?"

Tory hung her head and nodded.

The irony almost made Hannah laugh, would have had it not been so sad. Here, Tory thought her mother was dismissing her father's memory when it was Paul who had done the betraying. But Tory would never know that.

"Honey, I know how hard it's been since Daddy died. But life goes on. Your memories of him will always be alive in your heart. Nothing and no one could change that." She waited several excruciatingly long seconds.

"I know you're right, Mom. It's just kind of strange, you going on a date." Hurriedly, she added, "It's not that you're too old to go on a date..." Hannah raised a skeptical brow. "I mean, I hope you have fun. And... and if you have to go out, I'm glad it's with Mr. Murphy. He's really a cool guy."

"Thank you, I think." She gave her daughter a quick hug.

As if on cue, the doorbell rang. "That must be Sean. Do you have everything? Toothbrush? PJs? Clean underwear?"

Tory rolled her eyes. "Yes, Mother."

~ * ~

This time Sean brought truffles. "I heard somewhere that women must have chocolate at least once a day or they go into withdrawal," he said, with a mischievous grin. As he handed her the gift, Tory intercepted and slyly slid the box from her mother's hands, opened it and popped one into her mouth. Hannah didn't object. She was too busy drinking in the handsome sight of the man who could make her heart palpitate.

Like an unconscious thought dawning into realization, Hannah knew the more she saw him the more she had to see him again.

He greeted Tory with an easy warmth, kidded with her, but his rapport no longer stirred Hannah's suspicions. It had taken some time, but she'd accepted his explanations, partly because she wanted to and partly because of something she'd seen in his eyes, an almost desperate need to be believed. Short of hiring a private detective, which she couldn't afford, there was little Hannah could do to find out about his background. She'd had to rely on the opinions of others and her own judgment. She hoped that was good enough.

April met Tory as they pulled into April's driveway, and the two girls immediately started their usual chatter.

"Don't be late, you two," Tory teased as the girls broke into giggles.

"Cute kid," said Sean, watching his daughter as she walked off.

"Oh, she's cute all right." Hannah shook her head, her mouth curving into a tolerant grin. "They all have such smart mouths at this age."

"You're very proud of her."

His words caught her off guard and she looked at him in surprise. "Yes. Yes, I am very proud of her."

"I could hear it in your voice."

She returned his smile and continued her gaze as his eyes returned to the road. He was a beautiful man to look at. Coal black hair, so shiny and full, she knew if she touched it, it would feel like Tory's. The curved scar below his right temple added an attractive Indiana

Jones type of rakishness to the strength of his demeanor. And his eyes. Had she ever seen blue so deep or so penetrating?

Handsome. Sophisticated. Intelligent. Curiously urbane. Stirred together, they made a strong aphrodisiac that could drug any woman to lie down in surrender. Was she strong enough to resist? Did she want to?

Thirty minutes later, after making one stop at Hannah's request, Sean crossed the causeway to Sea Island, an exclusive enclave of expensive homes and old money. Hannah knew the only restaurant here was at The Cloister, one of the few resorts to boast a five-star rating.

"Oh, Sean, I don't think I'm dressed for The Cloister," she said, thinking he wasn't either, in Dockers and casual shirt.

"Sure you are. In fact, you may be too dressed."

When they parked in the lot and boarded a tram with a number of other people, she knew where they were headed.

"I hope this is all right," Sean said, as they reached the beach.

"It's wonderful! I haven't been to one of their beach parties in a long time. But I thought these dinners ended at the end of the summer."

"This is the last one for the season. I thought you'd enjoy it."

"You were right," she responded, with a slow smile.

He took her hand, helped her down and held on to it as they walked down the pathway. His skin felt good next to hers, comfortable and natural. The roughness of calluses, no doubt from his work at the stables, was an incongruous mark on a man who should be wearing Brooks Brothers instead of Dockers. But her suspicions had given way to avid curiosity and tonight she was determined to learn significantly more about him.

They walked down a pathway that led to a large open area filled with picnic tables topped with citronella candles and long tables filled with appetizers, entrees and The Cloister's famous desserts. Low country boil simmered in several wide vats that sat over cinder block grills, the savory aroma floating inward over a light ocean breeze. Numerous torches lighted the area, the orange luminescence casting a warm glow against a star-filled night sky.

"There's absolutely no way I could eat another morsel," Hannah moaned after finishing off a plate full of boiled shrimp, sausage, potatoes and corn on the cob.

"What? No room for dessert?"

She looked at him in awe. "You can eat dessert after three helpings?"

He winked at her and ate another peeled shrimp. "I'm gonna give it a good try."

She shook her head in wonderment. "You are truly amazing."

Hannah, thinking she'd have to diet all next week, took a deep breath to help settle her overly full stomach.

"Whew! Maybe I will pass on dessert," Sean said, wiping his hands on a napkin. "How about a walk down the beach?"

"That's a great idea."

Usually cold natured, Hannah didn't notice the chill in the night air. His fingers entwined in hers provided enough warmth inside her to withstand any sudden cold snap.

They walked on the hardened sand along the water's edge, careful to avoid the pools of water left by the receding tide. The sea was calm under the moonlight, the waves so small the water resembled a large lake rather than the Atlantic Ocean.

Unexpectedly, Sean bent down and picked up a small, delicate shell. "For you." He folded it in her hand. "A souvenir."

She gently fingered the perfect shape and, under the spotlight of a nearby security pole, admired the soft peach tone that turned to a deep gray when she turned it over. His gesture made her smile.

"I decorated Mrs. Burns' bedroom in these colors."

"Did she like it?"

"She asked me why I used orange and purple."

"How is that?" he asked, a flash of humor crossing his face.

"Mrs. Burns is eighty-six and color blind. I didn't know that beforehand. I had to change everything to pink and navy blue so she could see peach and gray."

He laughed with a deep, rich resonance, an infectious sound that made Hannah join him.

God, how she loved his smile. It slanted slightly, a sexy curve of pure masculine sensuality. She shocked herself with the urge to kiss him right there on the spot.

"How did you get into the decorating business?"

"Well, my first job was in a flower shop. I was right out of high school." Hannah could still see herself, an inexperienced, naïve country girl straight off the farm, determined to do something better with her life than waste away planting and plowing.

"I came to St. Simons looking for any job I could find. It didn't matter what job, I just wanted to get away from the farm. Mrs. Betty Ringle hired me as a gopher, and as time went on, I found I had some talent with colors and floral designs.

"When I married and gave up the job, I started helping friends decorate their homes. However, I never thought it would end up being my livelihood."

Sean spread the tablecloth he'd grabbed from a picnic table and they sat at the base of a small dune. "Did you meet your husband here?"

She nodded. "He came into the shop one day and..." She stopped. "No, oh no you don't," she said, with grinning accusation.

Sean looked around as if she were talking to someone else. "What?"

"You're not going to do it tonight. Every time we're together, I end up telling you things I usually don't tell anyone."

"I'm glad you trust me enough to talk about yourself."

Yes, it was becoming easier and easier to trust him and feel comfortable with him. And it was becoming just as hard for her not to hand him the key to her heart on a bolt of Waverly fabric. "Tonight, I want to hear about you." Hannah wrapped her arms around her knees, looking forward to prying loose some personal information. "So, where is home for you?"

"South Boston."

"Do you come from a big family?"

He shook his head.

"Brothers?"

"No."

"Sisters?"

"Nope."

She nodded, pursed her lips. "Any hobbies?"

He thought for a moment, then shrugged.

Raising a brow, she said, "I didn't realize this would be so difficult."

A smile tipped the corners of his mouth. "I'm sorry. I don't mean to be so cryptic." He laid back and placed his hands beneath his head looking up at the sky. Hannah was suddenly tempted to lie down with him. "Truth is, my childhood wasn't an *Ozzie and Harriet* script. My father was a drunk and my mother died when I was a teenager. I left home and never looked back."

"But how did you live? Where did you go?" Her heart went out to him and although her own childhood wasn't the best, she knew her parents had loved her unconditionally.

"I worked, stayed with friends. Joined the service for a few years, then worked my way through school and out of South Boston forever."

There was a familiar bitterness in his voice, she heard the whisper of it. She knew how some memories could prick the spirit to bleed painfully into the soul. Her prying obviously took him to a dark place he didn't want to be, and she didn't want him to relive something he'd rather forget.

Funny how he could make her want to spill her guts and feel so comfortable doing it. Yet, she couldn't make him feel the same way. "I'm sorry," she apologized. "I didn't mean to pry."

"Don't be," he said contritely, reaching out with a playful touch to push her bangs out of her eyes. "I was able to get out of a bad situation, made some great friends along the way and built myself a good business."

"Oh?" That bit of news caught her by surprise. "What kind of business?"

He hesitated as if in a dilemma. "It was a... small financial consulting firm."

That explained why he'd looked oddly out of place at a stable. However, the realization that her intuition had been right all along set off an uncomfortable nagging in the back of her mind. "You left a business you built from the ground up to give riding lessons?"

He gave a small laugh. "I needed a break. Some time to myself."

"You were lucky to have a friend to suggest St. Simons as a getaway place."

His brows drew together questioningly. "My...? Oh, yeah, right. My friend." He went on hurriedly. "I was working too hard. Never really connecting with people. Now I feel like I'm part of a community. And I have you to thank for that."

"Me?"

He nodded. "It would have taken me a year to meet all the people you've introduced me to."

"I doubt that. You would have done just as well without me. I've met a lot of new people myself this past year in my business."

"How is the business going?"

Hannah took a deep breath. "It's getting better. Cash flow is still a problem because people don't like to pay their bills."

"Is that why we had to make a stop at that house under construction?"

She rolled her eyes. "Builders are the hardest to collect from."

"Well, I have to say you were very professional. I especially liked the way you shook your finger at that guy."

She laughed, but felt a blush of embarrassment. "Maybe not professional, but effective. He gave me a check, didn't he?" She paused, then added, "I've had to do a lot of that in the past year. Actually I've learned how to do a lot of things this past year."

She glanced away quickly. "That sounded a little self-pitying, didn't it? I didn't mean for it to come out that way." Hannah looked out over the water, refusing to let her embarrassment demean everything she'd worked so hard for. "You know, when I think of all I've been through and everything I've accomplished, it amazes me. If anyone had told me I could set up a business and raise a child by myself, I would have said they were crazy. I don't even have a college education."

He rolled over to one side, propping his head in the palm of his hand. "But here you are."

"Yes," she said with a confidence that came all too rarely. "Here I am." She found him looking at her with just a slight smile in that way he had a habit of doing. "Why are you looking at me like that?"

"Like what?"

"Like you're trying to see inside me."

He waited a moment before answering. "Maybe because each time I look, I see more and more."

"Hmm. I might have to try that technique on you. I think I might be amazed at what I find."

He sat up abruptly, and shook his head. "Not much to find. What you see is what you get."

"Oh," she scoffed, "I doubt that."

"How would you like another client?" he asked, easily changing the subject.

"I can always use another client. Who is it?"

"Me."

Her eyebrows arched in surprise.

"My place needs some tender loving care."

The arch of her brow turned to a skeptical angle. "I don't come cheap."

"Hey, I'm good for it." His feigned indignation made her chuckle.

"I won't have to chase you down for a check, will I?"

Sean threw his head back and laughed and Hannah reveled in the sound. "No, you won't have to chase me, but I like the thought. I might enjoy being caught."

When she saw the suggestive teasing in his eyes, a tingling zap hit her stomach. She fast-forwarded, picturing them lying on the sand, kissing, touching, wanting more. He could make her feel alive with just a look and she wondered if what she felt was a schoolgirl crush. *I need more time,* her mind protested. *I have to be sure before...*

Sean leaned forward, his gaze zeroing in on her lips. Reason battled with emotions and in a moment of panic, she chose the wiser course and slowly pulled away.

"Then you have a deal," she said a little too loudly.

Sean blew out a pent up breath, letting the air fill his cheeks. "Next week?"

She nodded.

"Good."

A silent gap followed and Hannah knew if he continued to gaze at her that way, she wouldn't be in a sitting position much longer. "Well, it's getting late," she said, as she gathered her shoes and stood. Sean rose slowly to meet her and Hannah wished she could read him as easily as he seemed to read her. Perhaps it was better she didn't. She had to figure out her own feelings first.

He took her hand again and they walked back in silence. The crescendo between them had been building since they'd met and tonight Hannah felt they'd come close to a turning point. Where did they go from here? she wondered. Unable to answer, Hannah knew she'd just have to wait and see.

The anticipation sent a pleasant chill down her spine.

Ten

Sean stood on the balcony of his newly acquired townhouse, bracing an arm on the railing, his other hand holding a steaming cup of coffee. The Frederica River flowed peacefully but determinedly in front of him under a fog-shrouded sun. A large blue heron stood statue-like at the water's edge, blending into its natural surroundings. Sort of like what he'd been trying to do during the past several months. He took a sip of the strong brew and wondered if he'd succeeded.

He still had no idea why he'd bought this place. The modest apartment he'd been renting had been adequate for his needs, small, efficient, temporary. His studied, cautious approach on which he'd built his company was the same credo by which he'd lived his life. So where had this buying impulse come from?

"Doesn't matter," he said outloud, refusing to analyze his actions. "I can always sell it."

He turned around and leaned against the rail, looking through the glass doors into the almost-empty living area. A six-foot table served as a desk with computer, printer and fax sitting prominently on top. He'd managed to buy a bed, some bath towels and a supply of paper plates and plastic utensils, but the sparse decor only brought Hannah back to mind. Truth was, she hadn't been far from his thoughts since he'd dropped her off at her place a little after midnight.

On the surface, nothing had happened last night. They'd talked, held hands, and danced when they'd returned from their walk. He'd felt so protective with his arms around her slender frame, and he'd chuckled when she'd had to dance on tiptoe to accommodate his height. However, that small body contained a fortitude and perseverance that showed time and time again.

Something, however, had happened, something significant. *I could have had her last night,* Sean thought, *made love to her right there on the beach.* His heart rate picked up with the memory of how much he'd wanted to feel her under him. Could this be just a physical thing? No. He had known lust before, pure physical attraction that held no emotional element. What had happened last night was way different. He and Hannah had connected on a much higher level, and that had happened to him only once before.

With the exception of Angie, Hannah was the complete antithesis of all the women he'd ever dated. Not a socialite or corporate ladder climber, she'd carved a life for herself and Tory with talent, guts and determination. Not unlike himself, he realized. It was tempting to compare her to Angie but that meant dredging up painful memories. Angie was a closed chapter, one he refused to re-open.

Sean went back inside and walked slowly through the empty rooms, the echoes of his footsteps growing louder in his ears.

Now he had a big problem.

He'd found a child he didn't want to leave. And, he admitted with stunning clarity, he'd met a woman who fascinated and excited him. How the hell could he keep both of them in his life?

"I have to tell her," he whispered into the blank silence. But when? How? Would she be happy to learn he was Tory's father? *I doubt it.*

He could explain how this all came about, how he'd only wanted to make sure his daughter was safe and loved. That he'd come to love his child and lov... care for her mother. But no matter how he tried, his rationalization didn't eliminate his guilt. She'd be pissed, he knew for sure. If the situation were reversed, would he feel any differently?

One day at a time, he told himself, changing into sweatshirt and shorts and feeling the need for a solitary run on the beach. Yet, amidst his unanswered questions and confusing emotions, one thing was certain. Hannah and Tory were in his life to stay.

~ * ~

Fog rolled along the East Beach shoreline in various degrees of thickness, bringing with it a wet chill appropriate for the first day of November. Tiny sandpipers scooted along the water's edge, halting willy-nilly to grab a microscopic morsel with their thin beaks while a flock of hungry seagulls screeched overhead, dipping and diving over the water in hopes of spearing a morning tidbit.

Hannah drew the lapels of her jacket closely around her as she looked out over Pelicans Point, an aptly named spit of sand covered with a large number of the sleeping birds. The surf had picked up overnight, the soft roar of the waves a prelude of the storm that would no doubt follow. It brought a tingling anticipation that captivated her.

She hadn't slept well and had woken with the same sense of euphoria that had followed her to bed. Since Tory wasn't home and a number of things weighed on her mind, she had come to the beach where every subtle touch, every suggestive word from the night before came back to her, bringing a tingle to the pit of her stomach.

A deep breath of salty air filled her lungs as she inhaled happiness for the first time in months. When did it happen? What hour? What minute? Spreading her arms, she turned a pirouette on the sand and dismissed the rhetorical questions. They didn't matter.

She loved Sean Murphy.

It probably wasn't smart. It certainly wasn't logical. And not much in her life could be termed convenient.

She didn't care.

Nothing could throttle the dizzying current racing through her. Not even the little voice warning her to take it slow, be cautious. But Hannah rejected the silent warning. Sean wasn't like Paul. There was no pretense in Sean's caring manner, no airs or deception. He was simply a hardworking man who made her heart pound and her pulse race.

Can this really be happening to me? "Yes!" she cried out, then looked around quickly, relieved she was the only one on the beach.

Does he love me? She couldn't be sure, but a woman knows when a man is interested. And, thinking back on the look in Sean's eyes, Hannah knew he was definitely interested.

"Hannah?"

The sound startled her, but instantly she recognized the voice. It was the only one that could make her heart jump to her throat. Oh God, had he seen her acting like an idiot?

"Sean, hi. You're up early."

"I came out for a run and saw your car."

She nodded, suddenly aware as he walked toward her that his gaze was too intense, his gait too deliberate for a casual meeting. Her smile faltered just like her heart did. "I, uh, came for a walk myself."

He didn't answer.

"Th-thank you again for last night." What she read in his eyes wasn't 'you're welcome.' It was an invitation. Was he remembering their night on the beach? Did he want to finish what she knew deep inside would be inevitable? They faced each other sending unspoken messages, the air charged with excitement. With each pounding beat of her heart came a jolt of anticipatory excitement.

Propelled by her own need to touch him, Hannah reached out, but uncertainty stopped her in midair. Sean caught her hand before she could pull back and brought it to his lips. Without taking his eyes from hers, he kissed the soft skin of her palm, one spot, then another. Each kiss seared a permanent place in her heart.

When he took the tip of her index finger into his mouth, a stab of sheer wanting exploded through her. She couldn't think, couldn't breathe. His touch was almost unbearable in its tenderness and she felt the sting of happy tears. How her knees kept her standing, she didn't know.

Sean lowered her hand and closed the short distance between them. "Hannah," he whispered, "what have you done to me?"

She felt his hesitation and took it as if he sought her permission. She couldn't wait any longer to give him an answer. Standing on tiptoe, Hannah touched her lips to his. She lingered, savoring the moment and knowing she wanted more.

All of a sudden, he gripped her arms and pushed her away. Her eyes flew open and for a panicked second she thought she'd read him wrong. His pained expression only added to her confusion.

"Hannah, I have to tell—"

She shook her head. "Hush. Don't spoil this. Just kiss me. Please."

A low groan erupted from his throat and he crushed her to him. His kiss turned hard, demanding, sending new spirals of ecstasy through her. Locked in his embrace, her hands moved up his shoulders to curl her fingers in the thick silkiness of his hair.

When he slipped his tongue between her teeth, her mind went numb with the intimacy of it. Blood pounded, senses screamed, and a sharp ache pierced the lower part of her body.

When she thought she couldn't stand anymore, Sean cupped her head in his hands, and pulled back slightly, resting his forehead on hers.

"I think we have an audience." Hoarse and unsteady, his words finally sank in and Hannah came back to earth to the sound of giggles. She let out an embarrassed chuckle and waited for the two young boys to pass, hoping no one else had witnessed their momentary lack of sanity.

"Come on," he said. "Let's walk." He held her close with an arm around her shoulders as her heart drifted on a cloud of contentment. Today, there were no shadows of the past, no worries for the present. And she had bright hopes for the future.

~ * ~

Two days later, Sean stood bare-chested in front of the bathroom mirror, poured some aftershave in his hands and tapped each side of his face. Turning left, then right, he checked his slightly damp hair, thought about a hair dryer, then decided it would dry before Hannah got there.

He hadn't seen her since their shoreline kiss, only because her busy schedule hadn't allowed it. They'd talked by phone every day and even planned a day with Tory to explore Cumberland Island the next weekend. He wondered what Tory thought about his dating her mother.

Dating her mother.

His smile lasted only a second, then turned downward. He'd started to tell Hannah, wanted to before he'd lost himself in the feel of her in his arms. He should have insisted, he chastised himself, sat her down on the sand and told her who he was and how it was. Instead, he'd given in to the velvety sound of her whispered plea and fell into her kiss that left a burning desire for more.

"I'll tell her," he vowed, pulling on a shirt. "When the time is right."

It had better be soon, his conscience warned, before he could no longer shield himself from irresistible brown eyes that warmed with compassion and sparkled with laughter.

Before he got in over his head. Or was it already too late?

He finished buttoning his shirt when the doorbell rang. Frantically, he pulled on jeans and tucked in his shirt. "I'll be right there," he yelled down the stairway. Slipping into shoes, he ran down the stairs, yanked open the door—and stopped.

"What the hell are *you* doing here?"

Brian Cassidy dropped his bags inside the door. "Hey, buddy, good to see you, too." With an easy stride, he walked past Sean and glanced around the furniture-free room, raising a brow. "Nice place. Been here long?"

"I thought you weren't coming until next week." Frustration grew in Sean's voice. He'd opened the door expecting Hannah, not his executive vice president.

"I left you a message last week."

"Well, I didn't get it," Sean grumbled, running a hand through his hair. "I must have been moving that day."

"Why do I get the impression you're not happy to see me?"

Sean shook his head in annoyance and glanced at his watch. "You always did have lousy timing."

"Oh? Oh. Are you... entertaining?"

"Not yet."

Brian nodded. He walked around, hands on hips, looking in each room. "You got a bed?"

"Not that kind of entertaining." Although Sean liked the idea. "Look, she'll be here any minute and this might be a little awkward."

"Who's 'she?'"

Sean hesitated a long moment. "Hannah Stevens."

Brian dropped his hands and stared at him. "*The* Hannah Stevens? Mother of Victoria Stevens?"

"Yeah."

"Why is she coming here?"

Sean held up his hands in a defensive motion. "Long story."

"I've got all day."

"Well, I don't.

Brian shrugged. "How much longer do you plan to be here? Do you think it's time to come home?"

"Not yet."

"Okay," Brian said, with a casual nod. "Whatever."

"Is there a problem at the office?"

"Nope. I told you I was taking care of everything. Our investors are happy and content with their portfolios. All I need is your signature on some contracts I brought with me."

"Good, because I need more time here."

"To do what?"

Sean didn't answer.

"I still don't get it. You certainly should have found out what you need to know about this child by now." Brian brought his hand to his forehead, rubbed a spot below his hairline. Then his eyes narrowed suspiciously. "Or is there something else?" He paused. "Oh, shit. Don't tell me. Are you falling for this woman?"

Sean kept silent. It wasn't the time for explanations and he wouldn't know how to explain if he tried.

Brian shook his head, let out a short breath. "Is this your way of digging up the past or trying to make up for what you thought you had with Angie? Don't be a fool."

The sharp words took Sean by surprise.

Softly, Brian added, "Just don't make the mistake of thinking someone could replace her." He turned his head, sighed. "No one could." He paused. "Have you told her you're the father of her child?"

Both men looked to the door as the bell rang.

"No." Sean glared at his friend. "And neither will you."

~ * ~

Hannah smoothed her long skirt and checked her reflection in the side light windows of the front door. The morning had been filled with builders and clients, none of whom Hannah had been able to concentrate on. Every shade of blue she'd touched during the day reminded her of Sean's eyes and how they would change hue when he laughed or when he was angry. Or when he was about to kiss her.

Hannah took a deep breath to settle the nerves that jumped in her stomach like Mexican beans, then rang the bell. She turned a small half circle on the stoop and had to admire the setting surrounding the small enclave of townhomes. They sat back from the road, hidden by the beauty of meandering, live oak trees and sago palms. Tabby ruins of an eighteenth-century plantation worn black by time hid among the natural splendor, silent reminders of days long past. The row of connected homes, painted a pale yellow with green roofs, blended with a soothing warmth within the sage-colored greenery. With frontage on the Frederica River, she wondered how much the rent went for.

At the sound of the door opening, Hannah spun around, her heart stumbling against her ribs.

"Hi."

"Hi," Hannah said. God, it was sinful to look so handsome all the time. He probably looked great even when he got out of bed in the morning. "I hope I'm not late."

"Right on time. Come on in."

The heady smell of his aftershave filled the air as she walked into the small foyer. Instantly, she felt the symptoms of the spell he always seemed to cast over her. She grabbed for control and tried the professional approach. She glanced around the small foyer that led to the living room, taking in room layout and colors.

"I brought a number of samples for you to look—" Her eyes widened as he stepped closer to her and as he reached down for her valise, he dropped a light, loitering kiss on her lips.

The professional approach failed miserably.

"Will this take a long time?" His whispered voice gave her goose bumps.

She smiled, but swallowed hard. "Probably."

"Good."

His eyes teased her as much as his words excited her. Flirting wasn't her forte and even though she totally enjoyed the effects on her system, she felt out of her element.

She stepped away from his potent sensuality, afraid of what might follow if she didn't. "Maybe we should get on with this. Why don't you show me around?"

He took her hand and led her into the living area that had been out of view from the foyer. Her brows jumped in surprise as she slowed her gait. "Uh, Sean, you don't have any furniture."

"You know, it was your uncanny perception that attracted me right off."

She grinned but was still confused. "Didn't you bring anything with you from where you lived before?"

"It wouldn't look right here. So I want you to do it all. Top to bottom."

She still found the whole idea odd. "How long have you been living here?"

"Not long. I'd been renting a furnished apartment but when I saw this place, I had to have it."

A small itch of misgiving scratched at the back of her mind. Renting would have been expensive. However, townhouses like these, especially on the water, cost a small fortune. How could he afford it?

A movement from the balcony caught her eye. Believing they were alone, it startled her to see a stocky, red-haired man dressed in a business suit walk in. "Oh, I'm sorry," she apologized. "Am I interrupting?" She looked to Sean, wondering why he hadn't told her he had company.

"No." She saw a flash of irritation cross Sean's face. "Hannah, this is Brian Cassidy, a friend of mine from Boston."

"How do you do, Mr. Cassidy? I'm Hannah Stevens."

"My pleasure," he responded in a clipped Yankee accent.

Hannah surmised the man's round face would have taken on a friendly facade had his smile reached his eyes.

"Brian just happened to drop in. I wasn't expecting him until next week."

"Maybe I should come back another time and let you two visit."

117

"No, no," Sean objected. "Brian was just leaving. Weren't you?"

Unfazed, Brian seemed to enjoy Sean's displeasure. "But you haven't shown me around. I'd love to see it."

Sean leveled a glare at Brian. "Then you can leave."

Hannah began to wonder how much friendship existed between the two men.

The tour started upstairs with three bedrooms and two baths. The master bedroom had beautiful French doors that led to a balcony overlooking the river. She pictured a king-sized sleigh bed, antique armoire and chest. A reading corner would be nice, too, she thought, and for a fleeting second, she saw herself here, with him. And just as quickly, she dismissed the fantasy.

She continued to note room sizes and arranged furniture and colors in her head. Brian hung back, not offering any opinions, seemingly content to follow behind. Several times, however, Hannah caught him looking at her peculiarly, as if he was studying her.

They proceeded downstairs to the living area where the kitchen was narrow, but functional, with white appliances and cabinets. Did he cook? She opened a pantry door and grinned. Vienna sausage, macaroni and cheese and a tin of coffee. Emeril's worst nightmare.

The bottom floor held a den behind the one-car garage, which led to a small square of yard and a walkway to the river. She asked questions and made notes, and began to see bunches of dollar signs.

Before she could tell him the magnitude of the project, the telephone rang and Sean ran upstairs to answer it, leaving Hannah alone with Brian.

He walked casually around the room, alternately glancing out the sliding glass doors, then back to her. Maybe she was wrong, but she felt as though his attention was focused on her, and something in his demeanor sent up a caution flag.

"Nice place Sean has here."

She nodded. "Have you been to St. Simons before?"

"No, this is my first trip."

"I hope you'll enjoy your stay."

"I won't be here long. Just a day or two."

"Oh, well, maybe your next trip will give you more time to see the Island."

"Maybe."

He didn't make her feel comfortable with small talk, so she continued to make notes on her clipboard. The next thing she knew, he was standing next to her, touching her, looking over her shoulder at what she'd written. His closeness so disturbed her, she had to step away. "So, um, have you known Sean long?"

"Since we were kids. We grew up together."

"In South Boston?"

He nodded, seeming somewhat surprised.

"I'm glad Sean had a close friend when he was young. I understand his early years were kind of rough."

His brows shot up at her revealing statement. "Did he tell you that?"

"Er, yes." Suddenly, she felt the need to apologize. "Maybe I shouldn't have mentioned it. I just assumed since you've know him all this time, you knew about the problems he'd had."

He shrugged it off. "I'm just surprised he told you. Sean doesn't usually talk about his past—especially with a new woman."

A new woman?

He leaned against the door and folded his arms over his chest in a relaxed stance. The smile was still there, cocky, egotistical, deepening Hannah's uneasiness.

"You're not Sean's type."

His bluntness startled her. "Excuse me?"

"He usually goes for the tall, model types."

"It's none of my business what 'type' he goes for." His presumptuousness began to spike her temper.

"Really? After that kiss he gave you, I'd think you might want to know that."

"Our relationship is really none of your business."

He moved his shoulders in a dismissive gesture. "Just looking out for Sean's best interest. That's sort of been my job all these years."

Somehow, she couldn't believe he gave a flip about Sean's best interest. How could Sean call this jerk a friend?

"Tell you what," he said, "if you get tired of Sean, give me a call. I think we could have real good time together."

Now she could only laugh at the man's audacity. "Don't count on it." Shaking her head, Hannah started toward the stairs when Sean entered the room.

"What's going on?" he asked, seemingly sensing tension in the air.

"Nothing. Nothing at all. I was commenting on how well you seem to have settled in here."

Sean looked skeptical.

"That's right." Hannah plastered on a smile.

"Well, you two have a lot to do here. I'm over at the King and Prince, Sean. Give me a call."

Hannah kept the too-bright smile on her face as she watched Brian leave. Before he even reached the door, she decided to keep their conversation to herself. If Sean found out about their discussion, he wouldn't learn it from her. Besides, she wouldn't jeopardize this new relationship by coming in between two friends.

"Hey," he said, tipping her chin up, "are you all right?"

Brian Cassidy fled from her thoughts. When Sean looked at her that way, how could anything be wrong? *He must care for me,* she thought, wanting to lose herself in the safe confines of his arms. He couldn't touch her that way and not feel something for her.

"I'm fine," she answered, wondering again how she got so lucky to have this man in her life. "Do you play the lottery?"

His brows drew together at her out-of-the blue question. "No."

"Well," she said with a grin, "you'd better start. Winning it is the only way you're going to be able to afford what I'm going to do to this place."

Eleven

The bell rang after fourth period at Glynn Middle School, signaling the start of the morning break. Tory hoisted her backpack onto her shoulder and followed the crowd outside to the courtyard, looking for Henry.

"Hey, Tory." She turned and had to look up as tall, cute, popular Josh Logan appeared next to her. "Are you coming to the game this afternoon?"

Quarterback in the fall, basketball center in the winter and pitcher in the spring, he made every eighth-grade female heart flutter. And his father owned a Porsche.

Everyone had told Tory he liked her and at first, she had been flattered the most popular boy in the school wanted to go out with her. Yet, the more she got to know him, she wondered if that really was such an honor.

"Hi, Josh. No, I don't think so."

He looked stunned. "But I'm starting quarterback."

"So?" He could be so self-centered. "I have a big project to do."

"Oh. Well, I'll call you."

Tory looked around the courtyard. She had to find Henry before break was over. "Sure, whatever. I've gotta go. See you later."

She turned her back on him and walked over to where Henry and his friends always sat, in the back corner like a quarantined holding area for nerds.

"He likes you, you know," Henry said, inching over on the bench to make room for her.

"That's what I heard."

"Did he ask you out?"

She shook her head. "I think he's waiting for me to ask him."

He laughed. "Would you go if he did?"

All of a sudden it became important that Henry know. "No. He's a jerk."

Henry's eyes held hers as a slow grin spread over his face, making Tory smile in return. "What?" she asked.

"Nothing." He glanced over to Mr. Cool. "You should see the look on his face. Probably can't believe you're really talking to me."

For some reason, Tory liked hearing the satisfaction in Henry's voice. No longer did he stutter or drop his books or turn red every time Tory came within ten feet of him. She found herself seeking out his company more and more and really liked talking to him. "Forget him. Listen. I've decided I want Angela Jenkins' telephone number. Would you get it for me?"

"Sure." He paused. "What made you change your mind?"

Tory fixed her gaze at the clusters of students in the courtyard and squinted in the late morning sun. "I didn't change my mind, actually. I guess I needed some time to get my courage up." She shrugged. "And I still don't know if I have all the courage I need."

Henry offered her a handful of chips that he pulled out of a brown paper bag. "Are you sure this is what you want to do?"

His question surprised her. "Why?"

"Well, I've been thinking. What if this woman *doesn't* want to know you? I mean, I can't imagine she wouldn't, but I just don't want you to feel bad if she doesn't."

His kindness warmed her heart. He didn't look at her, just crunched on a nacho chip. "Do me a favor," he said after a long moment of silence.

"Sure."

"Don't call her unless I'm with you."

Her heart did a funny flip thing she'd never felt before and suddenly, Henry Pipkin looked very different in her eyes.

"Thanks, Henry," she said softly, wanting to say more yet not knowing how. The bell rang and students scrambled for books and backpacks. "Would you walk me to my next class?"

Shocked looks and whispered comments emanated their way as the two walked together through the crowd. The class beauty and the class nerd.

Tory noticed the stares, heard the buzz, but didn't even care.

~ * ~

"I'm sorry I'm late. It's been crazy today." Hannah slid into the wooden booth, automatically checking her watch. The Sand Castles Café was almost empty, too late for the breakfast crowd and too early for lunch, so it wasn't difficult to find Marsha. Her long graying hair reflected against the mahogany-colored paneling while her feather-shaped silver earrings caught the glint of the mid-morning sun that penetrated the diner.

"Well, you certainly don't look sorry," Marsha said, with a sly grin.

"What do you mean?"

"Big smile, flushed cheeks."

Hannah felt herself getting the once-over.

"Do I see a certain glow about you?"

"I don't know what you're talking about." Hannah hailed a waitress and ordered coffee, trying for feigned indifference but knowing it would be impossible to fool Marsha.

"Oh, yes, you do. Tell me about you and Sean Murphy."

Hannah raised an eyebrow in amusement. "Is that why you wanted to have coffee?"

"This is a very small island. You and he have been seen together quite frequently and I wanted to get it from the horse's mouth."

"Great." The idea of her and Sean being fodder for the gristmill wasn't appealing, but realistically, gossip was inevitable. Maybe it was better to set the record straight. Besides, she was dying to talk to someone.

"Okay. We've been seeing each other for the past few weeks."

Marsha nodded slowly. "How is he?"

"Fine."

"How fine?"

When she realized Marsha wouldn't let it pass, Hannah's defenses collapsed and she let out a sigh of pure contentment. "Real fine. Real, real fine."

"Ha!" Marsha laughed, slapping her hand on the table. "Tell me *everything*."

Hannah sat back in the seat and fiddled with the spoon, deciding to let it all out. "Oh, Marsha, I feel so incredible. My whole life has changed. When I get out of bed in the morning, I feel like I have something to look forward to. Every time I see him or hear his voice on the phone, my heart jumps to my throat. I find myself singing in the shower, whistling in the car and half the time, I can't concentrate on what I'm doing. When he looks at me, kisses me..." Marsha's eyes widened. "...the entire world stops turning." Hannah let out a short laugh of realization. "Either I'm losing my mind or I'm—"

"In love?"

Hannah gave Marsha one of those 'Oh, my God, what have I done' looks and nodded slowly. Then her fingertips flew to her temples. "It's awful. No. It's wonderful. Oh, God, it's scary as hell!"

Marsha broke up laughing. "Get a grip, girl. Love isn't supposed to give you a nervous breakdown. Have you told him?"

"Good Lord, no. I don't want to pressure him and I certainly don't want to look like a fool if he doesn't love me back."

"Surely he feels something for you or he wouldn't be in your face all the time."

Hannah shrugged. "I think he does, but I'm no expert in this area. I thought Paul loved me and look what happened."

"Paul is gone. Forget him."

"Hmm. Easier said than done."

"How is he in bed?"

"Paul?"

Marsha rolled her eyes. "Sean."

Hannah threw her a stern look. "I wouldn't know."

"Why not? You're two consenting adults."

"I haven't thought about it."

"Oh, don't give me that!"

"Well," Hannah admitted with a grin, "maybe I've thought about it, but we haven't progressed to that stage. To be honest, it would be awkward with my having a teenage daughter."

"What's that got to do with anything? Hannah, you're entitled to a life and you're certainly not obligated to tell Tory the intimate details of your relationship with Sean. And I know you'd be the soul of discretion. What does Tory think about you and Sean?"

Hannah shrugged. "The three of us have been doing things together and she and Sean get along so well. At first, she felt uncomfortable about my dating, but she seems fine with it now." She thought a minute. "Lately, she's been more... grounded, for lack of a better word. Not so moody."

"Maybe he's a good influence on her."

She nodded.

"I guess this means you no longer have doubts about him?"

Hannah let out a self-deprecating groan. "I can't believe I was so wrong about him. He's just a regular guy making a living. He's warm, considerate and hardworking..."

"Enough, enough! You don't have to sell me." Suddenly, Marsha sat up straighter. "You *did* make sure he isn't married, didn't you?"

Immediately, Hannah thought back to her conversation with Brian Cassidy. "He's not married."

"How can you be so sure?"

"A friend of Sean's came to visit him last week." She paused, shaking her head at the recollection. "His name is Brian Cassidy. He seemed nice enough at first, but when Sean was on the telephone, Brian started telling me what a womanizer Sean was, as if I shouldn't waste my time."

"Maybe he was trying to warn you off."

Hannah shrugged. "If that were the case, he could have come right out and told me Sean was married. Frankly, Sean doesn't come across as the playboy type to me.

"Then he got really obnoxious and came on to me!" She rolled her eyes. "I couldn't believe it."

"Did you mention this to Sean?"

"No, I couldn't. I'm not going to come between two lifelong friends. Besides," she said with a dismissive wave, "he went back to Boston. If he comes to visit again, I'll just make myself scarce."

Marsha reached over and touched Hannah's arm. "I'm so happy for you, honey."

"Thanks," she replied on a wistful sigh. "I never thought I could be this happy. But, you know, I wonder if this could become a problem. What if Tory gets too close to Sean? I worry that she'll be hurt if Sean and I go our separate ways."

"Hannah, what would you do if you didn't have anything to worry about?"

She chuckled. "You know me too well."

"Just take it one step at a time. If it's meant to be, it will work out the way it's supposed to."

"You're right." Hannah swallowed the last of her coffee and gathered up her purse. "Thanks for listening. I don't know what I'd do without you."

"Don't be silly. You'd do fine."

"What are you doing for Thanksgiving?"

"Probably staying right here."

"Why don't you come over for turkey? Sean's coming for dinner, too, so it will be the four of us. It'll be fun."

"Love to."

"Good. Listen, I gotta run. Did I tell you I'm decorating Sean's townhouse? He bought one of those on the river at the north end."

"Ooo, pricey."

"And beautiful. See you later."

"Bye. And stop worrying!"

Hannah smiled as she left the café. The day was beautiful. Life was great. And she was on her way to see Sean. Could anything be more wonderful?

~ * ~

A cold fall breeze swept through the stable, bringing with it a small cloud of twirling leaves. In the cramped office, Sean leaned back in the creaking chair and rested his boots on the desk. The dent from his heel only added another notch of character to the scarred and battered wood.

He laced his fingers behind his head, chuckling to himself as he looked around the room filled with dust, dirt and cast-off furniture. Quite a contrast to the elegant eighteenth-century furnishings of his Boston office. Far from stately, the room didn't emanate power or ooze success. He realized it felt right, an easy and comfortable fit. That's one reason he had bought the stable from Sam Haverty.

Sean closed the brown leather ledger, immensely satisfied with what the numbers told him. Sam had been on the verge of bankruptcy but now, only a few short months later, Sean was almost in the black. It had been a long time since he'd experienced the thrill of building something from nothing. And it had been a long time since he'd felt so at ease with his life.

Unbeknownst to them, Hannah and Tory were the reason. Their company had become routine, they had become a true threesome, a trio. Like... family. And as the word echoed in his head, guilt climbed all over him.

There hadn't been a good time to tell her the truth, he rationalized. He wouldn't do it tonight, either. A dinner-dance at The Cloister wasn't the right place. But soon.

He shook off the yoke of foreboding, remembering he had to pick up his tux before the store closed. Leaping up, he grabbed his keys and closed the door behind him. Thinking everyone had gone for the day, he was surprised to hear a voice, Tory's voice, coming from a nearby stall. He slowed, his footsteps silent on the sawdust floor.

"That's a good boy, Apollo. Now, if you'll just be still until I'm done, I'll give you this apple."

Sean grinned at her conversational tone as she brushed the animal. *I'll drop her off at home,* he decided, *and save Hannah a trip.* He walked toward the stall, then stopped in his tracks.

"Why do people have to lie, Apollo?"

His brows sunk into a deep frown.

"Why can't people just tell the truth?"

What was she talking about?

"She probably had her reasons, but it really hurt, you know? It wasn't right to keep it from me. I'm not mad at her any more, just disappointed, I guess. But I'm still going through with it. I hope she understands."

Who had lied to her? And about what? Sean heard the swoosh of each stroke as she brushed and he wondered what to do. His first opportunity to act like a parent and he didn't have a clue.

"Tory?"

"Oh, hi, Sean."

"I thought everyone had gone for the day."

"I told Jackie I'd brush Apollo for her. Mom's supposed to pick me up but I guess she's running late." She ran a hand down the animal's flank. "He looks so pretty when he's brushed."

He nodded. "You did a fine job."

"Thanks."

Now what? "How's everything going with you?"

She cocked her head. "Fine."

"School's going okay?"

"Uh huh."

"No problems?"

She laughed. "No problems. Why are you asking me?"

He shrugged. "Oh, no reason. I just thought... if there... was something I could help you with..." He held up his hands. "Anything at all?"

"No, but thanks."

That went well, he thought as his first attempt at parenthood fell flat. *How would Hannah have handled it?* he wondered.

Obviously parenthood took practice, but he decided, at least for the moment, against taking another stab at it. "Come on. I'll drop you off at home."

Twelve

"To the right, one, two, three, clap. Now to the left, one, two, three, clap. Back. Forward. Dip forward, now back. That's it, Sean."

Hannah danced next to him, giving instructions with a smile that stopped just short of outright laughter. He'd always considered himself a decent dancer, but the Electric Slide had him baffled.

Billed as The Cloister's biggest charitable affair, the Harvest Ball was the most elegant Island event of the year. No expense was spared on decorations, entertainment or dinner, and tickets always became scarce as hen's teeth an hour after going on sale.

When his buddies at the Huddle House had told him how popular it was, Sean had decided Hannah would love it. However, he hadn't expected her to balk so vehemently at his invitation. Two hundred and fifty dollars per person is ridiculous, she'd said.

So, he'd lied to get her to go, telling her a friend had given him the tickets. It had been just a small lie, but oh, how the words slid so easily out of his mouth. More lies. More deceit. It had to stop.

"No, no, Sean. Right foot. *Right* foot."

He tripped again and lost his balance. "I'm so sorry," he apologized as he stomped on the foot of the woman next to him. *Come on, you can do this.*

"If you bite your lip any harder, it's going to bleed."

Hannah's laugh broke through his concentration, and when he realized how foolish he must look, he laughed, too. "That's it, I give up," he surrendered. Luckily, he made it to the sidelines without getting an elbow in the ribs or crashing into another dancer.

Watching her finish the dance, he knew he'd been right to bring her. The lying part bothered him, but it was worth it to see how much fun she was having. She moved elegantly in time with the music, her red sequined gown clinging to every curve of her graceful body. A hot ache grew inside him, the sensation becoming more and more familiar every time he looked at her. He fantasized for several more seconds as short, quick scenes of her flashed in his head. Of her in his bed, moving under him, warm, tight. Suddenly the temperature in the room seemed to rise twenty degrees. He took a deep controlling breath.

It was inevitable they would make love, he knew it as surely as he knew his own name. But before that happened, he had to reveal his true identity. The how and when of that happening was still a problem.

"Why did you stop?" Hannah came up to him, her flushed cheeks almost as red as her dress. "You were really getting the hang of it."

He smiled ruefully. "Tell that to the woman whose foot I stepped on. Come on, let's take a break." They found a small table and ordered a drink. "Where did you learn to do the Electric Slide?"

"Would you believe Tory taught me? She learned it in her Phys Ed class. Oh, by the way, thank you for bringing her home today. I hit a snag that put me way behind this afternoon."

"What happened?" Sean crossed his arms and leaned forward on the table, enjoying their chitchat that had become so comfortable over the past several weeks. *She's a sensible woman,* Sean thought. *When I tell her I'm Tory's father, she'll understand. She probably won't be happy and it might take a while to get over it, but she'll come around.*

The rationalization felt good. Sort of.

"Where is Tory tonight?" he asked, after she'd run through the pitfalls of her day.

"She's at a lock-in."

"A what?" He made a face. "Sounds like she's been sentenced to prison."

"The youth group spends the night at the church. They eat pizza, listen to music and stay up half the night. She'll be dead tired tomorrow."

"Girls *and* boys?"

With a chuckle, Hannah raised a brow at his disapproving expression. "It's all very well chaperoned and no one changes into pajamas. Believe me, I checked it out thoroughly before I agreed to let her go."

Yes, he thought, *I'm sure you did.*

"It's hard to believe she's already thirteen," Hannah said, a warm look passing over her face. "Pretty soon she'll be going out with boys and getting her driver's permit."

Dating? Driving? A spark of panic flared up inside him. Not his little girl. My God, how could he protect her from drunk drivers and over zealous teenage boys? Unwanted reminders of his own adolescence made him wince. Drinking beer at Brian's when his parents hadn't been home. He and Colleen Delaney in the back of his old Chevy Camaro. He shuddered.

"Sean?"

"Hmm?"

"Don't look so upset. Tory will be fine." She gave him a reassuring pat on the arm. "It's sweet of you to be concerned about her."

You don't know the half of it. Sean swirled his scotch and water in the short crystal glass. "While we're on the subject, how has Tory been doing lately?" He didn't begrudge her the pride so plain in her smile. He did envy it, though.

"She's doing great and I'm so relieved. I was very worried about her at the beginning of school. She missed her dad so much and held in so much anger, first at him for dying, then at me. For what, I never did find out. But she seemed to work it out." Hannah covered his hand with hers. "I'd like to believe you had something to do with that."

"If I did, I'm glad." He paused, wondering if he should mention it. "By the way, I overheard Tory in the barn today. She was talking to Apollo while she brushed him and I guess she thought she was alone."

"What did she say?"

"Something about why did people have to lie and everyone should tell the truth. I got the impression she was talking from first-hand experience."

Hannah's smile faltered. "Did she mention any names?"

"No. She did say that she found out anyway and hoped someone would understand."

Her brow pulled downward and she looked away, her worried frown making him wish he hadn't mentioned it. "It's probably nothing. What do I know about kids, anyway?"

"What? Oh, well, it's probably just a tiff with a girlfriend. With kids this age, everything is a major catastrophe. I'll ask her, though. Thank you for telling me."

The smile didn't return to her face and Sean noticed that her color looked a little off. "Why don't we get some air? You look a little pale." As he got up from the chair, he looked over her shoulder to see a squat, bald-headed man walking toward them.

Oh, shit.

"Sean? Sean Murphy? Is this where you've been hiding?"

Sean stood slowly as the man pumped his hand. "Hello, Sid."

"I've been trying to get a hold of you for weeks. What did you do, quit your job?" Heads turned at the man's booming laugh. "I'm surprised to find you in this part of the country. How did you ever find your way to St. Simons Island?"

"Long story," Sean replied under his breath. Everything was becoming a long story. Long and complicated.

"We need to get together, Sean, as soon as possible," Sid said softly, leaning into Sean's ear.

"What about?"

"I've left several messages for that Cassidy fella, but he hasn't returned my calls. With all the money I've got invested in your company, I'd expect better service."

A blip popped up on Sean's mental radar. Ignoring Sid Goldstein's calls was not the way to do business. He made a note to call Brian first thing in the morning.

From the corner of his eye, Sean saw Hannah smile, but there were questions in her expression. "Sid, I assure you your money is being well taken care of." He put a hand on Sid's shoulder and turned him away from the table. "Don't worry about anything. If you'd like, I'll give you a call and we'll talk. Are you staying here?"

"No, no. I have a home on Sea Island. Why don't you come over—and bring your young lady."

When Sid turned back to Hannah, Sean saw no way out, so he made the introductions as quickly as possible. "It was good to see you, Sid. I'll call you." The man returned to his table, and inwardly Sean gave a sigh of relief.

Hannah's brows hit the ceiling. "Wow. How do you know Sid Goldstein?"

Here it comes, he thought. "He's done some business with my company. Would you like to have another drink? Or something to eat?"

"I thought you said you had a small company."

"Well, er, it started small. Would you like to dance?"

"Your company can't be that small if you have Sid Goldstein as a client."

Her questions made him nervous. Finding out what he really did for a living would only make matters worse. "Why do you say that?"

"The man has more money than God."

"I thought you didn't know him."

"I know *of* him. Who doesn't around here? He's the biggest philanthropist in the area."

"Sid took a chance on me, and when he realized what I could do for him, he stayed with me." Sean took her hand in his and leaned in close. "Hey, why don't we go back to my place? I'll fix us a drink and we can enjoy the view from the deck." He could almost see the wheels turning in her head.

"I didn't realize Brian worked for you. I thought he was just a friend."

"Friend and right-hand man." He nibbled on her knuckle. "I really don't want to talk business, do you? Let's enjoy ourselves tonight."

Her mouth curved in a smile. "Okay."

Her curiosity apparently satisfied, Sean breathed an inward sigh of relief.

Hannah rose from the table and took his arm. "Come on. Dance with me one more time before we go. And I promise, no fast dances."

He held her close, wanting desperately to lose himself in the feel of her skin and the fresh scent of her hair. But it didn't work. The weeks of deception had worn his conscience raw. He had to tell her tonight. *Damn, why couldn't life be simple?*

~ * ~

They held hands over the console as they drove from The Cloister, Hannah content in the amiable silence. She marveled again at how breathtaking he looked in a tux, and couldn't blame all the women who turned their heads in his direction. The evening had been wonderful and if she could be happier, she didn't know how. Yet, what Sean had told her about Tory came back to trouble her. Was it just an adolescent spat? Had one of Tory's friends lied to her about something?

Or had Tory somehow found out about Hannah's lie, the lie about Tory's birth parents?

Impossible.

Stop being paranoid, she scolded herself. The papers were safely hidden. Besides, Tory hadn't brought up the subject of her adoption since the beginning of school and she'd never been a child to snoop. Hannah had her reasons for not telling Tory; however, at the moment they all sounded like excuses.

Don't think about it.

She glanced back at Sean and noticed his hard stare at the road ahead. When she squeezed his hand, he turned to her.

"What are you thinking about?"

A smile spread over his face. "How beautiful you are tonight. I thought I was going to have to beat the men off with a stick."

"Really?" she countered in a teasingly haughty tone. "Seems to me a number of women were ready to give you their room numbers."

"Ah, but they paled in comparison."

Hannah held in a laugh, and acknowledged his courtly flattery with a nod. It may have been playful banter, but the result was intense. So much so that when he brought her hand to his lips and pressed a kiss to her knuckles, her heart flipped over in response. Desire, hot and fierce, sliced through her, making her pulse race with anticipation. Suddenly she longed to be loved, physically and emotionally. She wanted Sean to make love to her and fill the need left void for so many years.

When they arrived at Sean's place, Hannah couldn't help but survey the living room with a decorator's eye, then silently congratulated herself. Almost completed, it was a man's room, not overwhelmingly masculine, yet warm and welcoming. Leather and wood combined with soft, earthy colors of sage green, cinnamon and pale yellow with pictures of St. Simons and Kentucky Derby winners lining the walls.

She'd always enjoyed her profession, but choosing styles and colors for Sean's home had given her a sense of belonging, almost as if this was her home, and she had done it all with a touch of love.

"You like it?" he asked, as he poured them some wine. "I've got this great decorator."

She laughed. "The question is, do *you* like it?"

He handed her a glass. "I've never lived anywhere that felt so much like a home."

There was no higher compliment and her heart swelled with a feeling she'd thought long dead. A picture of him flashed in her mind, a boy alone in the world with no foundation on which to build a life and she was glad to be able to create a place where he could feel comfortable.

The November air prompted Sean to cover Hannah's shoulders with his jacket as they walked out on the deck. When she shivered, he drew the lapels together in front of her with several gentle but deliberate tugs. His eyes traveled from his hands to her shoulders, then to the top of her head. Everywhere except her eyes. So she captured his face between her hands.

"I hope I didn't step on your pride tonight," she said, wondering why he was so pensive. "It took *me* a long time to learn the Electric Slide."

He shook his head, his smile almost apologetic. "No, I enjoyed it, really." Softly, he added, "I enjoy all the time we spend together."

The admission should have sent chills sliding down her spine, but the worrisome crease on his brow puzzled her. "Sean?"

He didn't answer, only looked at her with a kind of torture in his eyes. To ease whatever troubled him, Hannah slid her arms up his chest and kissed him, hoping he'd sense her invitation.

"Hannah," he said putting some distance between them, "I have to tell you something. About me."

Something's wrong, she thought. Then it came to her almost immediately and silently she breathed a little easier. "If you mean about tonight, I know."

"You do?"

She nodded. "And it's okay. I figured if you had Sid Goldstein for a client, your company would have to be a lot bigger then you led me to believe. Which explains how you could afford to live in this place."

He made a stammering sound but she stopped him. "It's okay, I'm not angry. And right now, *I* don't want to talk about business." Like a sixth sense, she firmly believed that destiny had brought Sean Murphy here, to her, and now they would embark on a course that would change their lives. "I need you tonight, Sean. I want you." Her voice came from somewhere else, unrecognizable in its intensity. "Make love to me. Please." She had never been so totally vulnerable to rejection, even when she'd learned of Paul's infidelity.

When a troubled look passed over Sean's face, she stiffened suddenly. "If you're going to say no, do it quickly and let me leave."

Only for a moment did he hesitate, then his mouth crashed down on hers, his groan smothered on her lips, the sensation sending her stomach into a wild spin. She loved him with all her heart and soul, and tonight nothing could stop the overwhelming need to love him with her body.

His coat fell to the floor as she curled her arms around his neck and lost herself in his kiss. When he broke it, her small cry of protest turned to a gasp as he lifted her effortlessly in his arms.

"Tonight, Hannah, you'll be the most loved woman in the world."

Was this really happening to her? Every nerve tingled. And the small part of her that threatened to hold back, the part that refused to be hurt again, became lost in the struggle with loneliness, need, and newfound love.

Sean carried her to the room she'd lovingly decorated. How many times had she envisioned herself here with him? In his chair, his shower, his bed?

He let her down to stand at the side of the king-sized sleigh bed. No light was necessary. The blue-white light of the full moon flooded through the open drapes, casting an ethereal glow into the room. She swallowed hard under his intense gaze, afraid of loving him and desperate not to. His hands traced the hollow of her neck down to her shoulders and her heart pounded erratically.

"So soft," he whispered. "So delicate." When he kissed the path his hands had traced, she had to grip the edge of the mattress to steady herself. "Sean. Wait a minute."

"What?" He searched her face. "Second thoughts? I thought this is what you wanted."

"I do. It's just that I haven't done this in a long time." Her embarrassed laugh came out high and squeaky.

"I know it's been over a year since your husband died—"

"It's been longer than that." This wasn't the time for lengthy explanations and at the moment it wasn't important. "I just don't want you to be disappointed."

"I'm beginning to realize you could never disappoint me." His hands took her face and held it gently. "However," he teased huskily, "if you think you've forgotten how this is done, let me remind you."

This was it, the moment the bottom fell out and sent her into a free fall. The same sensation that came from losing your stomach on a roller coaster drop, exhilarating, petrifying, and wondering if you'll survive.

A shiver of excitement followed in the wake of his hands as they traveled up her arms. When his thumbs hooked under the thin straps of her gown and pulled them down, her breath hitched in her throat. He kissed her then, long and slow, until a dizzying haze filled her head, and the pulsating ache in the lower part of her body crescendoed to an exquisite pain.

She never felt him lower the zipper, but when he began to pull the gown from her, her arms flew up in natural defense.

"No, don't cover yourself. Let me see you."

Hesitation lasted only a second. Her past had taught her love and trust were as fragile as butterfly wings, yet for her, one without the other was impossible. And she loved him, more than she'd thought possible.

She let the top fall, boldly peeled it from her body and stepped out of sandals and panties.

"My God, you're beautiful. I knew you would be."

The blood echoed in her ears in uneven beats. A heady sensation came over her while his stare lowered from her eyes to her breasts.

Unexpectedly, he turned on a small table lamp, the dim light throwing shadows on the walls. He walked her to the mirror, stood behind her, her naked image becoming blurred under his erotic spell.

"Look how beautiful you are."

Their mesmerizing reflections brought out the sharp contract between them—so petite and tall, so fair and dark.

So male, so female.

He reached around her gently, outlined the circle of her nipples, then filled his hands with her breasts, making slow, lazy circles.

All reality escaped her. There was no mental anchor to hang on to as the most intimate sensations swept over her like a tidal wave. She leaned her head back against his chest as his lips caressed the sensitive curve of her neck, each kiss leaving its fiery brand.

Just when she thought her legs would buckle, Sean lifted her and placed her gently on the bed. His eyes never left hers as he hurriedly shed his clothes and lay down next to her. From the moment his mouth covered hers, Hannah's mind entered a new dimension of sensations and colors. She heard herself cry out in delight and felt the prick of tears at his tenderness.

He explored every inch of her, unlocking a treasure chest of unexpected pleasures. Never had she felt so feminine.

And she made discoveries of her own, like the way his muscles tensed when her fingers splayed over his chest and the sound of his breath as it caught when she held him in her hand.

How long they'd touched and tasted she didn't know, but it all lead to an urgency that had to be satisfied. Her back arched at his painful invasion and he stopped and caressed and kissed until she felt comfortable with his size. Then, slowly, the timeless rhythm overtook them and she met every thrust with her own. When the end came and she shook with wave after wave of ecstasy, the night exploded with his name on her lips.

Thirteen

Sean stared into the darkened room, hearing nothing but the steady rhythm of Hannah's breathing. She slept peacefully next to him in the crook of his arm like a long-time lover. Her arm fell over his chest and unconsciously, he caressed the top of her hand with his fingertips.

He had a lot on his mind.

Hannah had been wrong, dead wrong, if she thought she'd forgotten anything about making love to a man. He'd intended to be the seducer when in the end, she'd been the seductress driving him mad with her hands and mouth.

He closed his eyes and kissed the top of her head, desire warring with constraint and losing by the minute. He rubbed his leg over hers, kissed her forehead, her eyelids. She stirred slightly and when she lifted her face to his, he went to work on her mouth. God, he couldn't get enough. He wanted all of her, the honey sweetness of her lips and damp softness of her skin. The heat built more and more as he wrapped his arms around her, his mind reeling.

"Sean. Wait." Hannah broke the kiss, leaving him panting in agony. "I can't do this."

"What? Huh? Sure you can. You did it so well before." His body felt like it had hit a brick wall.

Hannah wiggled out of his arms and sat on the edge of the bed. "It's late. I really need to get home."

He appreciated the regret in her voice, but it didn't help. "No, no, no," he whimpered and dropped his head face-first into the pillow.

She chuckled at his antics, then ran a hand through his hair. "I'm sorry, but I do have to go."

Something about the way she rose made him grab her arm. "Hannah? No regrets?"

An eternity of seconds passed before he saw her smile and he could let out the breath he held. She shook her head. "Thank you for making me feel alive again."

If she kept looking at him like that, she'd be even later getting home. However, she didn't resist when he pulled her down for another kiss. "You could stay with me tonight. Tory won't be home until later in the morning."

"Hmm, that's very tempting, but I couldn't take a chance of her getting home before me."

"You could tell her you were at the store."

"In my gown?"

"Oh. Well, then, I could go home with you." His eyes followed his finger as he ran it slowly up her arm—then he flinched when he reached her scolding expression.

"And have her find us in bed?"

The tolerant smile she gave him made him feel like the teacher had just embarrassed him in front of the whole class.

"I have to set a good example for her. And I don't think having you walk out of my bedroom is the way to do that."

He nodded slowly in agreement. Somehow he had known what her answer would be, but he wondered if he'd asked her on purpose. Another test?

"You know," she explained, "sometimes it's necessary for parents to put their needs second to those of their children. This is one of those times. Besides, Tory likes you so much. I'm sure you wouldn't want to do anything to jeopardize that."

"No, no I wouldn't." Taking a deep breath, he cupped the back of her neck. "You are a remarkable woman, Hannah Stevens."

She jabbed him playfully in the ribs. "And don't you forget it!" With one last quick kiss, she grabbed her gown from the floor and headed for the bathroom. "I'd better get dressed."

He watched her walk naked across the room. She wasn't tall, just over five feet he would have guessed, the complete antithesis of the statuesque, model-like women he'd always preferred. And short hair had never appealed to him.

But if these were flaws, they had to be the sexiest flaws he'd ever seen.

As she closed the door behind her, Sean realized that her most beautiful attributes came from within, and they shined in everything she did, whether it was spending that extra thirty minutes with a client or giving up a Saturday to help build a home, or doubling as an in-house psychologist for her teenage daughter.

Their daughter.

Hannah had that rare quality of giving from her heart even at the expense of her own personal well-being.

He'd tried hard to find her guilty of being an unfit mother and had tested her at every opportunity. Each time she'd proven him wrong. Just like she'd done tonight. She'd put Tory first, not only out of parental duty, but out of love. He knew there could be no other mother for Tory.

Just as he knew there could be no other woman for him. He loved her.

It came to him simply, not a shocking revelation or earth shattering experience, but a realization that offered the kind of happiness he'd sworn Angie had taken from him forever.

He turned on another lamp and began pulling on a pair of jeans. The sound of Hannah gargling behind the closed door made him smile and he felt almost domestic. Then it all became clear—his future, their future—and it seemed so easy. Did she love him? Could she have given herself to him so completely if she didn't? Hannah wasn't the type for one night stands or casual relationships, he'd bet Sid Goldstein's millions on that. If she didn't love him now, she would by the time he got done with her.

His mind fast-forwarded. Hannah wouldn't have to work. She could stay home, get involved in charity events. Tory could go the best schools in Boston. He saw them all together as a family. *A real family.*

He pulled a T-shirt over his head and found himself chuckling. Everything was going to work out just the way he planned.

However, at the moment, it didn't include telling Hannah the truth. At least, not yet.

~ * ~

Ten days later, Hannah pulled the turkey out of the oven and wiggled a leg. *This had better be done,* she thought, feeling no confidence whatsoever in preparing a Thanksgiving meal. When was the last time she'd done this? Two years ago? Three?

The holiday had never been so special and she'd planned meticulously. The menu was pure Southern—cornbread dressing, sweet potato soufflé, giblet gravy, congealed salad, cooked-for-hours green beans, and pecan pie for dessert. She hoped Sean liked it.

But having him for dinner wasn't the only reason she felt so chipper. Three days ago, the telephone had rung with the chance of a lifetime and she couldn't wait to tell everyone.

"Mom! Hannah!" Tory's voice combined with Sean's as they called to her from the living room. "Come see the Rockettes." She hauled the bird to the counter top and let it sit. "I'm coming." Throwing the potholders Tory had made in the third grade on the counter, she made it to the television in time to see the signature high-kicking routine.

"I love watching the Thanksgiving Day Parade," Tory said. "We watch it every year, don't we, Mom?"

"Yup." They looked so natural, Tory and Sean, sitting next to each other, Hannah noticed. With the same dark coloring, they could pass as father and daughter. *What am I thinking?* The other day she'd found herself in a cloud of daydreams idly scribbling *Hannah Murphy* on a carpet order. *Stop acting like an adolescent.*

"Do you ever watch the parade, Mr. Murphy?"

Sean shook his head. "It's been a long time since I've seen it. Have you ever been to New York?"

"No."

"Well, maybe next year I could take you and your Mom to see the parade."

"Really? That would be way cool. Can we go, Mom?"

Hannah raised her brows. "It's a long time off. We'll see." She glanced at Sean and wondered what lay behind his words. Did he intend to be around for another year?

As they watched Underdog fly down Fifth Avenue, the doorbell rang and Marsha come in with two bottles of wine and a pumpkin pie. Hannah took her coat and eyed the pie suspiciously. "Did you make this?"

"You know very well I didn't. I got it at Sweet Mama's. They do great pies." She turned to Sean, who relieved her of the wine. "Sean, it's nice to see you again. Tory, come give me a hug."

After several minutes, Hannah left the threesome to small talk and the television while she went back to the kitchen. It wasn't very often she wished she had a real dining room and nice china, but looking at the tiny kitchen table barely big enough for four and the chipped, everyday dishes, she realized how much she'd missed the finer things in life, even if they had come with a price tag.

Hey, that's enough, she chastised herself. *You have the important things—a beautiful child, good friends and the man you love.*

With those things in mind, chipped plates didn't seem so important.

"Can I do anything to help?" She looked over her shoulder to see Sean lift his nose in the air. "Mmm, that smells terrific."

Her insides did a quick dance as he came up behind her and dropped a kiss on the side of her neck. "Mmm," he said, inhaling her perfume, "that smells even better."

"You're distracting me."

"I hope so."

She let out a laugh and turned in his arms, giving him a quick kiss in her own defense. If he nuzzled her neck one more time, she'd be a goner. Along with her dinner.

"How handy are you with a knife?"

He pulled back, his brows dropping into a deep V. "So much for romance. Why do you want to know?"

"I need you to carve the turkey for me while I dish up the rest."

He nodded slowly. "Carve the turkey. Sure."

The look on his face didn't give her a lot of confidence, but she set him up with a large fork, sharp knife and a platter. "Here you are. Go to it." She didn't know whether to step on his ego and show him how or just hope for the best.

As she rinsed out pots and cleared the counter to make way for the buffet, she made a point of not watching him perform surgery. Instead she concentrated on dishing up food, pouring wine and iced tea, and placing a bowl of fresh camellias on the table between two ceramic candlesticks.

When she turned back around, she almost laughed. Lips pursed and armed with knife and fork, Sean stood in front of the turkey studying it from several angles. He hadn't made one slice. "Uh, Sean? Can I help you?"

"No. No. I can do this."

"That's what you said about the Electric Slide."

He gave her a 'thank-you-Miss-Smarty-Pants' look that made her chuckle.

"Here. First you cut off the legs, then the wings." She placed the limbs neatly on the platter. "Then you cut under the breast, then slice down."

His arms came around her and trapped her at the counter, his warm breath teasing her cheek.

"Are you paying attention?"

"Uh huh. I'm concentrating very, very hard." He nipped her ear, sending a chill down her back.

"Good." She took a deep breath to gather her self-control, then ducked under his arm and patted his cheek. "Be sure to put the slices neatly on the platter."

Fifteen minutes later she called Marsha and Tory to the table, interrupting their game of Scrabble and an argument over whether or not 'dork' was in the dictionary.

Sean was silent when they held hands to say the blessing, and while clearly unfamiliar with the ritual, he didn't seem uncomfortable. He held chairs for each of them and the conversation that followed was light and humorous with Tory talking about upcoming exams and the annual Christmas dance.

"Do you have a date?" Marsha asked.

Tory nodded shyly while a soft shade of pink hit her cheeks.

"Who's the lucky boy?"

"Henry Pipkin." She looked at Hannah. "Is that okay, Mom?"

"Sure. When is it?" She passed Sean the gravy and immediately saw something in his eyes. He started asking Tory all about Henry and although he did it in a very casual manner, Hannah recognized grilling when she saw it.

"Mom, do you think I could get a new dress?"

"Well, we'll see what the budget looks like." She'd need new shoes, too, Hannah decided. She had a little money stashed away, but maybe Mrs. Gillis would decide to have those draperies made. No matter. Somehow Tory would get a new dress. Oddly enough, money problems didn't seem so upsetting lately. Financial insecurity still lurked over her shoulder, but Hannah didn't cringe from it anymore. She supposed it was all in how you looked at it.

And with Sean in her life, she looked at everything from a completely different viewpoint.

Lately, when happiness had threatened to explode inside her, Hannah had to grab control and remind herself this was just a relationship, keep it light, go slow. But of course, that all flew right out the window every time she got within ten feet of him.

The table conversation broke through her musing when Hannah heard her name. "I'm sorry, Marsha, what did you say?"

"I said I might have a new client for you. A customer of mine wants to redecorate, so I gave her your name."

"Oh, thanks. Every little bit helps."

"Have you had any new clients lately?" Marsha asked.

"Yeah." Hannah grinned at Sean. "Sid Goldstein."

Marsha choked on her green beans. "Sid Goldstein? How do you know him?"

"Sean introduced me."

Before Marsha could ask, Sean explained, "He's an acquaintance of mine."

"Well, I guess I can stop worrying about you now that you've got Mr. Money Bags as a client."

"It was just a small job. I'm not looking to retire any time soon." Hannah paused. "But I did receive an interesting phone call this week."

Sean looked up. "Who from?"

"Hook, Williams and McDermott."

"Oh, God, you're being sued," Marsha interjected.

"No, no. It's not a law firm. It's a decorating firm. In New York, Boston and Philadelphia. They're one of the biggest firms in the northeast."

Marsha looked impressed. Tory looked wary. Sean smiled benignly.

"What did they want, Mom?"

"They offered me a job. I couldn't believe it."

"No kidding," said Tory. "I wonder how they got your name."

Hannah shrugged. "They said one of my clients recommended me. It had to have been one of my Sea Island clients, although I only have a few of them."

"What kind of job?" Marsha asked.

"They didn't say exactly. Just that they had an opening in their Boston office and wanted me to come up for an interview."

Sean hadn't said a word, Hannah noticed. He smiled and looked interested, almost complacent, but the least he could do was show a little more enthusiasm.

"Hey, this could be the ticket you've been waiting for," Marsha suggested.

Tory stopped eating and slowly laid her fork on her place. "Does this mean we're going to move?"

She looked so upset, Hannah rushed to reassure her. "No, honey. I told them I wasn't interested."

"You did what?" Marsha raised a brow in bewilderment.

Sean looked more shocked than Marsha. Hannah definitely had his attention now. "But I did make *them* an offer. I suggested they open a branch office here and I could run it for them."

"Hey, that's a great idea," exclaimed Marsha. "Did they go for it?"

"They sounded interested and said they'd call me back. In the meantime, I'm going to write up a proposal for them to look at."

"Way to go, girl!" Marsha exclaimed.

As Sean nodded, Hannah basked in the admiration she saw in his eyes. "She's right," he agreed.

Hannah couldn't contain her excitement for the rest of the meal as she outlined her plans. Start locally, establish an identity, then branch out to Hilton Head Island to the north and Amelia Island to the south. Sean offered financial advice and Marsha suggested marketing strategies. Tory opted for a new house.

Too full for dessert, everyone agreed to pass for the moment, and as Marsha and Tory cleared the table and went back to their game, Hannah began washing the dishes, the excitement over this possible new direction in her life still bubbling inside.

"You seemed a little quiet at the table. You don't think my proposal is a good idea?"

Sean grabbed a dishtowel and began drying the dishes. "On the contrary. I'm very impressed at how you turned the situation around. You're really excited about it, aren't you?"

She washed a wine glass and set it on the drain board. "It's like the proverbial big break. It would be heaven not having to worry about money. I could get a regular paycheck and maybe even commissions."

"But how would you get your exercise if you aren't running down clients for checks," he teased.

"I'll take up aerobics. Besides, I don't think Hook, Williams and McDermott would approve of my collection techniques."

"Oh, but they haven't seen you in action. I could vouch for your effectiveness."

She laughed. "You're too kind."

"I'm curious, though. Why didn't you take the job?"

Wasn't that obvious? "Because this is our home, Tory's home. I couldn't uproot her, not now. She needs stability. She wants at least part of her old life back, and this opportunity could be the way for me to do that."

Sean wiped down the roasting pan and threw the towel over his shoulder.

Before she knew it, he turned her to him, his nearness spiking her pulse rate, a reaction becoming more frequent whenever he touched her.

"Oh, Sean, my hands are wet!" She stopped laughing in time to see the warmth in his eyes. It was the closest thing to 'I love you' she'd ever seen. And suddenly, she wanted to hear him say it.

"Have I told you what a special lady you are?"

"Not nearly often enough."

"Then I'll have to show you." He cradled her face in his hands and kissed her slowly, almost thoughtfully. Oh yes, he made her feel very, very special indeed. Her hands crept up his back as his kiss brought on a dreamy intimacy, and she floated on a wave of shimmering rapture.

Hannah didn't move when he pulled back. She kept her head up and eyes closed, wanting to stay in the center of her swirling emotions. When she heard him chuckle, she came back to earth and let out a shuddering breath. "A wonderful demonstration," she whispered.

And that was how Tory found them, locked in each other's arms. "Mom, how do you spell—"

Hannah's heart jumped to her throat. She jerked from Sean's arms, but he held her tight. A jumble of emotions—shock, confusion, embarrassment—swept over Tory's face. She took a step back, then half walked, half ran to her room.

"Oh, no, what have we done?" Hannah pushed away from him. "She won't understand this. I've got to talk to her."

Sean grabbed her before she could get away. "We haven't done anything, Hannah. Calm down."

"You're not a parent. You don't know about children. She's never seen me with anyone but Paul."

"Exactly, and it's a shock, but she knows we're seeing each other. Let her get used to the idea."

Frustration tangled with impatience. "Sean, you can't just ignore something like this. I *have* to talk to her."

"Then let me do it."

Hannah held up a hand and started to shake her head.

"Let me talk to her," he repeated.

Something in his voice, something she couldn't identify, made her stop and think twice. For several long seconds, she held his gaze and gradually gave in to the persuasion in his eyes. Inexplicably, she was willing to let this parental task fall into his hands, and it amazed her that she had few qualms about doing so.

"All right. But you have to be—"

"Trust me."

And, she realized, she did.

~ * ~

"Tory, may I come in?" She didn't answer his knock, so Sean turned the knob slowly and let himself in. Tory sat on the edge of the bed, shoulders slumped, staring at the floor. He didn't make a move to sit down, didn't want to invade her space. In actuality, he felt awkward and totally inexperienced.

"I'm sorry I interrupted you and Mom." She didn't look up and her apology held something close to an accusation.

"I'm sorry what you saw made you uncomfortable."

Silence.

"Are you angry with us?"

Shrug.

Now what do I say? he wondered. "I guess you've been through a lot of changes this past year. If it's any consolation, I know what it feels like."

"No you don't."

"Yeah. Yeah, I do." He took her desk chair, turned it backward and sat. "When I was a little older than you, my mother died."

Tory lifted her head a fraction.

"My father wasn't a very nice man. He drank a lot. Was drunk most of the time, and he... did other things. It wore my Mom down.

"I remember how I felt the day she died. Scared. Alone. And I hurt so much inside. A lot of things changed in my life then." He thought he saw a thread of communication in her eyes when she turned to him. "So you see, I know something of what you're going through. And I know how difficult it is when your life is turned upside down."

An uncomfortable silence followed, but Sean decided he'd said enough. The next move was hers.

"I guess it was kind of a shock when I saw you and Mom kissing. I've never seen her kiss anyone but Dad."

"I can understand that." How he wished he could make all of this easier for her.

Tory picked at a fingernail. "Do you like her?" Before he could answer, she added, "Well, duh, I guess you like her if you were kissing her."

He grinned. "I like your Mom very, very much. And I feel the same way about you."

"I just don't want her to forget Dad."

He took a hit to the heart. "She'll never do that. And neither will you. He'll always be with you." Sean meant his words, but on another level he wanted so damn much to tell her who he really was.

"I told Mom if she had to date, I'm glad she picked you."

That made him laugh. "Me, too. Are you going to be okay with your Mom and I seeing each other?"

"Yeah, I guess so. But would you mind not doing that in front of me or my friends? It's really embarrassing to see old people kissing."

He raised an ancient brow. "No problem," he said, dryly. "How about that dessert now?"

She nodded as he opened the door. "Mr. Murphy? Thanks for talking to me." Shock waves ran through him as she ran up and hugged him. He held his arms out, unsure, a giant lump clogging his throat. He squeezed his eyes shut, and in that long awaited moment, he folded her in his embrace and laid his cheek on the top of her head. "You're welcome, honey," he whispered hoarsely.

Just as quickly, she released him and headed to the kitchen.

Love exploded in his heart, and for the first time since the death of his mother, he felt the prick of tears.

Fourteen

The dawn broke cold and gray, bringing with it a steady rain that fell over the island as Sean drove down Frederica Road. It didn't hamper his mood, though, and certainly couldn't deter him from what he planned to do.

He'd checked in with Jackie at the stables that morning, and as usual, found everything under control. Making her manager had been a good decision. She'd kidded him about his good mood, saying his whistling would have every dog in a five mile radius howling. He'd just laughed.

Stopped at a traffic light, Sean glanced at his watch. Hannah would meet him at his place at 6:00 p.m. for dinner. A very special dinner. He still had a couple of hours to find exactly what he wanted. Maybe he should have flown back to Boston and had Brian help him find exactly the right stone. After all, he'd never asked a woman to marry him before. No, he couldn't wait. He had to ask her today, tonight.

He'd made his decision while eating a drumstick at her table, when she'd told everyone she'd turned down the job he'd arranged for her at Hook, Williams and McDermott. So much for wanting to help her. He'd been so sure she'd accept, it had caught him completely off guard when she hadn't, and then delighted him when she'd turned the whole situation to her advantage.

God, he loved her.

It can't get any better than this, he thought. The three of them, together. A dream come true.

Sean gazed out the driver's window, his thoughts wandering as raindrops fell lazily down the glass in haphazard paths, reminding him of another rainy day months ago, the day his life had really begun.

He supposed he should thank Elizabeth Jenkins for starting him down a path first of doubts, then of revelations. It rubbed his conscience that he hadn't contacted her, not even once. At first, anger had fueled revenge. He'd wanted to exact his pound of flesh and make Elizabeth pay for the secret she'd kept. Then, as the weeks had passed, she's drifted conveniently, if not easily, to the back of his mind.

Unfortunately, Angie's mother would have to wait a while longer. Until after he and Hannah were married.

After he'd told Hannah the truth.

The blare of a horn jerked him to the present, and he drove through the green light, letting out a troubled breath. Procrastination was never his style; there just hadn't been a good time to tell Hannah. Regardless, the longer he took, the harder it would be. Tonight was out, too. He couldn't ask her to marry him in one breath, then tell her he'd lied and manipulated her in the next.

When the time presented itself, he told himself again. She loved him. She'd understand.

She had to.

He pulled into Redfern Village, a unique shopping enclave in the middle of the Island, and parked in front of Caldwell's Jewelers. With a false sense of confidence, he pushed everything out of his mind except how to ask Hannah to marry him. Christmas was a great time for a wedding.

~ * ~

At 3:00 p.m., Hannah said goodbye to her last client, grateful she hadn't scheduled anyone else. Frequently during the day, she'd had to push Sean out of her thoughts and force herself to focus on colors, furniture and house designs. Smiling all the way home, she pulled up to her house, putting the finishing touches on her plans for a romantic dinner for two. She rechecked the contents of the overnight bag she'd packed, then made a call to April's mother to be sure Tory's sleepover plans were still in tact. Fifteen minutes later, she opened the front door and almost tripped over a brown envelope that sat on the doorstep. Her name was printed in big black letters. No doubt the fabric swatches Mrs. Goldstein had promised to drop off. In a hurry to get to Sean's, she threw the envelope into her bag then drove out to this townhouse.

The key was hidden under the planter outside Sean's door, as usual. Not a very safe place, but then, St. Simons was a small community. Small enough to where trust was still a matter of integrity. She let herself in, thankful she had three hours before he came home, time enough to surprise him with a candlelight dinner and the new negligee she'd ordered from Victoria's Secret.

She chuckled at how totally out of character this was for her. Too bold, too forward. Wicked. Daring. The thought gave her delightful goosebumps.

Pasta with shrimp, salad, French bread and wine—simple but elegant. Too bad the weather won't cooperate, she thought. A clear sky and full moon would have been so romantic.

She went about dragging out pots and pans and gathering ingredients, then started on the table. Beautiful gold-trimmed, white china and sterling silver place settings sat atop peach-colored place mats with matching napkins. Crystal wine glasses stood at each plate, silently waiting for a chilled Chardonnay, and the candlesticks would soon be joined by a simple arrangement of camellias and magnolia leaves.

All but the flowers were borrowed from the new party rental store in exchange for Hannah's passing out their cards to her clients. It helped to have connections.

She hummed as she washed lettuce and sliced tomatoes. Christmas would be here in several short weeks and because what to get him was still a problem, she realized there were some things she didn't know about him. Did he have any hobbies? Did he like brussel sprouts?

Did he want children of his own?

Her hands slowed as she arranged romaine on plates. She wondered what his reaction would be when she told him she couldn't have children.

You're not taking one day at a time, she reminded herself. *He hasn't asked you to marry him, has he?* Maybe he doesn't want to get married.

But she did. And the mental image of the two of them saying vows sent her heart into a tailspin.

"Stop it," she said outloud. "Just concentrate on today." She glanced at her watch. Forty-five minutes to make herself beautiful. Would they make love before dinner or after? She grabbed the small overnight bag she'd brought, and hurried up the stairs. A slow ripple of intimacy crept over her as she entered his bedroom, the feeling deliciously sensual. A pair of kicked-off tennis shoes sat in the middle of the floor and a shirt was tossed carelessly on the bed. She picked it up and inhaled his scent, then felt a slow burn in her belly. She ran a hand over the down-filled comforter and drew in a breath, not sure she'd survive the anticipation of what she hoped would be the most memorable night of her life.

Shaking herself back to reality, Hannah opened her bag and took out the black silk negligee. She held it up to her, liking the image the mirror reflected. Oh, yes, she thought, this should do very well. Sexy had never been a term she'd applied to herself, but looking at her reflection, maybe she should start.

She laid the nightgown on the bed then reached into her bag and took out the envelope she'd found on her doorstep. She wasn't going to give it a thought until she realized it wasn't thick enough to hold fabric swatches. Curious, she opened it and pulled out a picture of

Tory. She looked so cute, grinning in the obviously candid shot. Several more pictures were stuck together, shots of Tory at school, getting on the bus, talking with a group of friends. Suddenly, a chill ran down her back. These had been taken at school. Tory hadn't posed for these shots. It was as if she'd been observed. Watched.

He heart began to pound. She upended the envelope and a file dropped out. A file marked *Client: Murphy, Sean; Subject: Stevens, Victoria*. Her hand sprang back, not wanting to touch it, but afraid not to. She sat on the bed, opened it. What she read turned her blood cold.

~ * ~

"Hannah?"

She stared into the darkened sky as Sean came in, the sound of his voice hollow inside her. Rain fell heavily outside, sounding almost like storm waves pounding against the breakers as the wind threw sheets of water against the sliding glass door. A shudder ran down her back, but she knew it had nothing to do with the cold emanating from the glass.

"Whew, what a mess out there. Sorry I'm late." She heard his keys land on the foyer table. "I had a few stops to make."

A flash of lightning split the night sky, allowing a savage glimpse of the river. Each flash was a stab to her soul. Her mind had gone numb, but her heart pounded in death knell cadence.

"Hey, the table looks great. Are we eating in?"

She saw his smiling reflection coming closer. The smile she'd succumbed to. The smile of the man she'd given her heart and soul to. The man who'd betrayed her.

She'd thought she knew him, thought she'd answered all her own doubts and suspicions. *You fool. You poor lonely fool.* The charm, the sweet words. *You fell for all of it.* A sob worked its way to stop at her throat. No. Not until he told her everything. Then, when she was alone, she would let the tears come.

"Hannah?" Her whole body jerked when he touched her shoulder. "Hey, what's the matter?"

She stepped away from him, tiny tentacles of dread spreading vine-like through her gut. "Who are you, Sean Murphy?" she whispered.

"What? What are you talking about?"

Hannah heard his confusion, sensed a trace of annoyance. She turned to face him with the file clenched tightly against her chest. "Who are you?" Her voice gained strength as she fought the ache in her body with anger.

"I don't understand what you mean. Don't play games with me Hannah."

She let out a derisive laugh. "That's a good idea. Let's not play games. Anymore." She turned the file around and watched him. Something died inside her as guilt, stark and desolate, swept over his face.

Tightlipped, Hannah never took her eyes off him while she pulled out each photo followed by the typed report. The words she'd read held no emotion, no trace of the personal. Just the facts. With cold determination, she said, "Did you have this report done before you came here or after?"

"Hannah, I can explain. I wanted to tell you."

"Tell me what? That you're some kind of deranged stalker? Some kind of con man? What do you want from us?"

He reached out to grab her.

"Don't touch me! I swear to God, if you've hurt Tory in any way, I'll..."

"I'd never hurt her, never!" he shouted.

"How would I know? What is this about?" she yelled back, shaking the papers at him. "Who the hell *are* you?"

He hesitated only a moment. "I'm Tory's father."

The words didn't register. Her ears heard, but her mind couldn't, wouldn't, process. Then, confusion battled with a growing sense of panicked understanding. She stepped backwards, letting out a high-pitched, almost hysterical laugh. "Just because you've been playing Dad these past few months, do you think that makes you a real one?"

He caught her by the shoulders before she could get away, shook her.

"Hannah, I'm Tory's biological father."

The breath caught in her throat. Her head filled with a scream, desperate and denying. Tory's father hadn't been named on the birth certificate. It wasn't true.

"You're lying," she said hoarsely. "Just like you've been lying for months."

Sean shook his head. "I had a relationship fourteen years ago with a woman I thought I loved. But she left me and never told me she was pregnant. I never saw her again."

Angela Jenkins. Sean and Angela Jenkins. For some reason, Hannah suddenly felt on the tawdry end of a lover's triangle.

"Last March," he continued, "her mother came to see me and told me about the baby."

She wrenched out of his grasp. It all became clear now, frighteningly clear. "You want Tory, don't you?" She balled her fists at her sides, and when he didn't answer, she shuddered with fury and panic.

"You bastard!" She began to pace, her mind groping for reasons and answers. "You were so kind, so attentive." Tears weren't far away, but she had to hold on. If she looked at him, she'd lose it. "You made me fall in love with you. Why? You didn't have to go that far. Why didn't you just go to a judge? That would have been easy, but no, you had to come around every day, watching us, watching Tory, watching..." Her head raised up slowly. "...me." *Oh my God.* "You wanted to know if... if... I was a good mother." The realization hit her head on. "A *fit* mother."

Sean looked away, the silent admission a baseball bat to her gut.

Still, she held on. "If I'm an unfit mother, it would be easy to have Tory taken away from me, wouldn't it?"

"Hannah, please, listen to me. Things changed after I met you. I love you."

She didn't see his pain, didn't hear his pleading. "Liar!" she screamed, putting her hands over her ears. She grabbed her purse and ran to the door. "Don't you *ever* come near us again. Do you hear me? Ever! If I see you within a hundred feet of Tory, I'll... I'll... kill you!"

She ran into the storm, rain mixing with the tears she could no longer hold back. By the time she got to her car, she was soaked to the skin. Raw, primitive grief, as bitter cold as the December rain, tore fiercely at her heart. She held on to the steering wheel, took in huge gulps of air.

Ever so slowly, she gained control. Anger and rage rose to the occasion, surrounding her heart like a steel bandage.

No one will ever take my child away from me.

No one.

Sean stood rooted to the floor, watching his life fall apart as Hannah ran out the door. Going after her was useless, he knew. She wouldn't listen.

Where did she get the file? How could I have been so stupid and leave it out in the open? What have I done?

No, he couldn't let it happen. He loved her and had to make her understand he hadn't meant to hurt her.

Urgency propelled him out the door, the rain so heavy it pelted him with a punishment of tiny needles. "Hannah, wait!"

She must have heard him through the closed windows of the car because she turned toward him for a second.

He grabbed for the door handle as she started to back out of the parking space. "Let me explain. Please."

Hannah snapped her head around and her expression stopped him dead in his tracks.

Pain. Hatred. Misery.

He stepped back, stunned at the depth of his own unintended perfidy.

Tires squealed on the wet pavement as Hannah sped past him. Water sprayed in her car's wake.

He stared at the taillights, fists clenched into balls.

It wasn't supposed to happen like this.

He rested his head against the wet bark of an old oak tree and squeezed his eyes shut, taking in deep breaths to counter the sickening nausea that roiled in his stomach. Intense desolation and self-loathing twisted inside him like a white-hot knife, and for the first time, he cursed himself for coming here.

Thunder rumbled in the distance as the storm began to let up. The parking lot was littered with leaves and limbs, broken remnants of nature's violence. Sean returned to his condo, utterly oblivious to his sodden condition. His hand wrapped around the small jeweler's box in his pocket, making his heart break in despair.

He collapsed on the couch. Clear thinking was impossible, yet he had to come up with some way to make her listen and understand, make her forgive him.

He couldn't lose her, not like this. Not like Angie.

It won't happen again.

The vow gave him a spark of determination. He wouldn't go after her tonight. Maybe tomorrow. He got up and started to pace. Yes, tomorrow he'd begin the war to win her back.

He knew it would be the battle of his life.

Fifteen

Samantha Williams, Esquire, had a reputation for striking fear into the heart of any philandering husband, especially when the husband was the defendant in a divorce case. Tenacious and stubborn with a "don't leave him with a dime" credo, she was known as "the lady's lawyer" among the polite and "the ball buster" among the rest.

Hannah counted on that.

She sat in the reception area, wired to the point of exhaustion, hoping to be squeezed in between clients. It could take all day, the receptionist had told her when Hannah had arrived at 9:00 a.m.

She would wait.

Fatigue crept over her like a predator taunting her to close her eyes just for a minute. But when she did, Sean's image burned behind her eyelids. Handsome. Loving.

Deceiving.

Swallowing hard, she bit back the tears and focused on why she'd come here. Legally, there had to be something she could do to keep Sean away from them. A restraining order at least. Did he have any rights as Tory's biological father? That question had echoed ominously in her mind all night as she'd walked the floor, trying desperately to think clearly, calmly. Her emotions had run the gamut from anger to despair and every shade in between.

Nervously, Hannah smoothed the material of her wrinkled slacks, the same ones she'd worn to Sean's the night before. She hadn't changed clothes, hadn't even been to bed. By the time the sun peered through the kitchen curtains, an entire pot of coffee and one box of tissues were gone.

She'd been able to hide behind the excuse of a head cold when Tory had asked why her eyes were so red. How could she keep this from her daughter? Would Sean tell Tory he was her father? Could she keep Tory away from him?

Hannah took a deep breath and pushed back the panic. *How could he do this?*

"Mrs. Stevens?" The receptionist's voice jerked Hannah from her thoughts. "Ms. Williams can see you now."

With a sense of hope, Hannah walked into the office and shook hands with a strikingly tall woman wearing a stylish tan pantsuit. Her brilliant smile contrasted with her mahogany skin, bright gold earrings and necklace. Hannah sensed a warm and caring personality in the woman's handshake.

"Thank you for seeing me so quickly, Ms. Williams," Hannah said, taking the seat the woman offered.

"No problem, and please call me Samantha." The lawyer took her seat behind the desk. "How can I help you?"

The deep, soothing voice put Hannah at ease, but suddenly she didn't know where to start. Did she say she had fallen in love with a man who had lied to her, pretended to be someone he wasn't? Or maybe she should just admit she'd been gullible and naïve.

"I'm a single parent," Hannah began, "and I have a thirteen-year old daughter who is adopted."

"Are you divorced?"

Hannah shook her head. "My husband died over a year ago."

Samantha nodded and made a note on a yellow legal pad.

"My daughter takes riding lessons on the Island. Several months ago, the stable hand where she rides began giving her lessons." Hannah rubbed her throbbing temple as a headache made itself known. "I began to notice that he showed Tory—she's my daughter—more attention than the other students."

"In what way?"

"He'd give her more instruction and more encouragement. It made me uneasy. And he didn't look like he belonged at a stable," she went on to explain. "He didn't look like the outdoor type. I thought it was odd, so I started asking questions about him. But all the other parents of the riding students liked him and he seemed very... personable." Hannah stared at a point somewhere beyond the wall lost in a flood of memories she'd tried so hard to keep at bay.

She let out a small laugh. "He started coming around the house. Brought a pizza once and made repairs around the house." Sparkling blue eyes and jet black hair filled her mind. How could she have missed his resemblance to Tory?

"He was so caring," she said softly. *So loving.* A tear escaped and fled down her cheek. *Damn him for causing her so much pain!* Hannah wiped away the drop with an angry stroke.

She told Samantha her story, leaving out all her feelings of love and happiness and dreams. Just the cold, hard facts, the kind she'd read in the report she'd found in the envelope.

"Yesterday, I learned Mr. Murphy is Tory's natural father."

Samantha's head sprung up and she stared at Hannah for several seconds. "How did you find out?"

"He told me. After I found a report that had pictures of Tory and information on her, my husband and me." God, she felt so violated, victimized.

Samantha sat back in her chair, brows creased in question. "Let's back up here a minute. Tell me about the adoption."

"It was a private adoption," Hannah said, then let out a bitter chuckle. "Maybe it wasn't as private as I'd thought." She paused and took a cleansing breath. "The records were sealed. We were given general information on the mother, but there wasn't anything on the father. We'd thought perhaps the mother was an unwed teenager."

Hannah couldn't sit any longer. Rehashing old history unsettled her stomach and she started to pace, ended up leaning on the window sill looking out over the Brunswick River.

"My husband and I had wanted a private adoption. We didn't want to know or meet the mother. We thought that would be too confusing for a child."

Suddenly, Hannah felt the need to get it all out, all of her fears and insecurities.

"Actually, I didn't want any other woman to have a place in my child's life. It made me feel threatened." The admission sounded small.

"But there'd been one small glitch. When Paul and I had signed the adoption papers, the name of the birth mother was printed on the papers." Hannah shrugged. "Someone had made a mistake because as a private adoption, we weren't supposed to know the names of the parents. If Tory ever asked us if we knew them, we wanted to honestly say no.

"I realized there might come a day when Tory would want to find her natural parents. And I wouldn't object. But I wouldn't help her." Then she whispered, "I couldn't."

Hannah couldn't voice the fact she'd already lied to Tory. Hearing it outloud would only add to her shame.

She turned to see Samantha studying her intently, tapping a pen to her lips. "Did Mr. Murphy tell you why he waited thirteen years to see his child?"

"He said he didn't know about her until last March, and that the woman he'd had a relationship with never told him she was pregnant."

"How did he find out?"

"The woman's mother told him."

"Do you know where Tory's natural mother is?"

Hannah turned from the window as a new panic attacked her. "Oh, God, I hadn't even thought about her. What if she turns up here, too?"

Samantha held up her hand. "Hannah—may I call you Hannah?— let's take this one step at a time. Has this man threatened you in any way?"

Hannah sat back down, leaned forward. "Not directly. But I'm sure he wants Tory. Why would he go through this charade if he didn't? And that's why I'm here. I need to know what my rights are. Can I get a restraining order to keep him away from us?"

Samantha nodded slowly. "Perhaps. We'll have to show substantial cause. Stress to the child. His deception."

Hannah breathed a sigh of relief, but only for a minute.

"However, that's not going to solve your problem."

Dread returned and formed a hard ball in the pit of her stomach. "Why not?"

"I would suspect that if he's ingratiated himself into your lives, then he wants some type of permanence in your daughter's life."

"Do you think he'll want visitation rights?"

"At the very least."

"And if he wants more?"

Samantha shrugged. "He might sue for custody. How does your daughter feel about him?"

"She's crazy about him." By now, Hannah was numb with fear. "Could he win custody?" she choked out.

Samantha leaned forward, her brow creased in a sympathetic look. "I honestly don't know, Hannah. Adoption cases are tricky. The jury or judge may be sympathetic to the fact this man never knew he had a child. In that case, visitation rights would surely be in order.

"On the other hand, if he could prove, beyond a doubt, the child's home environment was not safe or not conducive to a healthy upbringing..."

"You mean, if he can prove I'm an unfit mother."

"Yes." Samantha gave Hannah a hard stare. "Are you?"

"No! I love my child more than life. I do everything I possibly can for her. But..." She hesitated. "What would constitute being unfit?"

"Well, if the child were left alone for long periods of time or if the mother was promiscuous in any way."

Hannah's rib cage shook from the force of the pounding of her heart, and she suddenly felt lightheaded.

"Hannah, what's wrong? Do you think you're unfit in some way?"

No! She opened her mouth, but couldn't utter a sound. When she found her voice, it sounded flat, dead.

"I have my own business. It's taken a lot of my time and effort and many times it's been a struggle just to keep food on the table. Sometimes I've had appointments at night and I've had to leave Tory at home by herself. And I'm rarely home when she gets home from school." She paused, not wanting to go on. "And... there's this man I've been seeing."

"What man?"

She didn't want to say it. "Sean Murphy."

Samantha looked confused. "What?"

"He was so kind, so caring," Hannah started to explain. "It was easy to fall in love with him." There were no tears now, only sadness and bitter recriminations.

"Did you have sex with him?"

No, I made love with him. "Yes."

"In your house? While Tory was there?"

Hannah shook her head hard. "Of course not. We were at his house, *never* at mine. I wouldn't do that." Hannah went back to pacing. She had to stay focused. "He made me fall in love with him."

Samantha looked dubious.

"I know that sounds irresponsible, even ridiculous, but that was his plan all along. He wanted to get close to see if I was a good mother." How could she have been so stupid?

"Well," Samantha said, stroking her chin, "this certainly is a twist."

Hannah didn't like the uncertainty that fell over the woman's face. "Tell me."

"We can get a lot of character witnesses, show you're a hardworking, single mother doing the best she can. Then we'll try to prove duplicity on his part. That should go a long way with a jury. And as far as your sexual relationship with him... Well, we'll portray you as being the victim. Hannah, I'll do everything I can to help you."

Hannah should have felt relief and at least a little confidence.

She didn't.

"But you can't be sure of the outcome."

Samantha shook her head. "I'll be honest with you. With all the precedents being set in adoption cases, you never know what could happen."

A cold wave of nausea crept up Hannah's throat, making her grab the desk for support. Samantha, obviously seeing Hannah's distress, jumped up and placed a comforting hand on her shoulder.

"Hannah, listen to me. I'm a damned good lawyer. They don't call me 'the ball buster' for nothing." She waited for a chuckle that never came. "I'll do everything in my power to help you. Believe me." She lifted up her hands. "But this may all be premature. You don't know for certain he'll sue for custody, do you?"

Hannah shook her head, but she knew. He would, she could almost bet on it.

"Okay, when or if he does, you come to me. In the meantime, I'll start on that restraining order."

Slowly, Hannah stood, gathered her purse and keys. "Thank you for seeing me."

"Keep your chin up."

Hannah nodded and walked out the door, her future and Tory's still in as much jeopardy as before.

She went to the beach, but didn't remember driving over the causeway or passing through the Village. The storm from the night before left a sunny, cloudless sky, but the stiff breeze held the chill of early December.

After parking the car, Hannah drew her coat tightly around her and sat on a flat rock. Usually, this spot gave her a sense of peace and solace, but not now. Today, she felt nothing but cold reality, as cold as the stone-gray water that crashed on the sand.

There were no guarantees in life. If she'd never admitted to that before, she certainly did now.

Tory is my life. The words seemed to echo in the wind. She wouldn't put her child through the trauma of a court battle and she wouldn't take the chance, no matter how remote, of losing her.

There was only one thing to do.

~ * ~

With a sour stomach and throbbing head, Sean drove by Hannah's house for at least the tenth time. He'd spent half the night with a beer in his hand, cursing his stupidity and rehearsing an apology. He couldn't remember the last time he'd read the report the PI had sent him. Hadn't he put it back in the file drawer? How could he have been so careless as to leave it out where Hannah could find it?

Sean shook his head, totally disgusted the he could have screwed up so badly. But he could kick himself later. His first priority was to face Hannah.

Finally, after the umpteenth driveby, he saw her car in front of the house and wondered where she'd been all morning. As he parked behind her and walked to the porch, he noticed the front door partially open. His already aching stomach lurched in alarm. Fearing a burglary, he took the steps two at a time and flung open the door.

"Hannah!"

She didn't answer, but he heard a commotion that drew him down the hallway to her bedroom. He stopped dead in his tracks in the doorway.

Hannah stood with her back to him, furiously yanking open drawers, pulling out clothes and throwing them into two open suitcases on the bed. So absorbed in what she was doing, she obviously hadn't heard him enter the house or call her name.

His relief over her safety veered sharply to disbelief, then to rage when he realized her intent. An apology was useless now. He crossed his arms over his chest and planted himself squarely in the doorway, blocking her escape.

"Going somewhere?"

Hannah whirled around, almost tripping over her feet. The scared stiff look on her face cut his heart in two.

"How did you get in here?"

"Through the door you left open. You should learn to lock it."

"Get out."

"I asked you where you're going."

"None of your business. I don't want you here and I don't want you in our lives."

If she'd only give him a minute to explain how things had changed since he'd fallen in love with her. But it was beyond that now. His desperation took a back seat to his mounting anger. She planned to bolt and no doubt take Tory with her.

He'd lost his daughter once. He wouldn't allow that to happen again. "How far do you think you'll get, Hannah?"

He watched her grab a negligee from a drawer, the Victoria's Secret tag still attached. Had she planned to wear that for him last night? Tightlipped, her eyes shifted with uncertainty, then she threw the nightgown on top of strewn socks and shoes and jeans.

Sean clenched his jaw, her determination fueling his fury. "Answer me, damn it!"

She jumped like a doe in the glare of headlights and when she spun around to face him, Sean faltered in agonizing guilt. Dark shadows hung like half moons under her eyes, stark evidence of strain and lack of sleep. Against her pale skin, the contrast was almost ghoulish.

He had done this. He'd caused the misery so blatantly etched on her face and for a moment he wanted to beg for her forgiveness. Yet, instinct told him if he gave in, he'd lose her and Tory forever.

"I'm getting as far away from you as I can. Don't you think I know what you want?" With hurried, jerky movements, Hannah zipped one suitcase closed. "You want Tory." With two hands she pulled it off the bed with a dull thud. "Well, you can't have her. I won't let you have her." Her voice shook, whether from anger or fear, Sean couldn't tell.

"You're going to be served with a restraining order," she told him. "And if you ignore it, I'll have you arrested."

That she'd gone to such lengths shocked him. Did she hate him that much? "Hannah, I'd find you no matter where you went. I lost thirteen years of *my* child's life. I won't lose any more."

Maybe it was the cold threat in his words that made Hannah slow her hurried pace, then drop the remaining suitcase on the floor. She stood up, rigid. "Don't do this."

"It wasn't hard to find Tory, you know. In fact, the private investigator found her in a matter of weeks. I just gave him a place to start and well, you know what they say. The rest is history."

She looked at him, a glazed look of defeat spreading over her face. "Please." She sat on the bed and lowered her head in dejection. As her shoulders slumped, Sean watched her tears fall.

"Please," she repeated on a sob, "don't take my baby away from me. She's all I have."

You have me! I love you! Sean turned his head, no longer able to watch her suffer the torture he had caused. But he couldn't stop until he made her see there was only one answer.

"There's a solution to this, Hannah. A way that would satisfy everyone." The urge to reach out to her was so strong, he had to physically restrain himself from taking a step toward her.

No, he had to play this out and pray to God it would work.

Hannah lifted her head to look at him with such helplessness, he almost lost his nerve. "Really," she said, disdain ringing through a half-sob. "And that would be...?"

"Marry me."

He kept a hard expression, staring at her for an eternity of seconds, his heart pounding wildly.

"Wh... what?" she sputtered, her tone so incredulous, he would have laughed if the whole situation wasn't so serious.

"Are you crazy? Have you lost your mind?" She shook her head as if wondering if she'd heard correctly. "Why? Why would I want to marry a man who lies and manipulates, who deliberately hurts people to get what he wants?"

Sean cringed inwardly at the accusation. "Don't make me take this to court and sue for custody of Tory. I'm sure a jury would be very sympathetic when they learn I never knew about my own child. Then, of course, there's the expense and emotional ordeal of a long, drawn-out court battle. I have lots of money, Hannah. Do you?"

Her eyes narrowed slightly, disgust mixed with astonishment. "What kind of man are you?"

"Then there's Tory. You know how much she likes me. I'm willing to bet she'd hate you for forbidding her to see me. Are you willing to take that chance?" Sean dropped his eyes. He couldn't stand to watch the effects of his treachery or to hear his own words.

"Why are you doing this?"

Her pleading questions tore at his gut but he didn't answer. If he didn't leave soon, he'd break down himself. "Think it over, Hannah," he said as he turned to leave. "I promise, you'll never have to worry about money for the rest of your life. And Tory would have every opportunity."

The knot in his chest made him swallow hard. What kind of heartless bastard would coerce the woman he loved into marriage? He forced himself to walk away before he ran back to say this was all a horrible, sick joke.

He'd had no choice. It was either force his hand or lose them both. A sagging emptiness filled him at that thought and he knew his life meant nothing without them. Hannah was right to despise him, but he loved her. And he'd show her just how much if only she'd give him the chance.

Silently, he walked down the hall and turned the knob on the front door, but his hand refused to pull. Squeezing his eyes shut, he leaned his forehead against the door and prayed to a God he'd abandoned long ago.

Please. Don't let them leave me.

Sixteen

"Olin, this isn't the color I picked out for this room. Sunrise Yellow was supposed to go in the family room, not the living room." *Couldn't these guys get anything right?* Hannah thought, suddenly wishing she were in a different business.

Olin, six-foot-six and three hundred pounds of pure Southern torpidity, towered over her like King Kong. From his back pocket, he pulled a worn, folded piece of paper. In the time it took to unfold it, Hannah could have had another cup of coffee. She counted to ten.

"Well, Miz Hannah," he drawled, "you put down here Sunrise Yellow in the living room."

Hannah scowled at him and snatched the work order from his hand, holding in the temptation to ask if he could read English.

"Olin, I know very well that I wouldn't tell you to paint the living—" There, in her handwriting, was exactly what she didn't need to see. How could she have made such a stupid mistake?

Hanging her head in embarrassment, she apologized. Normally, it wasn't her nature to be snappish. But then, nothing in her life had been normal lately.

She thanked Olin profusely for agreeing to repaint at no extra charge, then went through the rest of the spec house with clipboard firmly held against her stomach. Any more mistakes like that one would come out of her profit.

She rechecked window sizes and room measurements, but concentration was almost impossible. How could she keep her mind on anything except the situation she was in?

It had been a week since Sean had threatened her with marriage. Although he hadn't called or stopped by, Hannah knew he'd been watching her. Several times she'd seen him drive slowly by the house, like a silent stalker choosing his time to strike. And there wasn't a damn thing she could do about it.

She dropped her clipboard on the kitchen counter and stared out the window. She'd thought of running again, then almost laughed at that idea. If there was one thing she knew for sure, Sean wouldn't sleep until he'd found them. Grudgingly, Hannah admitted she'd probably do the same thing if the situation was reversed.

So, what now? Should she seek him out, try to talk to him reasonably and come to some kind of compromise? Or just avoid him, stay out of his way? She didn't have to wait long for an answer.

"I haven't heard from you."

Hannah jumped at the sound of Sean's voice. "Damn it, don't scare me like that."

He walked slowly into the kitchen, leaned against the counter. "Sorry."

He didn't sound it. "How did you know I was here?"

"I saw your car."

"In the garage with the door closed?"

He shrugged.

"Stop following me," she demanded.

"I'm just making sure you don't take a sudden vacation."

Hannah clenched her teeth and swallowed her irritation and anger. "Look, Sean," she said with as reasonable a voice as she could manage. "Surely we can come to some kind of compromise here. You can see Tory whenever you want. We can go on like before." Hurriedly she added, "Except we wouldn't... date... or see each other. And of course, Tory would stay with me."

He thought about it for a moment, but the look on his face told her he wasn't buying it. "What's the matter?" she snapped. "Can't you be fair about this?"

Sean pursed his lips, shook his head.

"I don't want to marry you," she yelled. "I don't love you!"

Sean pushed himself away from the counter and walked toward her. "Yes, you do."

Alarmed, Hannah backed up.

"You're angry with me and I don't blame you. But I'll bet you can't look me in the eye and tell me you don't love me."

She bumped up against the refrigerator with a start as he came within inches of her. Her eyes were drawn to his lips, firm and sensual, and instantly she hated her body's betrayal. Her heart beat wildly, wanting the feel of his kiss yet wanting to deny the shivers that pulsed through her.

"Tell me, Hannah. Tell me you don't want me to make love to you." His words drifted through her head on a soft whisper. "Tell me you don't want to feel me inside you."

She swallowed hard, panicking at how close she was to returning his kiss, how she wanted to drown in the feel of it.

"Stop it. Stop it!" With a last desperate grab at willpower, she blocked him with her arm and put a safe distance between them. A long silence ensued and when he spoke again, his voice was cold as ice water.

"I want an answer to my proposal, Hannah. Now."

She turned toward him, feeling a pillow of despair smothering her, but refusing to let her desperation show. She squared her shoulders, hating him for forcing her, hating herself for still loving him. "I despise you for making me do this." Brittle as ice, Hannah flung the words at him, but they made no mark. He only waited for an answer. "Yes."

"Good." He reached into his pocket and handed her a small black velvet box. She wouldn't reach for it, so he opened it himself.

In spite of herself, she let out a small gasp. The diamond, at least three carats, took her breath away. The morning sun shining through the window set off an explosion of color in the oval stone that appeared flawless. Involuntarily, she took it from his hand, wanting to react like any other woman who had just received a marriage proposal. But that was impossible. Elation came and went in an instant. She snapped the box closed and put it on the counter.

"You don't like it?" he'd asked.

"It's fine." She didn't look at him, refused to acknowledge the trace of disappointment in his eyes.

"Are you going to wear it?"

"Are you giving me a choice?"

His mouth straightened to a tight line. "No."

"Then I'll wear it. Anything else?" She'd be damned if she'd make this easy for him.

"We need to discuss wedding plans. You know, what church, who to invite."

She pursed her lips and shook her head. "No. You're the one who wants this marriage. You make the arrangements. I have a business to run."

His expression softened a bit, and she couldn't believe his audacity to look hurt. "It doesn't have to be this way," he said, the words sounding strangely like an expression of regret.

"Doesn't it?"

Their eyes locked for several long moments, neither of them giving an inch in the tug-of-war they played.

She grabbed her clipboard and moved to the foyer on her way upstairs.

"We need to talk about Tory," he said, following behind her.

Hannah stopped on the second step of the stairway. "What about her?"

"We need to discuss when and how to tell her about me."

"Do you mean tell her you're her father or tell her that you're a liar and the only reason you came here was to take her away from her mother? Or do you want to tell her you are going to take the place of her *real* father, the one she misses with all her heart?"

The disgust in her voice shocked even her and Hannah wished she could take it back. Too late, Sean's face registered the damage. She took a deep breath and walked down the stair to face him. Her stomach churned from too little food and too much anxiety. "I think we should tell her together, when the time is right. But I'll expect you to be honest with her, Sean."

He nodded, then looked away. The impulse to stroke his cheek came out of nowhere, and Hannah had to struggle to keep her hand at her side.

"I'll set the date for December twenty-eighth so it won't interfere with Christmas. We'll be married at Lovely Lane Chapel. Two oclock. Don't be late." He turned on his heel and left her there to stare after him.

She was going to marry the man she loved. How could that dream have turned into such a nightmare?

~ * ~

"I can't believe you turned down a date with Josh Logan to come to the dance with Henry Pipkin." April wrinkled her nose as she strung out Henry's name in exaggerated distaste.

Tory didn't appreciate her friend's tone and tried not to let it bother her. "He's really nice once you get to know him," she said, but her words were drowned out by the din of the entire eighth grade all crammed into the school gymnasium.

Tory and Henry had spent most of the day turning the gym into a wonderland of crepe-paper Christmas trees and cardboard Santas. The entire time, he'd joked around, teased her, held her hand as she climbed a ladder to tape red-cheeked elves to the wall. His company had taken her mind off the news she'd received that morning, news that had thrown her into the front seat of an emotional roller coaster.

When the other girls in the group began to snicker, Tory glanced over her shoulder to see Henry walking toward her with two soft drinks in his hands. She threw her friends a dirty look and turned her back on them.

"Thanks, Henry," she said, taking the cup he offered.

Henry didn't say anything for a minute, but Tory noticed how he hung his head and stared at the floor.

"Maybe you should have come with Josh. At least your friends wouldn't be laughing at you."

"They're jerks, Henry. I don't pay any attention to them and neither should you." She touched his arm. "You're the one I wanted to come with. Please don't let them spoil our evening."

Dejection slid from his face and Tory wondered at his ability to lighten her mood with just a smile.

As the deejay played a soft tune by NSYNC, Henry asked, "You wanna dance?"

She nodded and they moved to the edge of the dance floor, empty until now. Quickly, it filled with a number of couples, except for April and the group Tory had been standing with. They stood with their arms crossed, waiting unsuccessfully to be asked to dance.

Tory followed Henry's glance to the group and when he looked down at her, he said, "They're not laughing now, huh?"

She smiled and kept the giggle that bubbled up inside.

When the dance ended, they sat in folding chairs that lined the wall. Henry surreptitiously slid his arm around the back of her chair and her heart took a leap.

"Did I tell you how great you look tonight?"

Tory felt a blush creep up her face. "Yeah, when you came to the door to pick me up."

"Oh."

She felt grownup in her long red dress and it pleased her that Henry liked it, too. Lifting her wrist, Tory inhaled the sweet aroma of the gardenia corsage Henry had presented her with.

"You haven't mentioned anything lately about calling that woman, Angela Jenkins."

"Yeah, I know. I'm still thinking about it." At the moment, she had another topic on her mind besides her birth mother. Pausing, she wondered if she should tell him. She had to tell someone. "Guess what?"

"What?"

"My Mom is getting married."

At first he didn't respond, her statement was so casual. Then his eyes grew big. "Wow. Who's she marrying?"

"Mr. Murphy."

"No kidding?"

Tory shook her head and when she didn't volunteer more information, he said, "Are you okay with this? I mean, you like this guy, don't you?"

"Oh, yeah, he's really nice and I like him a lot." She shrugged. "I was just kind of surprised when they told me. I mean, we have a lot of fun together, you know, like a family. I knew they liked each other but I didn't think about them getting married.

"I was excited at first, but after I thought about it for awhile, it made me kind of sad. It's hard to picture mom with anyone but my dad." She shook her head. "Oh, I don't know. I get so confused. First I'm happy, then I'm sad."

"Well, look at it this way. Maybe you can move back into our neighborhood."

The thought sparked a smile. "Gee, I didn't think about that. That'd be cool."

"I guess your mom's real happy."

"I suppose so." Tory remembered Hannah's expression when they'd called her into the kitchen to tell her the news. Sitting at the table, Hannah had simply said she and Mr. Murphy were getting married. It had been Sean who'd jumped in to explain that he and her mom were in love and it was important for them to know if Tory objected in any way.

Tory felt strangely drawn to Sean like she had so many times in the past. Her initial surprise at their announcement had turned to teenage elation.

Yet, she couldn't figure out why her mother's smile looked so fake. And how come her mom had jumped when Sean had covered her hand with his own?

"When are they getting married?" Henry asked, breaking into her thoughts.

"Sometime around Christmas."

He nodded. "Are you going to be in the wedding?"

"I guess."

"Can I come?"

She let out a little laugh. "Sure."

He smiled at her then and the blush she'd felt before returned to heat her cheeks.

"Come on," he said, "Let's dance."

"But it's a fast dance."

"So?"

Guys don't fast dance, she thought as he pulled her to her feet. Wincing inwardly, she followed him to the dance floor, determined not to be embarrassed in front of everyone by how he danced.

She took a deep breath and moved to the music. When she finally got the nerve to look at him, her mouth fell open. Henry moved like one of the Back Street Boys on stage. She was amazed. A crowd started to form around them, everyone clapping and whistling. When Henry did a back flip at the end of the song, the crowd went wild.

"Henry!" she said as he walked slowly toward her with a cocky grin. "I never knew... Where did you learn...? How did you...?" Stunned, she couldn't get out a complete sentence.

"Guess I'm not a complete geek, huh?"

At that moment, her heart tripped and landed at his feet. For the first time in her young life, Tory fell in love.

~ * ~

"You want me to what?"

Sean heard disbelief crackle through the telephone line. He could picture Brian pinching the bridge of his nose. "I want you to be my best man."

"Best man for what?"

"I'm getting married, you idiot! Why else would I need a best man?"

"You're marrying Hannah Stevens? That's...that's impossible."

Sean let out a laugh. "Don't sound so shocked. Don't you think I'm good marriage material?"

"It's just that I figured she'd..." A long-suffering sigh hit Sean's ears. "Geez, Sean, you don't have to marry her to be able to see your kid."

"I know that."

"Then why are you doing it?"

"Because I love her and I love Tory." *And I want us to be a family.* Sean didn't hear anything for a moment, but he could sense Brian's disapproval. His elation at telling Brian the news dropped a notch.

"Did you tell her about Angie? And why you went down there in the first place?"

"She knows."

"What did she say when you told her?"

All excitement gone, the conversation triggered Sean's frustration and he let out a breath. "Well, I didn't exactly tell her. She, uh, found the private investigator's report."

"How did that happen?"

"Damned if I know. I must have left it out somewhere. Still can't believe I did that."

Sean felt a hollow ache in the pit of his stomach remembering the devastation on her face.

"Then what happened?" Brian asked.

"Just what you'd expect. She blew up. Said she never wanted to see me again."

"So how did you get her to change her mind?"

Sean didn't want to get into it. "It's complicated."

Brian snorted. "As usual. But then you always seem to get what you want."

Sean had hoped for Brian's support, not his disapproval. "Look, are you going to be my best man or not?"

"Sure, why not?"

Sean breathed easier. "Great. We're getting married on the twenty-eighth. Why don't you come down right after Christmas?"

"Okay." Brian paused. "Is there more to this story?"

"No," he answered too quickly.

"Come on, talk to me."

With the phone in one hand, Sean ran his other hand through his hair. He could never keep anything from Brian, even if he'd wanted to. No sense trying now.

"She was going to leave town and take Tory with her. I... I couldn't let her do it. Not after I'd found them. Everything I'd ever wanted was in danger of going down the tubes. I'd planned to tell Hannah, but there was never a good time."

"So how did you persuade her to marry you?"

Picking up Brian's habit, Sean rubbed the top of his nose, reluctant to voice the admission. "I told her if she didn't marry me, I'd sue for custody of Tory. And that I'd probably win."

"Well," Brian said after a suspended silence, "that's a hell of a way to get a wife."

"I'm not real proud of myself."

"Then why did you do it? Why marry a woman who obviously hates your guts?"

"She doesn't hate me, Brian. She's angry and upset, but I *know* she loves me. And this can work between us. I know it." The confident words fell just short of credible.

"You must have been pretty desperate."

Desperate, petrified and whatever else a man feels when his life is about to blow up in his face.

"I understand why you did it, Sean, but I hope you're not kidding yourself. You're really going to have to bust your ass making it up to her. Have you thought about what will happen if this plan doesn't work?"

"It *will* work."

"Right."

"Come on, Brian," Sean said, wanting more from his friend than skepticism. "Just be there for me, will you?"

"You know I will."

"Thanks."

After Sean replaced the phone in the cradle, he grabbed a beer from the refrigerator, all the while thinking about Brian's comments. Sean had never voiced his own doubts about a marriage based on threats even though his misgivings, clinging to him like a shadow, battled with his hopes and dreams.

Hannah loved him, he knew that without a doubt. Whether or not she would ever forgive him remained to be seen, but the only thing that kept his dream alive was his faith in their love for each other. He vowed to make amends every day of his life, if necessary, but he wouldn't let her go. He couldn't.

A layer of winter clouds hung in the late afternoon sky as he left the condo for some fresh air. The idea of a ride on the beach lured him to the stables where he brought Apollo out of his stall and began to brush him. The exercise massaged his mood and lightened his mental load.

"Excuse me."

Surprised, Sean looked up to see a tall, dark woman walking toward him.

"Are you Sean Murphy?"

He reached for a saddle blanket and threw it over the horse's back. "Yes. Can I help you?" From the looks of her trim, gray business suit, the woman obviously wasn't here for riding lessons.

She reached into her shoulder bag and pulled out a business card. When Sean read 'Esq.' after her name, his curiosity turned to suspicion.

"My name is Samantha Williams. I'm a friend of Hannah Stevens."

"A friend?" He tucked the card in his shirt pocket and lifted the saddle off the door of the stall. Hannah's lawyer? He wondered if he was about to be served with the restraining order Hannah had told him about. "Are you here in an official capacity or is this a social call?"

"More of a 'get acquainted' visit. Hannah's mentioned you several times."

"I bet she has," he murmured as he tightened the cinch. "I didn't know lawyers made house calls."

"I don't usually, but I decided to make an exception in this case."

"Lucky me." Sean figured her low, smooth voice did wonders with a jury, but he knew this was something more than a welcome call.

Samantha folded her arms over her chest and Sean could feel her eyes on him as he finished his task.

"Hannah came to me with a problem not too long ago."

"As a friend or a lawyer?"

When the woman didn't answer, he wondered if this was a last ditch effort by Hannah to discourage him from marrying her. Send a lawyer with a little intimidation and perhaps he'd back off. *Not likely.* "Tell me, Ms. Williams, did Hannah say that I was the problem?"

"Let's just say your name came up more than once." She pursed her lips. "I was helping Hannah with her problem when all of a sudden she tells me you and she are getting married."

"Oh, I get it," he said with a broad smile, "you're here to congratulate me." He knew he'd hit a nerve when her expression turned hard.

"I don't care for men like you, Mr. Murphy."

He snorted, not bothering to hide his contempt. "You don't know anything about me, lady."

"Oh, but I do." She crossed her arms, began to pace. "Mr. Sean Patrick Murphy, President and CEO of The Murphy Group, Boston, Massachusetts. Self-made man of one of the top investment firms in the country. Has taken over more than one business by playing hardball."

Sean turned to her, raised a brow.

"I don't usually take such a personal interest in my clients," she went on, "but when I found out about you, my curiosity got the better of me. I wondered what kind of a man—a man like you with money and power—would take advantage of woman when she's most vulnerable." Her eyes narrowed in disgust and she shook her head. "I defend women against men like you all the time. The kind that abuses women at every turn."

His temper hit the boiling point. "Just a damn minute. I have never raised a hand to Hannah. Who the hell do you think you are?"

"You should be asking yourself that question. You may not abuse her physically, but you're abusing her mentally. This whole marriage smacks of threats, blackmail and coercion. I'm here to tell you that all she has to do is say the word, and I'll come down on you with both feet. And I don't think the Boston financial community would be very impressed with the president of The Murphy Group once they read about you in *The Globe.*"

Sean stared at her coldly for a long moment. "That sounds like a threat, Ms. Williams."

"I never make threats. But I do keep my promises."

His temper, at first red hot, began to cool. Anger aside, he had to admire her nerve. She'd obviously done her homework. Had she told Hannah?

Sean turned from her and mounted Apollo in one fluid movement, making Samantha step back as the horse pranced nervously. "Thank you for being such a good friend to Hannah, Ms. Williams. I hope you'll be at our wedding." He rode out of the barn, not seeing the surprised, quizzical expression on the woman's face.

Haunted once again by doubts, Sean rode toward the beach, hoping to hell he was doing the right thing.

Seventeen

She'd always liked powder blue.

Hannah gazed in the mirror, taking stock of the woman who looked back. With the exception of the glazed, resigned expression, she did look like a bride.

The form-fitting, pastel gown with its simple lines and sweetheart neckline complimented her figure. A long-sleeved, short jacket gave the dress a stylish finish, and the faux pearls Hannah wore at her throat and ears added an elegant touch.

"It's perfect," Tory had said when they'd found it.

Perfect for Hannah's wedding day. The happiest day of her life.

She wanted to weep.

How could life be so cruel as to force her into a marriage with the man she both loved and hated?

"Mom?" Tory peeked in the doorway of the small changing room off the main sanctuary of Lovely Lane Chapel. "Are you okay? You look sad."

Hannah hurried to reassure her. "No. No. Not sad. Just... reflective." She stood, put a smile on her face and twirled around. "How do I look?"

"Stunning. Absolutely stunning," Marsha said, walking up behind Tory with three bouquets of flowers in her hands.

"Yeah, Mom, you look so pretty."

Hannah felt the sting of tears as her emotions swirled like a kaleidoscope. "Not half as pretty as you, honey." Marsha and Tory wore identical dresses of deep blue velvet with short jackets that mirrored Hannah's.

"Are you ready?" Marsha asked, passing Tory a multicolored bouquet.

Hannah took a deep breath but there was no happiness behind the smile she pasted on her face. "As ready as I'll ever be." Her answer made Marsha's brows draw up in an arch.

"Tory, why don't you go outside and tell Reverend Culberth your mom and I will be there in a minute."

"Okay."

As Tory left, Marsha laid her flowers on a small table and sat in a chair watching Hannah check her makeup one last time. "You know," she said, smoothing her gown over her knees, "when you told me you and Sean were getting married, I thought you were the luckiest woman in the world. And the most deserving. After what you went through with Paul, you've found a gorgeous man who obviously loves you and Tory and wants nothing more than to make you happy."

"Hmm." Hannah made a show of re-applying her lipstick. She pushed Marsha's comments from her ears. If she didn't think, if she kept her emotions in a protective cocoon, she just might make it through the day.

"Now I'm beginning to wonder if there's trouble in Paradise."

"Don't be silly." She threw Marsha a quick glance in the mirror. "It's nerves, that's all." She picked up the bunch of white roses, turned from the mirror and put on her most convincing smile. "I'm entitled. We'd better go. I wouldn't want to keep the groom waiting."

"Hannah." Marsha stopped her at the door. "I'm getting some very disturbing vibes. Something's not right here, but you obviously don't want to talk about it."

Hannah couldn't meet her eyes.

"If you have any doubts, for heaven's sake, don't go through with this."

I don't have a choice. The silence stretched into one long minute.

"Okay," Marsha said with a resigned sigh, "but if you ever need to talk or need a place to stay, you know where to come."

Hannah didn't trust herself to say a word. Instead she hugged Marsha fiercely then walked out the door to face an uncertain future.

~ * ~

The chapel was almost full with friends, clients and business associates of Hannah's and the few acquaintances Sean had made since coming to the Island. Not to be left out, Tory had invited a number of her friends, too, including Henry.

Sean had hired Mrs. Betty Nesbit, a Beacon Hill wedding consultant from Boston, to make all the arrangements and from the looks of it, the woman was worth every penny of her exorbitant fee. Flowers, candles and greenery artfully adorned the altar and pews, and a tastefully printed program was handed out. A four-piece chamber quartet played soft, classical pieces as everyone took their seats.

Everything was perfect.

As Brian spoke with the minister, Sean noticed his heart beating slightly faster then normal. Nerves, he determined, and why not? After all, it wasn't every day a man got married.

The thought brought him a smile, but it ended before it got started. Getting married wasn't the only reason for a case of nerves. He was scared to death. What if Hannah changed her mind? What if she left him standing at the altar?

What if she said "no" to the minister's "Do you, Hannah, take this man...?"

Sean squelched the panic with a dose of false reassurance and came back to the present when Mrs. Nesbit whispered it was time to start.

Sean took his place with Brian by his side as the traditional strains of the Wedding March rang through the sanctuary. His eyes followed Marsha as she came down the aisle, and he had to wonder at her stern expression. But it was Tory who brought a proud smile to his face. In her velvet gown and hair arranged in elaborate ringlets, she looked so grown up that his heart ached for the years they'd lost. He vowed to treasure every moment with her from now on.

Giving her a wink as she stood next to Marsha, he turned his attention to the far end of the aisle as the congregation came to their feet.

The sight took his breath away.

Perhaps it was the atmosphere, or the music and flowers, or the profound significance of this event in his life that made his heart clench. Hannah had never looked more beautiful than she did at that moment, walking toward him in an ethereal cloud of morning blue, to become his wife. His love for her, fierce and overwhelming, rocked him to the very depths of his soul.

Yet, his joy faltered a bit as she drew nearer. She stared straight ahead, not at him, and the smile she wore could have been carved from stone. There was no happiness in her eyes. She walked stiffly, almost reluctantly, as if walking an invisible plank. Suddenly, he wondered again if she'd go through with the ceremony.

Sean didn't hear the minister's words, he only knew he had to do something.

"We are gathered here in the presence of God..."

How could he show her how much he loved her?

"...to join this man and this woman..."

The words became lost in Sean's ears until he heard "Do you, Sean Patrick Murphy, take this woman..."

Suddenly, Sean held up his hand, cutting the man off, clearly astonishing the stalwart reverend. A soft buzz rippled through the chapel as Sean handed Tory Hannah's bouquet, then took Hannah's hands in his own. Knowing he had to choose his words carefully, he took a second, brushing his thumbs over her knuckles. When he raised his eyes to hers, he wanted so damn much to see love there.

"There has never been a lot of love in my life," he began, "and because of that, I don't think I've ever understood it, never knew how to handle it.

"Then you came into my life—not altogether by accident, I'll admit. And every day with you was a revelation. I saw what it meant to be a parent, to love unconditionally. How you created a business out of nothing but determination and still have time for those less fortunate. Was it any wonder I fell in love with you? You filled a void in my heart I never knew existed and opened up a whole new world to me. Then all I could think about was you and me and Tory as a family.

"I still have a lot to learn about love. About trust and honesty and the courage to do the right thing. But I'll learn, if you'll be patient with me."

He paused. "As God is my witness, you have my solemn vow that every minute of every day for the rest of my life, I'll do whatever it takes to make you happy. All that I have is yours—my home, my heart, my dreams. I love you, Hannah, and I'll love you 'til the day I die."

Without breaking his gaze, he kissed her hands to seal his vow.

Her bottom lip quivered ever so slightly and tears shone brightly as the words, as solemn and heartfelt as he'd ever spoken, came from deep within his heart. She looked away, but not before he saw the struggle playing out in her eyes. He searched for a weakening, any ray of hope for their future, and prayed that the wavering he detected might spark the love he knew she buried within.

Several silent seconds prompted the minister to ask the question again and Sean responded with a confident and resounding "I do."

Then it was Hannah's turn. Sean's pulse picked up as the minister asked her the same question, and when her silence became deafening, his heart spiked to his throat. *Say it. Say it!*

Reverend Culberth had to lean in to hear Hannah's less than audible "I do." Sean breathed again and with two deep breaths, he allowed his heart to fall back into place.

When it came time to kiss the bride, Hannah started to turn her head. Sean would have none of it. He framed her face with his hands and kissed her soundly, convincingly, meant to leave no doubt in her mind.

She was his. Always.

~ * ~

The ceremony lasted only thirty minutes and already Hannah was an emotional wreck. There'd been a moment, a second of indecision, when she'd almost succumbed to his words of love and commitment. She'd wanted to believe him, but the memory of his ultimatum was like a wound that wouldn't heal. With her tears had come a huge sense of loss for the life they could have shared.

Hannah walked down the aisle next to Sean, now husband and wife, both accepting congratulations from well-wishers. They posed for pictures and afterward, a long, black limousine took them to The Cloister for the reception. She noticed Sean had spared no expense here either, from the gleaming china and four-course dinner to the open bar and seven-piece band.

Yet with all the meticulous planning and money spent, Hannah kept Sean at an emotional distance, their conversation polite, but superficial.

"You look beautiful today," he said, as he led her to the floor for their first dance as husband and wife.

"Thank you."

"Did I do a good job with everything?"

"Very nice."

"You might be a little more enthusiastic." More people joined them on the floor.

She sighed. "Sean, let me make this clear. This is *your* wedding, not mine. The only reason I'm doing this is to keep my daughter."

His mouth tightened.

What did you expect? A declaration of love everlasting?

At that moment, Brian tapped Sean on the shoulder. "Mind if I cut in, ol' buddy?"

"Not at all." Hannah heard his annoyance and frustration. Sean stepped aside and handed her gracefully over to Brian's charge. "Be careful," Sean whispered to his friend, "you might get frostbite."

The strain of the day was taking a toll on Hannah as she neared the point of exhaustion. In Brian's arms, she relaxed a bit, feeling relieved to be away from Sean.

"When I get married," Brian said, "I hope my bride is as lovely a vision as you."

For the first time, she felt her tension lift as his exaggerated Irish brogue made her lips turn up. "Been kissing the Blarney Stone again, have you, Mr. Cassidy?"

"Just a touch of the truth, darlin.'"

Hannah didn't feel like talking and under the circumstances, it was easier not to.

"Sean's really outdone himself, don't you think?" Brian asked. "But then, he's never been known to do things in a small way."

She looked at him, wondering if she'd imagined the touch of cynicism. "When he told me he was making all the arrangements, I offered to help, but he said he had it under control." Hannah started to make an excuse for her lack of involvement, but decided not to. "I'm surprised he could afford it. This must have cost a fortune."

"Afford it?" His brows arched as if he wondered if she was for real. "He could pay for ten of these and never even feel it."

Her eyes narrowed, knowing immediately she'd been deceived again. "What does he really do for a living?"

When Brian gave her a quizzical look, she knew Sean had lied to her. Again.

"You don't know?"

"Obviously not."

"Oh. Well, maybe I should let him tell you that."

She sighed heavily. Would Sean ever tell her the truth about anything?

Lost in turmoil, they danced in silence until the music ended. He stepped away from her, his hand holding her arm. "Look, Hannah. Sean told me what happened between you and him. About Tory and this marriage."

Annoyance piqued at her. "I don't care to discuss my personal life, Brian."

"We're like brothers," he went on to explain. "We grew up together, laughed together, worked together. And went through some tough times together. We don't keep any secrets."

"Is that right? Tell me, did you know all about this from the beginning? Did you know he wanted to take my daughter away from me?"

When the admission spread over his face, she turned away, disgusted.

He grabbed her arm before she took a step. "I understand how you feel. You probably think Sean's a real bastard, and I'll admit he can be at times. I've seen his faults." He leaned closer to her ear. "He can be hardnosed and ruthless. But you can fight him. You don't have to marry him to keep your daughter. I know a good lawyer, if you need one."

She looked at him, totally confused. "I appreciate the offer, but I thought you were Sean's friend."

He looked away with a curiously sullen expression. "I am. I just don't want him to make another mistake."

What does that mean? she wondered.

"Do you love him?"

"I... I..."

"Do yourself a favor. Don't."

He walked off without another word. Suddenly she felt claustrophobic with Brian adding another layer to the conflicting emotions threatening to choke her. Desperately looking for an escape, she found the Ladies Room and to her relief, it was empty.

She sat on the chair and looked at herself in the mirror. The reflection held a shattering misery.

She covered her face with trembling hands and gave way to the agony in her heart.

Eighteen

Several hours later, Hannah stood on the balcony of the honeymoon suite, twirling a crystal flute between her fingers. The night was cold, but the champagne kept her warm.

They were spending their wedding night at The Cloister, so they didn't have far to go from the reception. The suite was beautiful, she'd noted, even if it did have only one bedroom. The pale beach colors blended softly with the white-washed furniture and the coordinating fabrics and paint colors complemented...

The thought faded. It was no use. The only thing she could think of was sex. Confrontation or consummation? She took another long sip of champagne, felt it trickle down the sides of her throat.

Surely he didn't expect them to be intimate. Well, she convinced herself with wine-fortified bravado, if he did, he was in for a rude awakening.

Yes sir, she'd set him straight in a minute.

The half moon cast enough light on the ocean to offer a path to the spot where Hannah stood on the balcony. The water lapped peacefully at the shore, but did nothing to soothe her fluttering heartbeat. Too much champagne, she thought.

"You look beautiful in the moonlight, Hannah."

She turned slightly at his words, but offered no response, only stared into the night sky.

"You can't stay out there all night. It's too cold. How could I explain a case of pneumonia on our wedding night?"

She didn't laugh, but knew he was right. Besides, she might as well go in and get this over with.

Sean stepped back to let her pass and although his flattering words hadn't fazed her, his appearance did. He wore black silk pajamas, the drawstring pants riding low on his hips, the shirt open down the front, exposing the well-defined chest she remembered so vividly. She dragged her eyes away, crushing the invading temptation.

Quickly, she moved to the large parlor area and mentally gathered her scattered determination. She sat on one of the two facing loveseats, immediately aware of the king-sized bed visible through a large archway.

"More champagne?" Sean stood at the bar and poured himself a brandy from a crystal decanter.

"No, thank you." She still had half a glass. Lifting it, she drank it down to one quarter.

The silence became heavy.

With a drink in one hand, Sean picked up a long thin box from the bar and handed it to her. "A wedding gift. I hope you like it."

She took it reluctantly, ran her fingers over the velvety case. The diamond necklace that lay inside was exquisite in its detail, breathtaking in its beauty. Yet, this time no gasp came from her lips.

"This must have cost a fortune," she said, closing the box slowly. "Your small company must be doing very well."

His brows drew together in a frown. Immediately, she saw his face fall. "Another lie, Sean?"

He didn't answer.

"What do you *really* do for a living? I mean, a wife should know what her husband's profession is, don't you think?"

Sean took the seat opposite her. He leaned back comfortably, legs spread wide, and it irked her that no guilt showed on his face. Only a defensive kind of arrogance.

"I'm the president and CEO of The Murphy Group."

"What exactly is The Murphy Group?"

"It's one of the biggest financial investment firms in the northeast."

She nodded, pursed her lips. "Sounds impressive. I suppose you make a good salary."

His left eyebrow rose a fraction, as did the corner of his mouth. "Don't worry, it's good enough to take care of you and Tory for the rest of your lives."

Oh no, she thought. He had another think coming if he thought she'd relinquish one more ounce of her independence. She stood, anger building, ready to stand her ground. "I don't want your money and I don't want your gifts. I plan to keep working, Sean. I've worked too hard to build my business to have you come along and 'take care of me.'"

"Whoa, whoa," he said, holding up his hands in surrender. "I just meant that I'm capable of making your life a lot more comfortable. I'd never interfere in your business."

She didn't know if she could believe him and comfortable was the last thing she felt at the moment. "Good. As long as we understand each other." She glanced at the clock with its hands closing in on midnight and chose that moment to make something else clear.

"It's getting late," she said conversationally, heading for the dressing room. "I'll take the bed. You can sleep on the couch."

She took several apprehensive steps. When she heard nothing, she took a few more and by the time she reached the dressing room door, Hannah grinned to herself. *Good job. Guess he got the message.*

Suddenly his arm shot past her, slamming the door. She spun around as he trapped her with his other arm.

"The only place I'm sleeping tonight is in that bed. With you." His voice, low and silky, held a sharp finality.

Hannah's stomach dropped to the floor. She battled her fright. Or was it excitement? Her head began to spin and she cursed herself for taking refuge in champagne.

His blue eyes caught hers and she swallowed hard at the desire she saw there. Grabbing for any shred of courage, she mustered a contemptuous laugh. "Do you honestly believe I'd be a *real* wife to you after what you've done? Read my lips, Sean, I don't want to have sex with you." The familiar woodsy scent of his cologne filled the air around her.

"I don't want to have sex with you, either."

Her brows drew together. Then why did he keep looking down at her lips? Why did she want to run her finger over his?

"I want to make love to you, Hannah. Long, slow, passionate love."

He inched toward her. She flattened her back against the door.

"I want you to beg me for more and beg me to stop."

Her heart jolted at his whispered, seductive words as a white hot spear of desire struck the lower part of her body.

No! No! her conscience screamed, but her body didn't listen.

Defensively, she pushed against him with both hands and instantly she knew it was a mistake. The feel of his chest sent shivers down her spine. Fascinated, she watched her fingertips run lightly over his chest, his muscles tightening under her touch.

He inhaled sharply and when she looked up, his mouth took hers, gently, his lips rubbing over the soft contours. He caught her face between his hands and kissed her, gently at first then hungrily. She welcomed him into her mouth, losing herself in a mindless pleasure that sent her senses reeling.

When he finished there, Sean trailed a line of kisses over her jaw and down her neck, slipped his hands inside and spread the jacket of her gown open, giving him more access to the slender line of her shoulder blade.

Hannah heard a moan come from somewhere, but couldn't determine who voiced it. She knew this was a mistake and would later only blame herself. Yet, on another level she wanted this, wanted him to make love to her again. God, she missed how he made her feel.

Her hands fell from his chest and she closed her eyes as his lips branded her skin. He reached around her and deftly pulled down the zipper, gently pulling the gown from the length of her. Her heart almost stopped when he unfastened her bra, but he didn't touch her. She watched as he knelt before her and slid down one thigh-high stocking, removed her shoe, then did the same to the other leg. Standing now only in panties, she gazed down at him through a passion-thick fog, her lips parted, breath unsteady. Was seduction fatal?

His eyes held hers as he hooked two fingers on each side of the white, lacey material and pulled slowly. Urging her legs apart, he found her center with his tongue.

"No, Sean, don't. I can't..." She gasped and grabbed the doorframe for support. He didn't stop, didn't yield, only drove her to unimaginable heights. Climax hit in wave after wave and with his name on her lips, she rode each to an awesome, shuddering ecstasy.

Her breath came in a long, surrendering moan, and unaware, she started to slide down the door. Swiftly, Sean caught her in his arms and carried her to the bed, laying her gently on the pale peach coverlet. Through passion-laden eyes, she watched him strip off the black silk shirt and pants. She loved the sight of him, tall, handsome and beautifully proportioned. The evidence of his desire sparked an urgent need and she reached for him. Blocking out all reason, with nothing in her mind except the necessity for a blind, satisfying completion, she guided him into her and rode the wave one more time.

And when it was over, when she felt him spasm within her, Hannah fell into oblivion, refusing to face the consequences of her own betrayal.

Nineteen

"Mine?"

The sight of Tory's eyes, wide as half dollars, forced a chuckle from Sean's throat.

"He's really all mine?"

Sean nodded and almost lost his balance when Tory flung her arms around his neck.

"Oh, thank you! Thank you! Sean, you're the greatest!"

Just as abruptly, she turned her attention to the huge horse, whose head hung over the stall. "Apollo, did you hear that?" She didn't hesitate to plant a kiss on his nose. "Now we can ride whenever we want."

"But remember," Sean added with a degree of seriousness, "owning a horse is a big responsibility. You'll have to clean out his stall every day, brush him, feed him and exercise him."

"I will, I promise." She pulled a carrot from her back pocket and held her hand flat while her new charge ate it with loud crunching sounds. "I've always wanted a horse of my own."

Her wistful tone wrapped around Sean's heart and squeezed ever so gently. He'd felt a lot of that during the past several months since he and Hannah had married, and he remembered hearing that tone when they'd moved into his townhouse. It had taken him every second of fifteen minutes to convince Tory the entire downstairs was hers. Then he'd tried to make it sound like a chore when he'd told her she'd have to pick out all of her own furniture. Even Hannah had had to laugh at Tory's speechless expression.

"Something wrong?" he asked, as he saw a shadow of worry cross her face.

"Do you think this will be okay with Mom? I mean, you know how she gets when you give me things."

"Don't worry about your Mom. I'll clear it with her." Sean mentally crossed his fingers. He and Hannah had had their discussions when it came to his giving Tory 'gifts.'

She *is* my daughter, he argued to himself, and it gave him great pleasure to provide her with things he'd never had. Besides, he never gave without attaching some degree of responsibility.

Did he spoil her? Maybe. Probably. Hannah thought he did and had told him so on a number of occasions. Always in private, always polite, always firm. And always distant.

Sean left Tory grooming Apollo and telling him what fun they would have now that he belonged to her. He walked outside into the spring sunshine, warm thoughts of Tory rapidly replaced with worry about his relationship with Hannah. His wife.

That was a joke.

He stopped in midstride, slipped his hands in his back pockets and looked up at the sky. She hadn't slept with him since their wedding night. Hell, they didn't even sleep in the same room. She kept her clothes in his closet, but she made a habit of working late, then sleeping in her office on the sofa bed. He didn't know how much more of this he could stand, wanting her so badly, loving her so much and yet, she kept her distance with polite conversation and smiles that never quite reached her eyes.

His concern for their future was quickly surpassing the confidence he'd felt on their wedding day. *Damn, I know she loves me.* There were times he'd catch her looking at him with a kind of longing in her eyes, as if she had locked away her love for him and thrown away the key.

He'd find that key if it took the rest of his life.

"Sean? You wanna go for a ride?"

He turned quickly at Tory's voice, then glanced at his watch. "Sure. But only for an hour. I told your mom we'd be home by six."

Tory saddled Apollo while Sean chose a chestnut mare, then they started down a wide trail flanked by a dense underbrush of palmetto bushes and sprawling live oaks.

It was times like this Sean treasured, when he and his child talked openly, making him feel more and more like a father. However, his thoughts flew back to Hannah as dark doubts of their being a real family crept up a notch.

As if she tapped into his mind, Tory asked, "Is something bothering Mom?"

The question jolted him. "Why do you ask?"

Tory shrugged. "She seems different. It's like she's always thinking about something. Sometimes I'll see her just staring. When I ask her if anything's wrong, she'll smile and say no, but I don't believe her." She paused. "She's glad she married you, isn't she?"

Shocked at her perceptiveness, Sean tried to steer her in another direction. "You're glad she married me, aren't you?"

Tory smiled. "Well, yeah. You're pretty cool. And all my friends think so, too. Mostly because they think you're cute."

Sean raised a brow, trying to hide a grin.

"But I like you cause you talk to me like a friend. Mom talks to me like a mom. And that's okay," she hurried to add, "but, well, it was hard on her when Dad died."

Sean nodded calmly, jaw clenched to prevent the words so close to his lips from spilling out.

I'm your Dad!

Sean hadn't broached the subject with Hannah about telling Tory the truth. He felt the danger of waiting too long to tell her, yet if he and Hannah didn't show a united, loving front, Tory would see through their sham in a minute.

"Your mom's been busy trying to get her business off the ground. That's all."

"I guess so," Tory said and although she nodded, there was a slight hesitation in her voice. "You two aren't fighting, are you?"

As Sean reined in his horse, it suddenly dawned on him how very perceptive this young lady was becoming. Maybe too much so. "Whatever gave you that idea?" He saw her cheeks flush a delicate shade of pink.

"Well," she began, staring at the leather reins in her hands, "I went upstairs to her office last week and saw the sofa bed out like she'd slept in it the night before." She threw Sean a quick, sideways glance. "And, uh, Mom and Dad used to sleep in the same room all the time."

Coming close to the awkward subject of sex shocked Sean into speechlessness.

"It's just that my friend's parents fought all the time and they didn't sleep together and now they're getting a divorce."

Sean heard the worry in Tory's loud, hurried explanation and he finally realized her concern. "Hold on there," he said softly, reaching over and covering her small hands with his big one. "Sometimes your mom has a lot to do. When she has to work late, she doesn't want to wake me up, that's all." Truth. "We're not fighting." Half-truth. "And we're not getting a divorce." Lie?

A smile grew on Tory's face and she leaned over and planted a kiss on his cheek. "I'm glad."

For a second, he couldn't speak, her childlike peck choking him with emotion. He cleared his throat, coughed into his fist. "I'm glad we straightened that out. Right now, we'd better get home. I've got a surprise for you and your mom."

~ * ~

The lunch crowd at Brogen's was gone by late afternoon. With her appointments finished for the day, Hannah stopped for coffee and

201

some much needed regrouping time. She took her cup to the second level verandah and sat at a small round table overlooking the Sound.

Taking a sip of hazelnut mocha, she closed her eyes and leaned back to chill out for ten minutes. Slowly, the tenseness in her shoulders and neck began to ooze out of her like the lazy current that flowed under the nearby pier. However, her solitude didn't last long.

"You don't look like a blushing bride."

Hannah snapped her head around. "Marsha! God, it's good to see you." She got up and gave her friend a hug. "Come sit with me. How have you been?"

Marsha took a seat and placed her iced tea on the table. "I'm fine, but good heavens, I haven't seen you in so long, I almost didn't recognize you."

"And I feel awful about that," Hannah said, with an apology in her voice.

"Married life must agree with you."

Hannah reached for her coffee. "Hmm," she uttered non-committally, taking a sip.

"Does that mean yes, it agrees with you or no, it doesn't?"

"It means I've been so busy getting the office set up for Hook, Williams and McDermott that I haven't had time to breathe."

"Oh." The word dangled in the air. "How's Sean?"

"Fine." She felt Marsha's scrutiny.

"And Tory?"

"Fine, too."

Marsha shook her head and added a small laugh. "Hannah, come on. I've known you too long. You are *not* a shining example of wedded bliss. You don't have that newlywed glow, you're not going on ad nauseam about your new husband, and I've hardly heard a word from you in months."

A long pause stretched into one very long moment. If Marsha could see through her, Hannah thought, could other people as well?

God, she was tired. Tired of living a lie and tired of the battle her heart waged every time Sean came near her.

"Sean is Tory's father."

"Well, I guess he would be," Marsha replied, "since you married him."

"No, I mean he's Tory's *biological* father."

Marsha's brows went from a V of confusion to an arch of shock. "Wait a minute. You'd better start from the beginning."

And so Hannah did. From finding the private investigator's report to Sean's ultimatum. Talking about it didn't solve anything, but she felt immensely relieved to confide in someone.

"Wow. Now I understand why you acted so strangely on your wedding day." Marsha shook her head. "I never would have pegged him for such a bastard."

"That's part of my problem. He isn't. Really."

"Huh? I thought you said—"

"Oh Marsha, I don't know what I'm going to do. When he forced me into marrying him, I didn't think I was capable of such hate. And if he was a bastard to live with, it would be easy to hate him." She gave a slight shrug of her shoulders. "The past few months he's been kind and considerate and charming. All the things that made me fall in love with him in the first place."

"Sounds like you still do."

"I don't know. Sometimes I think we could be so happy and just when I'm ready to give him my love, I remember why we're together in the first place."

"If you love him, why can't you forgive him?"

"Because," she said vehemently, then more softly, "because if he was so heavy-handed once, when will he do it again? It's like Paul all over again." She sighed sadly. "And I can't seem to get past that."

Marsha leaned forward, rested her arms on the table. "How can the two of you live like this?"

"Believe me, it's not easy. At home, we're polite and cordial and I smile a lot so Tory won't suspect anything."

"And in the bedroom?"

Hannah looked at Marsha and shook her head slowly. "I sleep in the room I use as my office. He sleeps in his own room."

During those nights when she could sleep, memories of their lovemaking had filled her dreams. Many times she'd wake, her body still consumed by a fierce longing. Then there were those times when she'd felt his gaze on her, so filled with desire, it had taken a mountain of willpower to resist. As much as she may be tempted, making love with Sean again wouldn't clear the barrier between them.

"How long do you think he'll put up with that?"

Hannah shrugged. "I don't know."

"How is he with Tory?" Marsha asked, going in a different direction.

"He's wonderful with her." A small smile broke through Hannah's troubled thoughts. "He spends a lot time with her and even helps her with her homework. It's obvious how much he loves her. The only thing I can fault him for is the way he gives her things. Money seems to be no object and every time I turn around, Tory has a new outfit or a new CD. He'll probably give her a car when she's sixteen. I don't want Tory to think that just because she wants something, she's going to get it."

Hannah sat back, brought a finger to her mouth and chewed on the nail. The hypnotic sound of waves meeting the shore brought her no solace. Sadly, she saw no solution to this mess.

"How long are you going to live this charade?"

The weight of that question felt like a ton on her shoulders. "I have absolutely no idea. If I leave him, he'll sue for custody and with his money and influence, there's a good possibility he'd win. That's too big of a chance for me to take."

"I don't understand his reasoning," said Marsha. "Would you have shared custody or agreed to visitation rights?"

"Of course, and I told him so. But he didn't want that, either." Anger stirred and mingled with a sour taste in her throat. "He wanted both of us."

Marsha raised a brow, pursed her lips. "I think he really does love you."

Hannah's eyes widened incredulously. "I don't call that love. It's blackmail. Emotional extortion of the worst kind. And if he thinks he can..."

"Whoa, whoa," Marsha interrupted, putting a comforting hand on Hannah's arm. "I didn't say what he did was right. But from a bystander's point of view, he may have thought it was the only way to keep both of you. He didn't want to lose either of you."

Hannah opened her mouth to object.

"Wait. From what I know of Sean—which is not much I'll admit—he seems like a decent man."

Hannah rolled her eyes.

"I've seen the way he looks at you and quite frankly, I wish I had a man to look at me like that."

Hannah didn't respond.

"He's not Paul, Hannah. Forgive him before you lose him."

Hannah didn't want to hear any more. She wanted sympathy and a shoulder to cry on. Not words that rang with an element of truth.

"Thanks for the advice," Hannah said, in a clipped tone. "I've got an appointment. I'll call you soon." She grabbed her purse and left, not noticing the worry on Marsha's face.

~ * ~

The white two-story house stood in the classic New Orleans style, each level wrapped with a porch and black, wrought iron-railing. Shiny black shutters and boxes filled with colorful impatiens adorned each window, offering a warm, homey welcome.

The beautifully landscaped yard boasted a neatly manicured lawn and trimmed palm trees. All it needed, Hannah thought, was a paddle wheeler steaming down the Frederica River that flowed fifty feet behind the house.

Hannah didn't know whose house it was and couldn't imagine why Sean had wanted her to meet him here. She parked next to his Explorer, got out and admired how the house sat so peacefully in the late afternoon sun.

"Hey, Mom! Up here!"

Following the sound, Hannah located Tory on the balcony. "What are you doing up there?"

"You've got to see this place. It's so cool! It's got a pool in the back and a boat dock!"

"Wait a minute," Hannah called out, but Tory disappeared through the double doors. At the same time, Sean walked out the front door. He wore his achingly familiar smile she outwardly resisted and inwardly adored.

"Hi," he said, leaning over to kiss her. She turned her head and felt his lips brush softly against her cheek. The feeling was exquisite. So much for evasive tactics.

"What's going on? Whose house is this?"

Sean spread his hands openly. "You like it?"

She laughed slightly. "What's not to like? It's beautiful."

He walked to the middle of the circular driveway, hands on hips, and surveyed the property. "I thought we could move in next week."

Her brows shot skyward. "What?"

"Mom!" Tory called again, this time from the front door. "Come see my room. It's huge!"

"Yeah, Mom," Sean said, taking her arm. "Come see her room."

Hannah let herself be led, too stunned for words. Had he bought this house? Without even consulting her?

Sean must have mistaken her silence for pleasant surprise because he grinned through the entire tour. Tory was so excited, Hannah didn't want to burst her bubble, so she kept her short comments as enthusiastic as possible.

"Well, what do you think about it?" Sean asked when they all came back outside. "I thought you'd have a great time decorating it."

"It's quite something."

"We knew you'd like it, Mom. Can we do my room in purple and white?"

"We'll see."

"This has been such an awesome day," Tory chattered on. "Guess what? Sean gave me Apollo today. Now he's all—"

Sean threw Tory a quelling glance.

"Uh, well..." she stammered. "I... I have to take good care of him everyday," she tried to explain.

"Really?" Hannah's anger built to the seething point, but she kept it in, except for the accusing tone that came through anyway. "Why don't we go home and discuss this?"

Not waiting for an answer, Hannah turned and walked to her car. She didn't see Tory's pleading glance or hear Sean's whispered, "Don't worry."

Hannah saw nothing but the confrontation that waited for her at home.

~ * ~

Tory chose to ride back to the townhouse with Sean. *Probably because she knows I'm not happy about this,* Hannah decided.

Once again, she felt Sean squeezing her into a corner. Buying a house without telling her. Giving Tory a horse when he knew how she felt about showering Tory with 'things.' Every time she objected, it made Hannah look like the bad guy and only made her relationship with Tory worse.

She felt like a bit player needed for the production, but last on the list of credits. She couldn't live this way. She wouldn't.

"Did you buy that house?" Hannah asked after they'd arrived home. She spoke to Sean privately in her office, on her own turf, and had ignored the anxious look on Tory's face.

Sean nodded. "I thought it would please you. Although," he muttered, "I'm beginning to think nothing pleases you." He faced her in a defensive stance, arms crossed over his chest, feet apart. "What's the matter, don't you like it?"

"Under different circumstances, I'd love it. However, I don't like people deciding things for me. Or forcing things on me." She saw his jaw tighten as the accusation struck home. "Didn't you think this was important enough to discuss with me? Husbands and wives usually make such a big decision together."

"But we're not the usual husband and wife, are we?"

"No, no, we're not. Most husbands don't usually blackmail their wives." She knew, from the tight line of his mouth, the intimation was not lost on him. "And I've asked you before not to keep giving Tory things. She's going to grow up thinking all she has to do is ask and all her wishes will be granted."

"Everything I've given her comes with a responsibility. Either she has to earn it or take care of it."

"And that makes it all right?"

"Damn it, Hannah. I want her to have the things I never had. After all, she's *my* child, too, remember? I *am* her real father."

"A fact you never let me forget."

Sean threw up his hands. "Look Hannah, I'm sorry. If you don't want this house, we'll get another one and we'll do it together."

No! Doing that would bring them closer and her willpower was only so strong. She looked away from him.

Sean's shoulders dropped. "I've done everything I possibly can to make you happy." He paused. "Is there no way I can atone for my sin?"

She didn't answer him and the silence stretched out between them.

"Is this going to work, Hannah?"

The question pierced her heart. She didn't have an answer, yet after living with him every day, she realized losing him would be as unbearable as living like a couple on the verge of divorce. "I don't know," she whispered.

"Well, while you're making up your mind, remember this." He closed the distance between them in two long strides, grabbed her by the shoulders and kissed her. Hard. He'd never treated her like this, with a roughness that frightened her. Her eyes widened for a long second, then slowly closed under the escalating excitement. Each thrust of his tongue hinted at anger... at first. Then he seemed to sense something. Maybe the desire to match his own.

She grew warm. Her skin tingled under his touch. The blood pounded in her ears and somewhere deep inside throbbed with carnal awareness.

She didn't fight him, nor did she invite him. She wanted his hands on her. Everywhere. Conscious thought blurred under his onslaught and in no time, he pushed off her jacket and unbuttoned her blouse. His hands closed over the lacy cups of her bra and Hannah moaned as he squeezed and gently molded her breasts. She let her head fall back waiting for him to unhook her bra, anticipating his next touch.

"No other man could make you feel like this, Hannah Murphy."

Suddenly, he dropped his hands and it all ended as abruptly as it began.

Hannah blinked as she groped for control. His face, so close to hers, came into focus. His voice was amazingly calm, but there were lines of strain around his mouth. His cold blue eyes held her still. "Remember that the next time you have any thoughts of leaving me."

He left her alone, trembling. She pulled the sides of her blouse to cover herself. As with Paul's betrayal, she felt her self-esteem slipping away. She had no control then and she had no control now. The only difference was, this time she was in love with the man who manipulated her.

Dropping to the couch, Hannah hung her head and felt the sting of tears.

Twenty

Sean left the house, his anger a mask for the dread that ate at him. He put the Explorer in gear and just drove. It didn't matter where; he had no destination in mind. All he could think about was the chance he'd lose Hannah and Tory. That meant losing everything. He'd been so confident, known in his gut that Hannah would eventually recognize how much he loved her. But instead of growing closer, their relationship was spiraling out of control and he felt helpless to stop it. Her words had shaken him, but what terrified him more was what she hadn't said. Would she divorce him? Had he pushed her to that point?

As he pulled into a parking space at East Beach, his cell phone went off. He decided to answer only when he recognized the number of his Chief Financial Officer, Dan Nelson. "Yeah, Dan, what is it?"

"We've got a problem."

Not now, Sean thought. "Take it to Brian."

"Er…I think this is for your ears only."

"What is it?"

"We've been doing a pre-audit check on the books and I've found some discrepancies."

"Such as?"

"Payments for services never performed, questionable investments with client funds, strange tax write offs." The man paused. "It looks like embezzlement."

Sean's mind started to race. "Can you tell how long it's been going on?"

"Not exactly, at least not yet. We probably wouldn't have noticed anything if one of my people hadn't stumbled across a payment to a company that turned out to be bogus. That's when I started digging."

Sean's stomach rolled. "How much?"

"So far, over two million."

"Shit!" The ramifications to the company, his company that he'd worked his ass off to create, could be disastrous. "Who's the son of a bitch doing it? Get the Legal Department involved right away. I don't want this bastard getting off on a technicality. And let Brian know about this as soon—."

"Wait a minute," Dan interrupted. "Let's just keep this between you, me and Legal, for now. I'd rather not let this out to anyone else."

"Why not?"

"Because I'm not… absolutely sure… who's doing it."

Sean heard the hesitation in Dan's voice. "But you have an idea."

"Yes."

"Then tell me!"

"Not until I have all the facts."

Dan's blunt refusal gave Sean a dark premonition. "All right. Do what you have to do, but do it fast. And keep my posted." He hung up, torn between staying in St. Simons to save his marriage, or going to Boston to save his company.

~ * ~

"It will be beautiful, Mrs. Thigpen. Trust me." Hannah stood, eagerly gathering her swatchboards and paint samples. "And I promise it will be ready for your Garden Club party at the end of the month."

It was close to five o'clock, and although she hadn't wanted to spend the entire day with this one client, Hannah had to be sure the woman liked her choices for the new decor.

After piling her paraphernalia into the back seat of her car, Hannah turned the key, only to hear the engine cough and sputter like a smoker with emphysema. She grimaced and tried again. Finally, the engine came to life and she breathed easier.

Please last for another month, she prayed. By then, she would have the down payment for a new car. Or, she could just accept

Sean's offer to buy her one. The shiny, red BMW convertible he'd seen on a dealer's lot. He'd tried to convince her it would go a long way in advertising her business. She'd silently agreed and under normal circumstances, she would have loved to accept a gift from her husband.

But their circumstances were far from normal.

Before putting the car in gear, Hannah let her head fall against the headrest and closed her eyes. Lately, it seemed she was tired all the time, even in the morning after eight hours of sleep. Vitamins, she decided. With iron. That's what she needed.

Or maybe she needed an assistant. A fleeting thought, Hannah didn't dwell on the probability of that happening any time soon. Besides, there were other more pressing problems to deal with.

She drove down Frederica Road, glad she had no more clients but not looking forward to going back to Sean's condo. He had been uncharacteristically quiet after their discussion/argument of several days before. They hadn't talked any more about the house or their situation, and their silence added to a wall of tension that was quickly becoming insurmountable.

Tory was another problem. Sullen one moment and almost weepy the next, Tory had been acting strangely again, even with Sean. He couldn't solicit a smile or a giggle, and Hannah had noticed how Tory looked at Sean as if he were a stranger.

Hannah pulled into the driveway, turned off the car, and sat there, stressed to the max yet too tired to move.

How long are you going to live like this?

The question plagued her more and more frequently and although she never voiced the answer, it was always there, a whisper of the inevitable. Her decision came with quiet determination. No tears or histrionics. Just a stark realization of what had to be. Not even for Tory could she live with a man who lied and manipulated with the same skill as her dead husband. She had to take control of her life and the only way to do that was to stay away from him. If they continued on this course, Hannah was in danger of falling under his spell, and his lies and deceit would chip away at her self-respect until she was nothing more than a clone of her former self.

Divorce?

The thought sent her heart plummeting. As much as she hated him, she also loved him. And that was the saddest part of all.

If he followed through with his threat to sue for custody, she would fight him to the end, no matter how much money and influence he had. As for Tory, Hannah could only hope she would understand.

Wait. One step at a time. How would he react when she told him she and Tory were leaving? No matter. The first step had to be taken and she gathered her courage for an ugly scene.

Looking around the parking lot, Hannah didn't see Sean's Explorer in its space, but she knew he and Tory would be home soon from the stables. She gathered her materials from her car, entered the townhouse and plunked everything on the kitchen counter. As she put on a pot of coffee, she heard the front door open.

"Hannah?"

Would she always feel her stomach drop when he entered a room?

"Hi," he said, the smile she'd always loved sending a knife to her heart.

Not seeing Tory directly behind him, she grabbed the opportunity, but it took her a second to bolster her courage.

"Sean, we need to talk."

His arm slowed in mid-air as he threw his keys on the nearby table. An audible sigh left his mouth. "Look, if it's about the house, we'll just forget about it. It's okay. In fact, why don't we go out together?"

"It's not about the house." She took a cup from the cabinet and concentrated on pouring the coffee. "It's about us."

Her heart pounded as a dead silence filled the air. When he didn't respond, she glanced up to find midnight blue eyes challenging hers, wary and apprehensive. Swallowing hard, she went on.

"This isn't working, Sean. With us. You must know that. I can't live this way any more." She steeled herself for his reaction.

He leaned back, bracing himself against the counter in a defensive stance. "What way?" He spread his arms to encompass the room. "Isn't this better than that shack you and Tory were living in?" His voice rose an angered octave.

"It's beautiful," she answered softly, "but that's not what I mean, and you know it."

"Then what? I've done everything I can to make you happy."

Hannah recognized the desperate pain in his eyes that his anger tried to hide. The same anguish filled her heart day after day, tearing her apart.

She stiffened as he began to walk towards her. "You can't force someone into marriage and expect them to be happy. Love isn't measured by how much money you have or how many things you can buy or give."

He ignored her comment and stopped with inches between them. "I know what it is," he said, his voice hard and menacing. "I haven't made love to you enough. And it's about time I changed that." He grabbed her and crushed her to him. His lips were hard against hers, demanding, punishing, and exciting. Yet, with every ounce of willpower, she resisted. She fought to keep her arms at her sides while her hands fisted tightly for control. As her lips remained motionless under his onslaught, tears pooled behind her eyelids.

After what seemed an eternity, he pulled away. When a tear fled down her cheek, his expression changed from anger to agony. He let go of her, lifted his palms as if in surrender. "Hannah, I'm sorry. I'm so sorry. I didn't mean that."

She moved away from him and wiped her cheek with the back of her hand. Had their relationship brought them to this?

Sean stared at the floor, his hands in his pockets. "You can't let it go, can you? I was wrong, I know that, but I'd hoped in time you would forgive me." His shoulders slumped dejectedly. "Guess that's not going to happen, huh?"

She didn't trust her voice to answer him. God, how she wanted to forgive him. What was wrong with her? Had Paul ruined her for any man?

"Please, Hannah, don't do this. I love you."

Her heart broke in two jagged pieces while the pain inside her grew to a sick, fiery gnawing. "And I love you, Sean," she whispered, her voice fragile and shaking. "But sometimes love just isn't enough."

She watched in torment as shocked defeat and despair filled his eyes. She started to reach for him, to comfort him, but the gesture came too late, the chasm between them too wide. This is what she'd wanted, wasn't it?

Tears threatened again and she inhaled deeply to keep them at bay. "We'll have to talk about this later," she said softly. "I know Tory's right behind you and I don't want her to hear us."

"Tory's not with me."

"What?"

"She spent the day at April's."

"Oh." Hannah could've sworn Tory said she would be at the stables with Apollo all day. It wasn't like Tory to change her plans and not tell Hannah or leave a note. She picked up the phone to call April's house.

"Hi, Sue. It's Hannah. May I speak to Tory please?"

"Tory's not here."

"She's not? Sean thought she was going to spend the day with April."

"No. April had a case of smart mouth and she's grounded this week."

A flicker of alarm ignited inside her. "He must have misunderstood. Thanks, Sue."

Hannah replaced the telephone in the cradle. "She's not there." Sean now stood next to her, brows drawn together in a frown. Without another word, Hannah dialed Sara's house and got the same disturbing response.

"Where is she?" Her alarm started to turn to panic.

"I'm sure she's fine," Sean said, laying a comforting hand on her shoulder.

Hannah shook her head. "This isn't like Tory. Why would she tell us two different stories?"

"I don't know," he answered, his face showing signs of serious concern. "Did she leave a note?"

Hurriedly, Hannah cast a quick glance around the kitchen. "I don't see one."

"I'll check her room. What about that boy she sees?"

"Henry Pickens?"

"Yes."

"I'll call him." Hannah picked up the phone again as Sean went down stairs. There was no answer at Henry's and she had no luck when she called several of Tory's other friends.

Think. Think. Hannah paced the floor to keep herself focused, but she could easily fall to pieces if she allowed her imagination to run wild. *Maybe she left a note in my room.*

As Hannah turned the corner of the bar to go upstairs, she heard a rustle under her foot. A huge wave of relief washed over her as she picked up the folded piece of paper addressed to:

> *Mom,*
>
> *I'm sorry I've been a brat lately. But you see, I've known for a long time that you lied to me. It bothered me at first because we always said we would be honest with each other. I guess you had your reasons, but it was important to me and I thought you knew that.*
>
> *Anyway, I found out what I wanted to know, or at least part of it. When Sean came along, things got better for us and it didn't seem so important.*
>
> *Then Sean lied to me, too. Well, maybe not lied. He just didn't tell me everything. He should have. Why didn't he? Why didn't you?*
>
> *It doesn't matter now. Today, I'm going to find out everything. Don't worry about me.*
>
> *Tory*

A chill ran a ragged course down Hannah's spine, the shock leaving her light-headed. She reached to the counter to steady herself.

"Hannah," Sean called, coming up the stairs. "I didn't find a note, but here's something... What? What is it?"

Her voice trembled with the agony of every parent's worst nightmare. "Tory's run away."

~ * ~

I'm not late, Tory thought, glancing at her watch. Having ridden around the Village three times, she parked her bike in the rack next to the old oak tree.

Maybe she didn't come. Maybe she changed her mind and decided she didn't want to meet me.

Nervously biting her lip, Tory looked around the playground. Parents were busy pushing their kids on swings, watching them slide precariously down the slide or scolding troublemakers throwing sand. No one seemed to be expecting her.

Disappointment edged in next to her determination as she made her way to the pier. Sometimes old people gathered on the benches to talk. But only a few sat there today and no one seemed interested in her.

Not willing to give up yet, Tory decided to wait a little longer just in case she'd given the wrong directions. As she walked back to the playground, she noticed a white-haired lady sitting alone on a bench facing the water. Tory stopped, her heart suddenly pounding in anticipation. *Is it her?* If not, she'd feel foolish and for a second, Tory almost lost her nerve. In an instant, the speech she'd practiced flew out of her mind, yet with hesitant steps she approached.

"Excuse me?"

The woman turned and gasped as if the face she saw belonged to someone else. "Ang—Victoria," she said, softly. Tears gathered in the woman's eyes and inexplicably, Tory felt the sting of her own.

"Are you my grandmother?"

"Oh, my dear, dear child." Elizabeth Jenkins reached up and with only a moment of uncertainty, Tory slid into her embrace. Her grandmother smelled like lavender and the arms that held her offered a peaceful haven.

They sat there for a long time, silently healing their years apart with the joy of discovery.

~ * ~

"She knows." Sean's stomach tightened as he read the note. "Tory knows about me. Damn," he whispered, running a hand through is hair.

"We should have told her months ago," said Hannah, shaking her head.

"I agree. But it's too late for that now." All of his plans, all of his well-meaning intentions took a back seat to finding Tory. Finding her alive and unhurt.

"We've got to find her. We've got to call the police."

Sean, seeing the frantic look in Hannah's eyes, grabbed her by the shoulders. "We will. But not until I know what's going on. What did Tory mean when she wrote you lied to her?"

Hannah's face crumbled. "It's my fault. Oh, God, it's all my fault. She'd wanted to know who her parents were. I told her I didn't know, but I did." In anguished tones, she poured out the story to him about the clerical error on the adoption papers and how she could never forget the name of Angela Jenkins.

"After Paul died, Tory started asking all kinds of questions about where she came from. I told myself she was too young to know. But that wasn't it at all.

"The thought of Tory finding her mother scared me to death. I couldn't handle the thought of losing my only child." She shrugged defenselessly. "I always knew there might come a time when Tory would want to find her biological parents. And I thought I was okay with it. But deep down inside, the fear was always there. I just chose to ignore it."

Sean drew Hannah into a chair and held her hands across the table. "Tory will never find her natural mother, Hannah."

"Really? How do I know Angela Jenkins won't show up here wanting to claim her child?"

Just like you did hung in the air, but Sean refused to acknowledge the silent accusation.

"Because she's dead."

Hannah inhaled sharply, startled at the news. "Oh, Sean. I'm... sorry." She hesitated, then reached out and laid a hand on his arm. "You must have loved her very much."

Sean felt the comfort in her gesture and knew it was genuine. Her compassion had always defined her, and she offered it even in the midst of difficult circumstances.

"Yes, I did. But that was a lifetime ago." He didn't want to get into it, not now. Finding Tory was paramount.

"I should have been honest with her," Hannah admitted. "I should have told her the truth. If anything happens to her..." She squeezed her eyes closed, a tear trailing a wet path down her cheek.

So many lies, Sean thought. His, Angela's, Hannah's. All born out of a panicked sense of self-serving preservation. All so destructive.

He lifted her chin with his finger. "We'll find her, Hannah. I promise." With that, he leaned over and sealed his promise with a kiss.

~ * ~

They agreed to split up. Sean took the north end of the Island while Hannah rode the south end. If they couldn't find her in two hours, they would call the police.

Hannah canvassed several beach areas where Tory and her friends liked to go, but not seeing Tory anywhere only increased her panic. *Thank God for Sean,* Hannah thought as she drove to the shopping center to check out the movie theater. She felt a tug at her heart, knowing his love for Tory was as strong as hers. Maybe more so. Had she ever really thought of him as the *father* of her child? In fact, had she ever stopped to put herself in his place to discover he had a child he knew nothing about?

He was a good father, she knew that, and he'd always be there for Tory. Just as he'd always been there for her. Just as Hannah knew he would love her... forever. Her hand flew to her lips, so sudden was the realization.

All these months, she'd let her anger overshadow the feelings she'd tried to bury. They couldn't stay buried any longer.

I can't let him go.

Twenty-one

"I guess she didn't want to meet me." Still anxious for the answers to all her questions, Tory inched away from her grandmother. "My real mother," she added. "She didn't come with you."

Elizabeth reached up and pushed a lock of hair behind Tory's ear. "No, she didn't come. But not because she didn't want to." She sighed and looked out over the water. "Have you been happy, Tory?"

Tory shrugged. "Well, yeah. Except when my dad died. I missed him a lot. Mom and I had to move out of our house and she had to go to work. It was hard for her and sometimes I wasn't much help." Tory hung her head. "I didn't mean to give her a hard time. I just missed my dad so much."

"Sometimes life can be hard, especially for young people," Elizabeth whispered.

"Then Mom got married again and things were a lot better. Sort of."

"You never told me how you got my telephone number."

"I found my adoption papers. Angela Jenkins' name was on them. I gave her name and the name of the hospital where I was born to a friend of mine who's really good with computers."

Elizabeth raised her eyebrows.

"You can find anything with a computer," Tory said. "It was the only way I knew to find her."

"What about your natural father? Was his name on the papers, too?"

"No, but it turned out it didn't matter. My Mom married him."

Elizabeth's eyes flew open. "What?"

Taking a deep breath, Tory said, "His name is Sean Murphy. I heard him and Mom talking and that's when I found out he was my real dad. I decided to call you the next day." Anger mixed with disappointment. "They should have told me. I'm old enough to know."

Elizabeth waited a long minute before saying anything. "Tory, not everything in life is black and white. Adults make mistakes even when they believe deep in their hearts what they're doing is right."

"You mean like Angela giving me up for adoption?"

Elizabeth nodded slowly.

"Why did she do that? Didn't she love me?"

A look of torment swept over Elizabeth's face as she sat up and turned to face Tory. "Oh, honey," Elizabeth said, taking Tory's hand in her own. "Angela loved you more than anything in the world. Don't ever think she didn't. Giving you up was the hardest thing she'd ever done. But she wasn't married and she wanted the best for you, a normal family with a mother and a father. I know there wasn't a day in her life that she didn't think of you."

Tory sat for a moment, the pieces of the puzzle fitting together faster than her adolescent mind could handle. "Wait a minute. If Angela is my real mother and Sean is my real father, then, do you know Sean?"

Elizabeth nodded.

"And he knows you?"

"Yes."

Tory's thin shoulders slumped. "Seems like everyone knows everything except me." Confusion took over and it was impossible to stop the questions flooding her head. "Why didn't Angela come to meet me?"

Elizabeth squeezed Tory's hand. "Because... because," she said softly, "she passed away, honey. Over a year ago."

Tory looked up sharply, the words shocking her into silence. Fate had ended her quest with a cruel twist and even though she would never know Angela, Tory felt a strange kind of loss. Sadness ran to guilt, then to anger—all too much for a thirteen year old. Her grandmother's comforting hug helped to ease the jumble of emotions that threatened to explode.

~ * ~

"Tory? Tory!" Driving through the Village, Hannah spotted her sitting on a bench. A rogue wave of relief crashed over Hannah as she parked the car. Then she ran, seemingly oblivious to the car that just missed her or the people who stared after her. It took only a minute for Hannah to reach Tory and grab her in a fierce hug.

"Thank God. Thank God you're all right." Hannah held on, afraid to let go. "I thought you'd run away. You scared us to death."

Tory slowly pulled away and looked to the elderly woman who stood several feet away. Hannah's brows creased in confusion when Tory reached for the woman's hand.

"Mom, this is Elizabeth Jenkins. My grandmother."

It took only seconds. Just seconds for her relief to hit a brick wall of shock and realization. Hannah heard the anger and accusation in Tory's voice, each sharp word openly exposing the guilt Hannah had covered for months.

"How did you...? I don't understand," Hannah stammered.

"Why did you lie to me when I asked you about my real mother?"

"Tory—"

"And you knew about Sean, too. Were you ever going to tell me he's my real father?"

Hannah's eyes widened. "Of course. Of course we were. We just wanted to find the right time. Come on, let's go home and we'll talk about it."

Tory shook her head stubbornly. "No, I'll never believe anything you tell me. Not ever!" She backed away, then turned and ran.

No! No! Hannah's world started to disintegrate. Panic licked at her heels as she started after Tory. Heart pounding, she ran down the sidewalk determined to tell Tory everything. No lies, no omissions. Hannah opened her mouth to call to Tory, but nothing came out. Suddenly people and cars moved in slow motion. Her legs felt like two tree trunks. Everything blurred around her. Then, her knees buckled and she fell through a world turned gray.

~ * ~

Sean was headed over to Henry's when he got the call on his cell phone. The nurse wouldn't tell him anything except that Hannah had had an accident. All the way to the hospital he barely managed to keep his worst thoughts under control.

Jerking the Explorer to a stop, he ran into the Emergency Room and caught sight of Tory sitting stiffly in a chair. At the sight of him, she ran into his arms.

"I'm sorry. I'm sorry. I didn't mean it," she wailed.

He held her tightly, vowing never to let her out of his sight again. Easing her away, he said, "Tell me what happened."

"We were at the Village. And... Mom and I argued. I told her I didn't believe anything she told me and I ran to get my bike. When I looked back, she was on the ground and people were all around her." Tory's eyes fixed on the floor as if reliving a nightmare. "She looked so pale and she wouldn't wake up."

Sean hugged his sobbing daughter. "It's not your fault, Tory. It was an accident, do you understand? An accident." He looked around for a nurse, or anyone who could tell him about Hannah. "How did you get here?"

"My grandmother called the ambulance and we rode with it."

Confused, he said, "What grandmother?"

"This grandmother."

The voice came from behind him and when he turned, he received yet another shock for the day.

"Hello, Sean."

"Elizabeth. What are you doing here?" He looked down at Tory. "How do you know this woman?"

"It's a long story," Elizabeth answered, "that we can talk about later. Right now, your wife is the most important thing."

"Did you see what happened?"

Elizabeth nodded. "It seemed like she just collapsed, hitting her head on the sidewalk to boot."

Just as she finished, Sean saw a man come through a set of double doors, shirt sleeves rolled up to the elbows, tie loosened around the neck. His only identifying mark was the stethoscope hanging around his neck. "Mr. Murphy?" he asked, walking up to the threesome. "I'm Dr. Tucker."

"How's my wife?"

"Well, she hasn't regained consciousness due to the bump on her head. But she's stable. We're going to run some additional tests and then we'll move her to a room. I'll let you know."

A cold, numbing fear ran through him. He couldn't lose her, not this way. Why hadn't he ever told her how much he loved her and needed her? That his life was nothing without her?

Elizabeth, consoling a distraught Tory, raised her eyes to his with a compassion he didn't deserve. Tory was wrong, she wasn't at fault. He was, for the lies and deceit that had brought them all to this. As he watched Elizabeth kiss his daughter, he recognized that all the important things he'd fought for in his life—money, wealth, power— were just a veneer, a thin layer of insignificance. How could he have been so blind for so long?

I won't lose them.

~ * ~

While Hannah was being moved to a private room, Sean, Tory and Elizabeth sat in the nearby waiting room. Sean had said little to Elizabeth, but how she'd found Tory still remained a mystery. Had she hired someone to find Tory? That was the only explanation he could think of, but if that were the case, she wouldn't have to come to him to find her. And what had she told Tory?

Sean sat with Tory in the crook of his arm wanting, like every parent, to protect her from the harsh realities of life, inevitable as those were. Failure had never been an option in his life, but suddenly, his success at being a dad and a husband was in serious doubt. He couldn't change Hannah's condition anymore than he could the past. But he could change the future and it was time to start.

He crossed a leg over a knee, played with a strand of Tory's hair. "Tory, there are some things I need to tell you." She looked at him with a troubled face that almost broke his heart. She sat up slightly and nodded.

"A long time ago, when I was a lot younger, I met a wonderful woman." He smiled, seeing Angie looking back at him like he'd done so many times, when Tory cocked her head a certain way or flashed a quick smile.

"We fell in love." He paused. Oddly, saying the words no longer brought the old pain or bitterness. Instead, he smiled slightly at the sweet memory. "I thought we would get married and live out our lives together. But it didn't work out that way."

"She didn't want to marry you?"

Sean shook his head.

"Why not? Didn't she love you?" Sean didn't seem to notice the sudden interest in Tory's face.

He shrugged. "I thought she did, but later I found out she didn't think I'd make a good husband." *Sometimes love just isn't enough.* Hannah's words came back to haunt him.

"What was she like?"

The question seized his heart in a slow, vice-like grip. How did he tell his child about the mother she'd never know? A long minute passed as he allowed the memories, sweet and sad, to escape the locked doorways of his mind.

"She was warm and loving. And funny," he added, with a laugh. "She was a teacher and loved kids. Most of the time, she acted like they were all her own."

His heart started to pound as the truth came closer. "She had a beautiful smile. Just like yours," he whispered, hoarsely. So concentrated on his own words, Sean didn't see the flicker of guilt that touched Tory's face. "Her name was—"

"Angela Jenkins."

The name sounded strange coming from Tory, but it didn't surprise him. No doubt Elizabeth had told her about Angela. Still, he fought for the words, any words, that might explain his feelings, his motives for not telling her himself.

Another realization hit him hard. If Tory knew about Angela, then... "Did Elizabeth tell you?"

"About Angela?" Tory shook her head. "I found my adoption papers. Angela Jenkins was listed as my real mother."

He couldn't breathe. "And your father's name?"

Tory didn't answer. She didn't have to because her face said it all.

"You know, don't you?"

She looked at the floor, picked at a fingernail. "That you're my biological father? Yes. But your name wasn't on my adoption papers. I overheard you and Mom talking... Well, it was more like arguing, last week."

He would have rather faced a hostile takeover than endure the silence that followed. Finally, he said, "Your Mom and I were waiting for the right time to tell you. Guess we should have done it sooner."

She nodded, but didn't look at him.

"Your Mom realizes she should have talked to you about Angela, but after your adoptive dad died, she was afraid of losing you, too." He paused. "That's what's been bothering you all these months, isn't it?"

She nodded again.

"And now?"

She sighed and straightened, her eyes still filled with a type of sad resignation. But as she lifted her head, Sean saw something else. A look of understanding that matured her beyond her thirteen years. "I'm not angry any more. I should have put myself in her place. And in yours." Her voice cracked. "I've been such a brat. This never would have happened if I hadn't made such a big deal about it." She started to cry. "I've lost a mother I never knew. I can't lose another."

Sobs shook her slender shoulders and his heart ached with sharp regret. "First, your Mom is going to be fine. We have to believe that." His gut twisted and he said a quick prayer. "And second, we've all made mistakes." His remorse hit rock bottom. How had everything gotten out of control? All the secrets and lies of omission, as well-intentioned as they might have been, now only served to destroy the family he so desperately wanted.

Taking a deep breath, he plunged in. "There's a lot more you need to know, Tory. It's time you knew it all."

He started from the day he'd learned of her existence, his feelings when he'd seen her picture, and the reasons he'd come to St. Simons. It was difficult at first, to explain his motives, good and bad, but as the words came out, he freed himself from the weight of countless lies and secrecy.

"Why did you marry Mom?"

The question surprised him, yet he realized how imperative it was that she believe his answer. "I married her because I love her, Tory. More than anything in the world. Except maybe you."

"You didn't marry her just to be with me?"

He shook his head. "I couldn't marry someone I didn't love." And that was the truth.

He went further, taking the calculated risk of telling Tory why Hannah had agreed to marry him. He told her the complicated story as simply as he could. The risk paid off.

"Gee, Dad. If you hadn't done that, we wouldn't be together now."

Her logic astounded him. He glanced up to see Elizabeth in the doorway, two drinks in her hand, a warm smile curving her mouth. She handed Sean and Tory each a cup.

"I owe you an apology, too, Elizabeth," Sean said. "I should have contacted you a long time ago. Guess I was still angry with you for not telling me sooner about Tory."

"Just like Tory was angry with *you* for not telling her sooner?"

"Yeah," he said, the irony not lost on him. "I hope you'll accept my apology."

Elizabeth sat next to Tory. "It's not important now, Sean. I have my granddaughter. I know she's loved, and nothing could make me happier."

As Elizabeth gave Tory a hug, the hair on Sean's neck tingled. He looked around quickly, sensing more than seeing a presence. For an instant, he felt Angie's closeness in the warm glow of contentment that engulfed him.

He watched grandmother and granddaughter, all the anger and hurt that had plagued him for so long disappearing in the knowledge that Elizabeth would always be the connection between Tory and Angela. That part of his life was finally at rest.

"What do you say we go down to the cafeteria and get something to eat?" Sean asked.

Tory hesitated. "What if the doctor comes in and we're not here?"

"I'm not hungry," Elizabeth said. "I'll come get you if there's any news."

Grudgingly, Tory walked with Sean to the elevator. "How about a nice big cheeseburger and a chocolate shake?"

Tory nodded, but Sean could tell her heart wasn't in it. As he tried to think of a way to cheer her up, Sean saw Dr. Tucker walking toward them.

"Mr. Murphy, I'm glad I caught you. Your wife has regained consciousness and it looks like she'll be just fine."

Sean closed his eyes tightly, let out a huge sigh of relief. "Thank God," he whispered.

Tory's face lit up like a beacon. "Can I see her?"

Smiling, the doctor nodded. "She's in room four-twelve, third door on your right. But only for a few minutes," he called out as Tory ran off in a flash.

Pulled by the urgency to see Hannah himself, Sean started walking backwards toward her room. "What were the results of the tests? Do you know why she collapsed?"

The doctor shook his head. "Everything seems to be normal. Has she been under any stress lately?"

"Yeah. She has," he admitted, his guilt returning.

"Well, that fact coupled with the pregnancy could certainly bring on a fainting spell. But I assure you, Mr. Murphy, the baby is fine."

Twenty-two

Baby?

Stunned, it took a moment for Sean's confusion to clear. Then his jaw dropped as shock plowed into him like a freight train. He stared, speechless.

A baby?

He started to smile, felt a laugh of pure elation rumble deep inside.

A boy? A girl?

But his joy crumbled in seconds as something inside him died. His world shattered, the jagged pieces of his hopes and dreams slicing his heart in small, even pieces.

She didn't tell me. She knew and she didn't tell me. Thoughts flew through his mind like a hurricane. *Does she hate me that much?* He replayed their earlier conversation in his mind, the words she'd spoken, and more importantly, the words left unsaid.

Divorce.

She'd intimated and hinted, but he'd refused to accept it. Had she planned to divorce him and not tell him about his child? Or would she have used this as a lever so he wouldn't sue for custody of Tory as he'd threatened?

"Mr. Murphy?"

Blame battled with outrage, the war stirring up a familiar feeling of deja vu. Angie had had his child and never told him. Now Hannah...

No, not again. This can't happen again.

Surprise registered on the doctor's face. "You look a little shocked. Didn't your wife tell you she was going to have a baby?"

Sean raised his head slowly to meet the doctor's eyes. He should have been happy, ecstatic. Instead, a sharp pain of despair swallowed all his euphoria. "How long has she been pregnant?" he asked, holding out hope this was all a huge misunderstanding.

"I'd say two to three months."

The door to his dreams slammed shut. Long enough to know she was pregnant, Sean thought. Long enough to make plans to leave him.

Just like Angie.

~ * ~

"Mom?"

Tory's voice reached Hannah through a veil of exhaustion. Her head throbbed horribly and her arms and legs felt like four poles of lead. With monumental effort, she opened her eyes, the sight of Tory sending a rush of relief through her.

"Hi, honey," she said, the words raspy through a dry throat.

"Are you okay?"

Hannah managed a weak smile. "I am now that you're here."

Tory stood just inside the door, keeping her distance as if afraid to approach without permission. When Hannah held out her hand, Tory ran to the bedside and started to cry. "I was so scared you were going to die," she said through hiccuped sobs. "And it was all my fault... and I'm so sorry for being such a jerk."

"Shh, it's all right, honey." When Hannah had woken to find herself in the hospital, it had taken a nurse's explanation to clear up her fragmented recollections. When she did, the memory of finding Tory and the scene that had followed came back in vivid detail. "We never would have argued if I'd been honest with you about your mother from the beginning. I was afraid if I did, I'd lose you to her."

As Hannah stroked Tory's long dark hair, the fierce love that welled in her heart brought tears to her eyes. Biological or not, the bond with her child could never be threatened or broken, no matter what the circumstances of Tory's birth. Hannah felt the sting of remorse at how long it had taken to come to that realization. "That was silly, wasn't it?"

Tory nodded, sniffled.

"There's something else you need to know," Hannah said, fighting the fatigue that pulled at the edges of her consciousness. "About Sean."

"You mean about him being my real father? I already know. He told me about Angela Jenkins, too, and why he came here. He told me everything."

Hannah's eyes widened.

"And it's okay. Really. I'm glad he told me. Right now, I just want you to get better so you can come home."

Home. Did they still have a home? Where was Sean? Suddenly, she needed him desperately. Needed his strength and the comfort of his arms.

Needed to tell him she loved him.

Surely it wasn't too late for them. She only hoped he loved her enough to listen and accept her apology. *When he gets here, I'll tell him how wrong I've been,* she decided. Then everything would be fine. They could all be a family.

"Tory, we'd better let your Mom get her rest."

Hannah's gaze flew to the door and her heart swelled at the sight of him. "Hi," she said with a smile, barely able to keep her eyes open. "I have to talk to you."

Sean walked up behind Tory, stopping a telltale distance from the bed. "How do you feel?"

His bland, distracted smile sent a chill of apprehension through her. "Tired. And I have a whopper of headache," she told him, letting out a little laugh. What was wrong? Wasn't he glad to see her?

"The doctor said you'll be fine," he said, the tone disturbingly flat.

"Sean's right, Mom. I don't want to wear you out." Tory stood and wiped her wet cheeks with the back of her hand. "We'll be back tomorrow. Okay?"

"You'd better."

Tory kissed her mother's cheek. "Bye."

"Bye."

Fully expecting Sean to stay, at least for a few minutes, Hannah's mind reeled with confusion when he followed behind Tory.

"Sean?"

He stopped, hesitated before turning around.

Please hold me, she begged silently. As he came to her, tears of regret threatened to spill down her cheeks. He leaned over her and she lifted her face for the feel of his lips on hers.

The cold kiss on her forehead jolted her.

"Sleep well. I'll see you tomorrow." With that, he left, leaving her mind congested with doubts, uncertainty and a pending sense of loss.

He's probably tired, Hannah rationalized, fighting down her unease. Yes, that was it. And he wanted her to get well as quickly as possible. Tomorrow he'd be his old self again.

Everything would be fine.

It had to be.

~ * ~

The next morning, Sean woke with the sun glaring through the deck doors, the brightness blinding behind his eyelids. Sitting in the same chair where he'd fallen asleep, he wiped a hand over his bearded face, then massaged the crick in his neck. He'd sat in the dark long after Tory and Elizabeth had gone to bed and fallen asleep somewhere between heartbreak and torment.

Hannah had been right. Their marriage was a farce. He'd asked too much of her to forgive him his sins.

You're a fool.

He'd kidded himself to think his love for her could fix anything, and the only thing he'd accomplished was to make her despise him enough to hide her pregnancy.

Just couldn't be honest with her, could you?

He'd paid the price the first time. Now he would pay again.

Sean stretched out the stiffness in his legs, then went to the kitchen for coffee. He found the filters, placed one in the basket of the coffee maker. Looking around for the coffee, he remembered Hannah always kept it in the refrigerator. *Keeps it fresh,* she'd said.

His hand froze on the door handle as his stomach twisted into a knot. He pictured her here, in her terry cloth bathrobe, fixing coffee, making Tory's lunch for school, calling to her not be late for the bus.

He squeezed his eyes shut, the loss so great, it took his breath away.

"Good morning, Sean."

He started slightly and shoved the pain deep inside as Elizabeth came into the kitchen. "Morning. Would you like some coffee?"

"Please."

He didn't trust himself to face her, in case a shred of emotion still showed on his face, so he busied himself with pouring water into the coffee maker and reaching for cups in the cabinet. The silence stretched into several long minutes.

"Well, it was quite a day yesterday," Elizabeth said, breaking the uncomfortable lull. "I'm glad Hannah will be all right."

Sean nodded. He braced his hands on the counter, watched the stream of coffee fall into the carafe. "So am I. And I'm glad you were there to help her. Thank you." He felt Elizabeth studying him as he poured the steaming liquid.

"Sean, I can understand if my presence here is causing you and Hannah a problem." Before he could answer, she added, "However, to be honest, I couldn't stay away from my granddaughter for anyone."

He detected a defensive note in her voice, but didn't take umbrage. "I understand, Elizabeth, and it's probably best you are here." He let out a long breath. "Helps to get everything out in the open."

While he poured the steaming brew, it occurred to him there were a number of unanswered questions where Tory and her grandmother were concerned. "How did you find Tory?"

"I didn't. She found me." As Elizabeth recounted how Tory had contacted her and their subsequent meeting, Sean had to admire his daughter's tenacity but made a mental note to speak to Henry Pipkin about the consequences of computer hacking.

"And when I saw Tory—my granddaughter—" Her voice softened. "Oh, she looked so much like Angela. I just held her in my arms."

Sean knew the feeling. He remembered his own shock upon seeing Tory's picture for the first time, and how Angie's image had stared back at him.

"We talked about Angela," Elizabeth continued. "Tory had so many questions."

"Like what?"

Elizabeth shrugged. "Oh, what Angela was like, why she'd given Tory up for adoption, how she died. And I answered them as honestly as I could."

"What was her reaction?"

The older woman thought for a moment. "Pensive. Thoughtful. And sad, I think. But she seemed to accept my explanation. I asked her if she was happy here and she told me about Hannah and her father who'd passed away." She raised her brows. "And you can imagine my shock when she told me you had married her mother."

He nodded, once again feeling the burden of guilt. But he couldn't change his past actions or the circumstances that had brought them all to this point. He could, however, set their course straight and do what was best for all of them. No matter how much it hurt. "I would have contacted you eventually, Elizabeth," Sean said, hoping to convince her. Then he paused. "Hannah and I were trying to smooth out some rough spots." He looked down into his now-cold coffee, not intending to elaborate and not seeing Elizabeth's look of concern.

"Did Tory say she was happy?" Sean tightened his grip on the mug, braced himself for the answer.

"Yes. Yes, she did, in spite of what's happened. She knows you and Hannah love her and I'm sure she loves both of you. So it seems everything has worked out for the best, wouldn't you say?"

If only that were true. The heaviness that settled on his chest made him inhale deeply. *At least she's happy,* he thought. Maybe he'd done something right after all.

"Sean, I've decided to stay for a while and take some time to get to know Tory. I hope that's not a problem with you or Hannah. I can stay a local hotel if you could recommend one. And if Hannah needs anything when she comes home from the hospital, I'd be happy to help."

"Thank you." That would probably be best, he thought glumly, since he probably wouldn't be around for Hannah's recuperation. He pushed himself away from the counter. "I'd better wake up Tory. I know she'll want to see Hannah first thing this morning."

~ * ~

Tory, Sean, and at Tory's insistence, Elizabeth, reached the hospital by late morning. All along the way, Tory chatted constantly, happily pointing out interesting Island landmarks to her grandmother. Sean added a comment here and there and did his best to mirror his daughter's light-hearted mood. Tory didn't need to know the plans formulating in his mind or the consequences to come. Best to let her have this time now.

The hospital lobby was busy with Sunday visitors, volunteers and the assorted hospital staff. "I hope Mom likes these," Tory said, holding a bouquet of red-tipped yellow roses. "Do you think she will, Dad?"

His stomach clinched. Would he ever get used to her calling him 'Dad'? Would she stop after he and Hannah divorced? "She'll love them because they came from you."

As they neared Hannah's room, Elizabeth decided to wait for Tory in the waiting room and Sean excused himself to go to the nurses' station. "I'll be there in a minute," he told Tory. "If your Mom's asleep, be careful not to wake her."

The day nurse told Sean that Hannah had had a restful night, and although the doctor hadn't made rounds yet, all indications were that Hannah would be fine. Despite what was to come, Sean breathed a sigh of relief. He waited before going to see Hannah. Tory needed some time, some happy time with her mother. At least that's what he rationalized.

When he couldn't put it off any longer, Sean started toward Hannah's room. He felt like a dead man walking.

Twenty-three

"And when you come home, I can take care of you," Tory said, leaning so close to Hannah, she almost sat on the bed.

Hannah had woken early that morning feeling remarkably refreshed. She'd slept soundly for the first time in months and came awake with a smile on her face and Sean lingering on the edge of her dream. When reality set in, the smile slipped somewhat as she remembered Sean's visit of the day before.

There'd been no warmth in his smile or in his eyes and the kiss on her forehead had left a cold imprint. Even a casual acquaintance would have shown more concern, she thought, but an icepick of apprehension chipped away at her annoyance. Had she accomplished what she'd set out to do and pushed him so far away it was too late for them? No. She wouldn't—couldn't—accept that.

"You won't have to take care of me, honey. I feel wonderful. Besides, your exams start next week and you'll need to study for them."

Tory nodded enthusiastically. "And I will, too. My grades will be the best ever. You'll see."

Hannah's brows drew together at the too-eager words. "You don't have to convince me. Something wrong?"

"Oh, Mom, I'm just glad you're okay." Her adolescent voice cracked. "I'll never forgive myself for giving you such a hard time and acting like a brat. This was all my fault. But I promise to do a lot better from now on."

"Come here," Hannah said, drawing her into a hug. "And I'm sorry, too. For not being honest with you and for not facing my own fears. Starting today let's promise we'll never keep secrets again, okay?"

"Yeah," Tory agreed.

When Tory pulled away from her, Hannah saw a trace of newfound maturity in Tory's face, and a warm sense of pride filled her heart. Pride for the promise of the woman Tory would become and a sense of sadness for the passing of time.

"Did the doctor say when you could come home?"

"No, I haven't seen him yet, but I feel so good, I don't see why he would want to keep me. Maybe I can come home today."

The longer they chatted, the more Hannah eyed the door and finally, she couldn't hold back any longer. "Is Sean with you?"

Tory nodded. "He went to the nurses' station and said he'd be here in a minute."

Long minute, Hannah thought.

Tory hesitated a second. "And my grandmother is here, too."

"Oh?"

"She's really nice, Mom. When you fainted, I was so scared. I didn't know what to do. She called the ambulance."

"Well, then, I'll have to thank her for helping you." Hannah had forgotten about the elderly woman who'd been with Tory at the park. How would her presence affect Tory's life? All of their lives? "Tory, how did she find you?"

"I found her. It's a long story."

Halfway through the details, Sean walked in with a small bouquet of flowers. Hannah's heart leaped at the sight of him. He gave her a brief smile but his expression only escalated her nervousness.

He placed the flowers on the bed stand. "You look much better," he said, standing behind Tory, his hands on her shoulders.

Something isn't right, Hannah thought. "I'm hoping I can go home today."

He didn't make a move toward her, not to kiss her or even to touch her. "Tory, it's getting near lunchtime. Why don't you and Elizabeth go down to the cafeteria and get something to eat?"

"Okay. Mom, can I bring you back something?"

"No, thanks, honey."

When Tory left, Sean sat in the blue naugahyde chair in the corner of the room. He steepled his fingers under his chin, stared at the floor.

Hannah's heart thumped hard several times. "What is it, Sean? What's wrong?"

His incredulous look coupled with a scornful laugh. "You can cut the act, Hannah."

What act? "Look, Sean, I know we've had our problems and maybe we haven't shared much—"

"That's an understatement."

He wasn't making this easy. She tried again. "I've done a lot of thinking since we talked yesterday. I was devastated when I found out you were Tory's father and then when you forced me to marry you, it was so hard to forgive you."

"So you decided to make me pay for it... in spades."

"No!" He wouldn't listen. How could she make him understand? "I mean... well, yes, I thought then that our marriage wouldn't work out and I couldn't see any way to save it."

"You mean you want a divorce." The line of his mouth tightened and she saw a muscle jump in his jaw.

"Maybe then I did, but I was wrong. With everything that's happened, I've realized one important thing. I love you, Sean. I've loved you from the day you came to my door with a pizza in your hand. Please. Let's try again." For several interminable seconds, her whole world teetered on a precipice.

His chuckle was humorless. "If you'd said that two months ago, even a week ago, I might have believed you."

The words slapped her in the face.

"What's going on, Hannah? Did all of this throw a kink in your plans?"

She shook her head in confusion.

"Stop it," Sean said, his voice frigid with contempt. He sat motionless, his hands gripping the chair arms as if holding in a violent reaction. "You don't have to pretend anymore. I know all about it."

Frustration hit full force. "About what? What are you talking about?"

"The baby!" he yelled, then more softly, "Our baby."

Baby? Tory? Tory wasn't a baby.

"The doctor told me, Hannah."

Told you? About a baby? She felt like Alice trying to decipher reality in the Looking Glass.

"When were you going to tell me you were pregnant?"

Hannah opened her mouth, then shut it. *Impossible.* She blinked in bewilderment.

"Before... left... or after...?"

His words didn't register, only bounced off the walls of her brain. *They told me I'd never have children.* Could it be? With cautious amazement, her hand slid downward over her abdomen as an unexpected warmth spread through her.

"...the divorce?"

Thoughts spun, feelings soared.

"It doesn't matter... blame myself..."

Her tiredness, the nausea. Why hadn't she recognized the symptoms? Because she'd never been pregnant before.

"...deserve it."

She and Paul had decided to adopt after months and months of disappointing fertility testing. After Tory had arrived, they'd never tried to have other children.

"I'll give... divorce... what you want."

"Oh my God," she whispered to herself. *A baby.* Sean's baby. Suddenly, there were no shadows across her heart, no wall of recrimination to separate her from the man who filled her whole being with love.

Hannah squeezed her eyes closed and again moved her hand over her stomach, mentally imagining the child that grew within. Their child. She started to smile.

"But I won't be separated from my children, Hannah. I want full visitation rights."

At that moment, the steely tone of Sean's voice sliced through her euphoria like a sword. *Visitation rights?* She looked up to be jolted by the stony mask of his face and instantly all of the words he'd spoken rose from her subconscious to surface in chilling detail.

A small, panicked laugh escaped her as she tried to explain. "Oh, no. No, Sean, you don't—"

"Don't tell me no!"

He jumped to his feet with such force, she drew back in fear. "Don't think you could ever keep me from Tory or the child you're carrying," he threatened, his pointed finger emphasizing every word. "You'll never do that to me." He walked backward to the door, fury in his eyes.

"No, Sean! Wait!"

And then he was gone.

~ * ~

"I'd really like you to get to know my mom," Tory said, as she and Elizabeth returned from the cafeteria. "She's the best mom in the whole world." Tory looked down at the plastic wrapped package in her hand. "Mom loves brownies. I hope these are as good as hers." Tory quickened her pace. "You are going to stay for awhile, aren't you, Gran? You can stay with us. I'm sure Mom and Dad won't mind."

Elizabeth smiled. "Yes, I'd like to get to know your mother. No, those brownies probably are not as good your mom's. And I'm certainly going to stay for awhile, but we'll see about staying at your house."

Tory laughed. She knew she talked too much, but she didn't care. Like the Scream Machine at Six Flags Over Georgia, she'd ridden an emotional roller coaster over the past several days and was glad to finally get off. Her spirits soared now that her mother was going to be all right.

"Gee, I didn't bring Dad anything to eat," Tory realized as they passed the nurses station. "Well, he can share this with Mom."

They walked the short distance to Hannah's room and opened the door. Sean's words stopped them cold.

"Don't think you could ever keep me from Tory or the child you're carrying!"

His back was to Tory but that didn't hide the anger in his voice. Tory winced when he jabbed his finger in the air. Then he brushed past her and Elizabeth not sparing them a glance.

"Mom?" Hannah's stricken look started a rumble of panic in Tory's stomach. "What's the matter with Dad? Why's he so mad?"

Hannah collapsed against the pillow and let out an anguished sigh. Then, as if wanting to reassure her, she gave Tory a weak smile and reached out to take Tory's hand. "It's just a misunderstanding. That's all."

"What kind of misunderstanding?"

Hannah inhaled deeply. "Well, it seems I'm going to have a baby."

Tory's mouth dropped. "Wow."

"I didn't realize I was pregnant," Hannah explained, letting out an embarrassed laugh. "Guess I had too many other things on my mind."

Still shocked, Tory took a long minute. She'd always wanted a brother or sister. But now? How would a baby change their family? she wondered. What would her friends say?

"You don't look too happy," Hannah said, her worried frown causing Tory a minute of guilt.

"I guess I never thought about you and Dad..." She gestured with her hand. "You know." Tory felt a heat wave hit her squarely in the face.

"Having children?"

"Yeah." *Please don't go into the birds and bees thing,* Tory said to herself. *How embarrassing.*

"I'll need a lot of help when the baby comes."

Tory only nodded.

"And you can help pick out baby furniture and baby clothes."

Tory nodded again, this time with a little more enthusiasm. "That'd be cool."

"And you have at least seven months to get used to the idea."

Tory couldn't help but chuckle at Hannah's cajoling. "Yeah, I guess." She gave Hannah a sly grin. "Will I get paid if I have to babysit?"

Hannah laughed at the typical teenage question. "We'll see," came the typical parental response.

Then it dawned on Tory. "I still don't understand why Dad was so mad. Why would you want to keep him away from me?"

"I don't, honey." Hannah's smile faltered. "I'd never do that. This is all a misunderstanding. There are some things Sean doesn't understand." For a second, her expression stilled. "But don't you worry. I'm going to straighten everything out when I get home."

Somehow, Tory wasn't convinced.

~ * ~

"Sean Murphy, you stop right there!"

The harsh command, just above a whisper, cut through Sean's bitter-cold despair but didn't stop him from pushing the elevator button. He turned to see Elizabeth advancing toward him like the commander of a Minutemen brigade.

"Where do you think you're going?"

He watched the lights on the elevator panel. "This doesn't concern you, Elizabeth. There are things you don't know about."

"I know your wife is going to have a baby."

He couldn't stop the sarcasm. "Did she tell you that? She sure as hell didn't tell me. Does this all sound familiar?"

Elizabeth's mouth tightened. She planted her hands on her hips. "Hannah said she didn't realize she was pregnant."

"Right." He shook his head, ran a hand through his hair. "Look, Hannah and I... we just couldn't make it work." God, he wanted to get away from there. "Things have happened you don't know about."

"Well, that may be true, but I'll tell you one thing, young man. You lost a child and a woman you loved once before. If you don't go back in there and clear this up, you'll lose again."

Sean hung his head as the elevator door opened. "I've already lost." He stepped on, then caught the door as it started to close. "Elizabeth... Hannah may need some help."

She nodded curtly.

He moved back into the elevator and watched the door close slowly on his life.

Twenty-four

The late afternoon sun hung lazily over the horizon, streaked by layers of pink-purple clouds. The last rays of the day filtered through the leaves of the century-old oaks, casting a soft luminescence against the row of townhouses that lined the Frederica River.

A knot rose in Hannah's throat as the cab, carrying her, Tory and Elizabeth pulled into the parking lot.

Home.

Her emotions hit a peak as she swallowed hard past the lump that threatened to choke her. So many times she'd dreaded coming here at the end of the day, knowing she'd have to walk the tightrope between love and hate.

Today, love had won the long, internal battle and there wasn't a place on the planet she'd rather be.

"I don't see Dad's Explorer," Tory commented, craning her neck to check his usual parking space.

Hannah caught the note of misgiving in Tory's voice. "He's probably at the stables. I'm sure he'll be home soon." *I hope.*

"He should have brought us home."

Hannah silently agreed. And she was sure he would have. If they had a marriage. If he still loved her.

From the corner of her eye, Hannah caught the frown on Elizabeth's face. "It doesn't matter, honey. We'll surprise him when he comes home."

Tory nodded, but her expression mirrored her grandmother's.

Hannah had been determined to get home as soon as possible after Sean had walked out of her hospital room. She'd hounded the nurses to see the doctor and when he'd come, she'd cajoled, argued and browbeat the little man into releasing her. He had, but only on her solemn vow to rest when she got home. The promise had come with her fingers crossed under the sheet. Her first priority was to set things right with Sean. To do that, there would be no time for rest.

Elizabeth graciously paid the cab driver and the three walked into dead silence.

"Dad?" Tory called out.

No answer. Hannah's foreboding doubled.

"Mom, I'm going to change and go down to the stables and tell him we're home."

"Okay." *Once he's had a chance to calm down,* Hannah told herself, *he'll understand.* Wouldn't he? A jumble of worrisome thoughts crowded her mind as she went to the kitchen, and by rote, moved the used coffee cups from the sink to the dishwasher. Should she wait for Sean to come home or go to the stables and demand he listen to her? She ran a dishcloth over the countertops.

"Hannah, come sit down. I can do that." Elizabeth took her arm and led her to the couch. "You're supposed to rest."

Exhausted though she was, it came to Hannah that this woman posed yet another problem. She lowered herself slowly to the couch and through half-closed lids, Hannah watched the elderly woman prepare two cups of tea. Tory was obviously infatuated with her newly found grandmother and Elizabeth certainly looked the part with her plump figure, blue-white hair and sensible black shoes.

But what did she really want? Did she have some kind of ulterior motive where Tory was concerned? After Elizabeth had witnessed Sean's outburst, would she try to take advantage of Hannah's vulnerable state?

Hannah closed her eyes, laid her head against the back of the couch. She didn't have the fortitude to deal with both Sean and Elizabeth. Maybe with a little luck, one problem would go away.

"Here you go," Elizabeth said, handing her a cup.

"Thank you." Hannah took a sip. "I haven't had a chance to thank you for helping Tory and me." She smiled, although the words came out with a slight edge.

"I'm glad I could help."

"Now that you and Tory have met, I suppose you'll be leaving St. Simons?"

Elizabeth blew on the hot liquid. She looked over the rim, brows raised, and waited an obvious second before answering. "Actually, I've decided to stay for a while. Spend some time with my granddaughter."

They stared at each other, the line drawn in the air.

Slowly, Elizabeth laid her cup on the table. "Hannah," she said gently, "I'm not here to intrude on your life or cause any kind of rift between you and Tory." She leaned back in her seat. "I was beginning to lose hope of ever finding her. She's the only link to Angela I have. I can't give that up."

Hannah felt like a heel. Her confrontational mode vanished in a second as her heart went out to this mother who'd lost her only child. She couldn't doubt the sincerity in the woman's words. Wouldn't Hannah do the same thing if the situation was reversed? She chastised herself for allowing old fears and insecurities to surface again. Those days were gone.

Elizabeth chuckled, but Hannah saw the sheen of tears in her eyes. "She's a wonderful young lady and you deserve all the credit for that. When I first saw her, it was such a shock. I wasn't prepared to see so much of Angela in her. And when we started talking, well, I could tell she'd inherited at least one my daughter's traits. Headstrong."

Hannah laughed. "And I thought she got that from Sean."

"But she's sensitive and caring, too," Elizabeth added.

"I should have been honest with her when she asked about her birth mother."

"Hindsight is always twenty-twenty," Elizabeth replied with a shrug. "But I believe everything happens for a reason. Perhaps this has brought you all closer together."

Hannah smiled benignly. "It's brought Tory and me closer and I'm thankful for that. Sean, however..." She shrugged in a helpless gesture. "I guess you know we're having some problems."

Elizabeth nodded gravely. "I surmised that."

"Mom? Mom!"

They both turned quickly at the sound of footsteps running up the stairs. Tory burst into the room, a piece of paper in her hand. "It's Dad. He's gone!"

Instantly, Hannah felt the blood drain from her head. "What do you mean?"

"He left me this note. He said he had to go to Boston to take care of some business. Why would he do that when you just got home from the hospital?"

Hannah's hand trembled slightly as she read the note. Something had come up. He had to return to Boston. He'd call soon as he could.

Nothing about coming back.

Hannah turned her back on them, walked slowly to the sliding door that faced the river.

"Mom?"

She pressed her lips together. *You bastard.* Her initial panic turned slowly to anger, then to fury of the first kind. How *dare* he leave them?

"Dad is coming back, isn't he? Mom, tell me what's going on, please. I'm old enough to know."

He had made her fall in love with him, forced her to marry him, got her pregnant, and now he leaves? No way, Hannah vowed. He'd come back here if she had to drag him. But how?

Hannah dropped the note on the coffee table, then looked at Tory. "Your dad thinks I don't love him anymore."

"Is that why he left?"

"I think so, yes." Hannah's heart sank. She'd hoped she would never have to see that troubled expression on Tory's face again.

"So you don't really know if he's coming back."

"No, but—"

"I am *not* going to lose another father."

The statement held a plea that rang out clearly. Hannah took Tory by the shoulders. "No, you're not. I'm going to take care of this." She folded her arms around Tory hoping to instill a confidence she didn't quite feel herself. "Listen to me," she said. "I don't want you to worry about anything. Why don't you go down to the stables and make sure Apollo is all right? I'm sure he'll be looking for the candy you always give him." When Tory didn't budge, Hannah lifted her chin with a finger. "I promise. He'll be back."

As Tory left, Hannah crossed her arms over her midsection and did a slow pace across the room. "He didn't listen," she said to Elizabeth. "All he had to do was listen, and this could have been avoided."

"Can't say as I blame him."

Hannah stared at Elizabeth. "You think he was right to just walk out?"

"Now, I didn't say that. But maybe you should try to look at this from his point of view."

"Which is?"

Elizabeth paused. "You're upset. Come sit down."

Begrudgingly, Hannah took a seat on the couch.

"You probably know that my daughter never told Sean about Tory. At the time, I'm sure Angela did what she thought was best. But it wasn't right. Every man should know when he's going to be a father. The day I told Sean he had a child... Well, I'll never forget the look on his face. There was shock, and wonder, and most of all, hurt. Hurt that the woman he loved thought so little of him as to not tell him of his own child.

"Can you image what he thought when he found out you were pregnant? That such a devastating thing should happen to him again with a woman he loved?" She shook her head. "Yes, he should have listened, but can you blame him for not?"

"But I'm not Angela," Hannah said.

Elizabeth nodded. "Exactly. And Sean isn't your former husband."

"I don't understand what you mean. What do you know about Paul?"

"Only what Tory told me. That he left you in a bad way when he died. Makes me wonder if the ghosts of Angela and Paul are a big part of what's standing between you and Sean."

Elizabeth's words sunk in with a clarity Hannah couldn't deny. As wrong as Sean's actions were, he loved her, and if they were going to make it, Hannah would have to put Paul to rest once and for all.

At the same time, Hannah thought of Sean and how all of this must have seemed like a bad re-run. She had to go to him, make him listen, and stop the hurt that she knew had to be killing him.

"I have to make him understand." She looked to Elizabeth. "I just don't know how to go about it."

Elizabeth rose from her chair and stood erect. "Mrs. Murphy, I think it's time for that stubborn husband of yours to realize just what kind of stuff his wife is made of. I believe we need a plan."

Hannah grinned. It suddenly occurred to her that Elizabeth might turn out to be a very, very strong ally.

~ * ~

For the third time, Sean picked up the gold pen, his hand hesitating over the black line. Then, with a vicious sweep, he scrawled his name, closed the file and shoved it across the massive mahogany desk. He sunk back in his chair, the soft leather offering no comfort.

His lawyers had been diligent. But then, that's why he paid them a huge retainer. Fast service. It had taken only two days to have the papers drawn up. Two days to bring his life to a grinding halt.

Sean stood up and took a deep breath, cleansing the mental claustrophobia. He walked to the expansive window and took in the panoramic view of Boston Harbor. The first time he'd looked out this window, he knew he'd really made it. The top floor, the corner office, the big desk—success.

'Lonely at the top' suddenly took on a whole new meaning.

"I usually don't put much stock in rumors, but I had to see if this one was true. Damned if it isn't. Sean Murphy is back."

Sean turned from the window to see Brian in the doorway. "I see you still don't knock."

Brian gave him a lopsided grin. "Old habits die hard. Damn, it's good to see you, pal."

Sean smiled weakly. "Yeah. It's good to be back."

"I've got a lot of things to talk over with you. How long are you planning to stay?"

Sean opened his mouth, then was saved by the buzz of the intercom.

"Brian?" said Sean's assistant. "You have a call on two."

"Who is it?"

"I don't know. She wouldn't give her name."

Brian's brows creased. "Tell her I'm busy. Get her name and number and I'll call her back later."

"Okay."

He turned back to Sean. "So, are Hannah and Tory with you?"

"No.

Brian made a pained face. "I guess that means you won't be here long. I was hoping to go over some things with you then take some time off. Maybe go down to the islands. Get a little sun."

"No problem. You've earned it."

"Thanks. So, how is Hannah?"

Sean stared at the floor. "I'm filing for divorce." He let it all out then. The marriage, the baby, his deception. Brian was the only one he could talk to.

Brian shook his head. "I'm sorry about this. But I didn't think it would work out from the start."

Sean had hoped for a little more sympathy. "Is this where you say 'I told you so'?"

Brian shrugged. "Should have listened to me from the start, ol' buddy. This is one time you just couldn't come out on top."

Sean cocked a brow, annoyed at Brian's glib remark. "Gee, thanks."

The intercom buzzed again. "Brian, would you *please* talk to this woman? She's called back three times."

"Oh, all right." To Sean he said, "We'll talk about this later. When I get back."

Sean felt like Brian had slapped him upside the head. He must have vacation on the brain, Sean rationalized. What other reason could he have for being so short?

Before Sean could dwell more on his friend, his private line rang. He was tempted not to answer, but only a select number of people had the number. Whatever it was had to be important.

"Yes."

"Sean, it's Dan Nelson."

Sean put thoughts of Hannah aside, glad for the interruption. Ever since he discovered money disappearing from the company, Dan had been updating Sean almost daily on his progress toward finding the thief. "We found him." He paused. "But you're not going to like it."

"You're damn right I'm not going to like it," Sean said, anger building. "Who is it?" When Dan answered, Sean felt his world fall out from under him. He fell into his chair, choking on his shock. "You're sure?" The words came out in a hoarse whisper.

"Yes. There's no doubt. He was clever, and it took some digging, but between my people and security, we found several accounts in the Cayman Islands all leading back to him. I've contacted the police." He waited a second. "I'm sorry about this."

Sean wiped a hand over his face. "Yeah, so am I." He hung up, feeling the pain of betrayal all over again. It cut to the quick, paralyzing, numbing, leaving a trail of desolation in its wake.

~ * ~

Hannah tapped a finger of one hand on the kitchen counter, the portable phone held to her ear with the other. She'd thought twice about calling Brian. She didn't particularly like him, perhaps because she couldn't quite figure him out. He would profess to be Sean's friend, closer than a brother, then he'd ply her with a laundry list of Sean's shortcomings. Maybe Brian was protecting Sean from what he thought was a second doomed love affair. If that were the case, Hannah couldn't blame him, but something still seemed off, something she couldn't put her finger on. Maybe it was a personality thing and he just didn't like her. However, if this plan was going to work, Brian had to be a willing participant. She needed an ally.

Elizabeth had insisted Hannah rest at least two days before going to Boston. While she'd rested, they'd debated and discussed and finally decided that a straightforward, simple plan was the best. Confront Sean head on. Tell him why she hadn't known about the baby. Make him listen. Somehow. She could be as stubborn as he and she'd stay in his face until he believed her.

However, she had to be certain Sean wouldn't throw her out of his office. To be sure he didn't, she needed Brian. After another minute, he came on the line.

"Wanda, I told you this wasn't going to work out. You like Mexican, I like Italian. You like chick-flicks, I like Stallone—"

"Brian? Brian, wait a minute! This isn't Wanda."

"Oh," he stammered, sounding embarrassed. "It isn't? I'm sorry. Who is this?"

"It's... it's Hannah Murphy."

Whether his silence was surprise or antipathy, she didn't know.

"Hello, Hannah. This is unexpected, but I'm glad to hear you finally took my advice."

A hint of complacency reached her ear. "What do you mean?"

"I spoke to Sean today. He told me he's filing for divorce."

"A divorce!" The news sent a blow to her heart. If Sean had already seen his lawyers, there was no time to waste.

"Brian, I need your help."

"Sure. I know a good divorce lawyer."

"No, you don't understand, I don't want a divorce."

Complacency turned to disgust. "Oh, for God's sake. Look, I don't have any more time for your love life for Sean's. Call Dr. Phil."

"I thought you were his friend. Don't you want the best for him?"

When Brian didn't answer, she went on. "I have to talk to Sean, make him understand. And I need your help to do that."

"I'm going out of town tomorrow afternoon."

"I can be there first thing in the morning."

"I don't know what you think I can do."

"Just get me into his office. That's all I ask."

She held her breath waiting for his answer as his sigh of annoyance hit her loud and clear.

"If I have time. And I won't guarantee anything."

With irritation simmering just below the surface, Hannah gave him a curt 'thank you' and hung up. His attitude bugged the life out of her. What did Sean see in this guy that she couldn't? But at the moment, the question was irrelevant. Obviously, Brian's help wasn't a sure thing. Once in Boston, she'd have to do her best to convince Brian how much she loved Sean and wanted him back. From Brian's tone, she knew it wouldn't be easy.

~ * ~

The following morning, Elizabeth accompanied Hannah to the airport. Not knowing how long she would be in Boston, Hannah went prepared with a week's worth of clothes. She hoped she wouldn't have to wear all of them.

She checked in at the gate, then sat with Elizabeth and waited to board. "Tory should be home around four," Hannah said, mentally going through her checklist. "She may go to the stables to help Jackie with the horses, but you might want to remind her to do her homework. And I've notified all my clients that I'll be out of town, but I'll check my messages every day. There's plenty of food in the refrigerator—"

Elizabeth patted her knee. "Hannah, honey, everything will be fine here."

She let out breath. "I know it will. Guess I'm a little nervous." She hadn't slept much the night before. She'd paced the floor, trying to decide how to approach Sean. Defiant and angry? No, that wouldn't work. Meek and repentant? Hardly. After all, she still had a little pride. Finally, around 5:00 a.m., she'd decided to play it by ear.

Hannah yawned and rounded her shoulders in a stretch to ward off the fatigue. She unzipped the side pocket of her suitcase, checking to be sure the file she'd picked up the day before was still there. Glancing at Elizabeth, she noticed a definite frown on her face. "Something wrong?" she asked as she heard her flight being called.

Elizabeth stood up with her. "No, not really. I was just thinking maybe you should have a backup plan in case ours doesn't work."

Hannah picked up her carry-on. She wondered if she could handle the original plan let alone a backup. "Like what?"

"Seduction."

Hannah did a double take. "Huh?"

"Did you bring a negligee?"

"What? No. Just a T-shirt." Hannah didn't know if she should laugh or be shocked.

"Buy something sexy when you get there. A T-shirt won't get the job done. Black. Get a black one. If all else fails, put it to good use."

Hannah grinned and let out a small laugh. How could she have ever thought badly of this wonderfully warm and understanding woman? Dropping her luggage, she put her arms around Elizabeth in a fierce hug. "Thank you," she whispered. "Thank you for coming into our lives."

With that, Hannah picked up her bag and walked onto the plane, her confidence at a new high.

Twenty-five

The elevator opened directly into the reception area of The Murphy Group and Hannah was immediately struck by the stunning view of the city. She couldn't admire it for long, however, for fear of running into Sean, so she quickly asked the receptionist for Brian. The bouncy young blond pointed with a purple tipped finger. "Down this hallway, last door on the right." Hannah's pulse quickened every time a man walked toward her and she took several calming breaths to soothe her jittery nerves.

There was no one at the desk in Brian's outer office, so she tapped lightly on his door. When he didn't answer, she turned the doorknob but found it locked. She knocked louder.

"Who is it?" The sharp edge in his voice made her start.

"Hannah Murphy."

It took an entire minute for him to open the door and when he did, his eyes held a suspicious glint through the crack. "I forgot you were coming." He looked past her, right then left, almost as if to see if she'd been followed. Then he glanced over his shoulder into his office. "Come in."

The room was a disaster. A number of file drawers were open, files sticking out at odd angles. The floor was spotted with strips of paper, the bulk of which lay next to a shredder. A large briefcase sat in the middle of his desk, almost full of manila folders. Hannah raised her eyebrows, totally astonished at the sight.

"Sorry about the mess," Brian said, closing the briefcase. "I'm doing some housecleaning before I leave town." He sat at his desk and opened the bottom drawer.

Hannah got a bad feeling. "Do you still plan to help me see Sean? I've got to tell him—"

"Look," he said, rifling through the drawer, "I don't have time for this. Make an appointment with his assistant."

"Right. Just like that. You know he'll refuse to see me." She shook her head, exasperated. "I don't get you. You're supposed to be his friend, the one he's counted on, looked to, since you were kids. I would have thought you'd want the best for him."

"The best for him," Brian repeated, his expression grim. "Sean Murphy always gets the best. Don't you know that by now? He's the golden boy, always coming out on top. And where have I been? Always behind him, always number two." He snapped the briefcase shut. "I only wanted one thing," he whispered, staring, as if remembering. "But he made sure I couldn't have her."

Hannah's eyes widened. If colors were true, his were shades of hatred. Her jaw dropped, too shocked to say a word. For years Sean had thought of this man as a brother, never realizing the depth of Brian's bitterness. She knew Sean would be devastated when he found out. So many things went through her mind at once. Why was Brian telling her this? Did he expect her to tell Sean? And why was he in such a hurry?

Brian looked sharply at his watch. "Sorry I couldn't help you," he said, lifting the briefcase off the desk. "But I don't want to miss my plane." He took two steps before the door to his office opened.

"I couldn't let you go without telling you to have a good time." Sean stood in the doorway, a hard expression settling on his face. He glanced at Hannah, didn't look surprised to see her. Brian, however, stopped short.

"Hey, buddy." Brian clutched the briefcase tighter, the nervous smile not quite covering the tenseness in his eyes. "Thanks."

"Taking work with you?" Sean asked.

"Just some things I wanted to go over." Brian turned as Dan Nelson entered the room followed by two uniformed police officers.

"Dan," Brian said, the smile dropping from his face. "What's... what's going on?"

Sean casually walked toward Brian's desk. "How long were you planning to be gone? A week? Two? Or were you ever planning on coming back?"

Hannah saw Brian swallow hard.

"I don't know what you're talking about."

Sean reached under the lip of the desk. "Sure you do." He pulled out the small round listening device and held it up between two fingers. "Let me take a guess where you're going. The Cayman Islands? With two million dollars of company money?"

Hannah gasped.

Brian froze, then dropped the briefcase and gave Sean a cold stare. "What's two million to you? Nothing. You wouldn't even miss it."

A flash of pain crossed Sean's face and Hannah's heart went out to him. He'd thought she'd betrayed him, and now he had to suffer the betrayal of his closest friend.

"Why?" Sean asked, the word filled with anguished confusion.

Brian's laugh held unmistakable contempt. "Sean Murphy, the number one man. The original rags to riches story. Who helped you get there? Me. Me!" he said, jabbing his thumb in his chest. "Oh, I'll admit I didn't mind being number two." He paused. "Until Angie came along."

"What do you mean?" asked Sean.

"You never loved her, not like I did. All those times you cancelled dates and I stood in for you. You never really appreciated her, her inner beauty, her kindness. You just took her for granted, believing she'd always be there." His voice softened. "But she liked me, I could tell, and I knew if I could just get you out of her mind, she'd come to me."

Hannah watched Brian, sadness creeping into his eyes.

"I showed her pictures of you and other women, told her how you cheated on her."

"That's a damn lie," Sean said.

Brian smiled, smug and satisfied. "I doctored the pictures, told her I couldn't let you do that to her. After all, I was her friend." He dropped into a chair. "But then she left and she didn't come back. She would have loved me. And there I was, number two again.

"So I started taking a little money here and there. Figured I earned it after being your lackey all these years."

Before anyone could stop him, Sean lunged. "You son of a bitch!"

"Sean, no!" Hannah yelled.

Sean's hands were around Brian's throat in a second, as the two hit the floor. It took Dan Nelson and the two police officers to break them apart.

"Get him out of here before I kill him," Sean said, face red with rage, chest heaving.

"Take it easy, Sean," Dan said, still holding him back. "Take him out," Dan directed the officers. Subdued and cuffed, Brian was led to the door. "Wait," Brian said. He turned, the smug smile returning. "Hey, Sean, guess who made sure Hannah got the private investigator's report?"

Hannah saw Sean's jaw tighten as Brian's laugh echoed down the hallway.

"Are you going to be all right?" Dan asked.

Sean nodded.

"Call if you need me."

"Thanks, Dan."

Hannah stood alone with Sean. He ran a hand through his dark hair, walked to the window and stared for a long moment. She wanted to comfort him, but wasn't sure he'd let her. She walked slowly up behind him.

"Why did you want to see me?" he asked still staring out the window.

Hannah hesitated. "How did you know?"

"We've had Brian's office bugged for some time. I was listening when you came in."

"Oh." She wished he'd turn around, look at her. "I wanted to talk to you. About us."

He shook his head. "There's nothing more to be said."

"You don't understand."

He laughed without humor. "You're right there. I don't understand. Anything. First Angie, then you, now Brian. Funny, I never thought of myself as a fool."

She felt his pain, but knew he wouldn't let her console him.

"The divorce papers are on my desk. Pick them up from my assistant and sign them on your way out." He didn't even turn her way when he left the room.

Hannah hung her head and sighed heavily. She certainly hadn't expected this turn of events. Now, in the face of Brian's treachery, getting Sean to listen to her would be doubly hard. The anguish on his face made her wish she could physically feel the pain for him. But she wouldn't give him up, even though she didn't have a clue as to what to do next.

She made her way to Sean's office, intuitively knowing he wouldn't be there. His assistant handed her a manila folder, yet, there was no way on God's green earth she would sign the papers inside. "I'll bring them back tomorrow," Hannah said, then asked the woman if she could arrange for a room for the night.

Hannah took a cab to a small, elegant hotel off Boston Common. The service was impeccable and the room was beautiful, tastefully done in eighteenth-century furnishings, complete with a separate sitting room, canopied bed and a view of a colorful rose garden from the small balcony. Any other time she would have admired the décor, but the only thing on her mind was Sean. Exhausted and mentally drained, she didn't bother to unpack. Instead, she laid on the bed and within minutes fell sound asleep.

~ * ~

The third empty glass of scotch stared up at Sean as he sat at the bar at Paddy's Tavern. Late afternoon found only a handful of customers at the pub that had been in existence since Sean could remember. He looked at his watch and debated over another scotch before happy hour started. No sense in being here then. He had nothing to be happy about.

He hadn't meant to end up in South Boston, the old neighborhood where he vowed never to return. But after hours of soul searching and aimless walking, he hoped the answers to Brian's betrayal might be found in their roots. How had this happened? *What did I do,* he wondered, *to turn Brian against me?* They'd played together, laughed together, told each other things they'd never admit to anyone else. And they'd loved the same woman. Was that when Brian had started to hate him? Why hadn't Sean seen it?

For the second time in as many days, guilt and pain cut through him. He'd lost his lover and his best friend and he could only blame himself. He'd deceived Hannah and had taken Brian for granted. *What kind of person am I?*

Disgusted with himself, he paid the tab and left the bar. He yanked off his tie, opened his shirt collar and threw his suit coat over his shoulder. He walked again and soon found himself standing in front of the house where he'd grown up. The only good memories were of him and Brian, playing street hockey, sharing a clandestine cigarette. Life had not been simple then, but Brian had made it bearable.

Sean's breath hitched in his throat as he felt himself drowning in a sea of loneliness and alienation. One part of him wanted to reach for his lifeline, the other held back. If he reached, would she still be there?

~ * ~

It was early evening when Hannah opened an eye. The last vestiges of twilight came through the window casting a gentle glimmer over the furnishings. She took a diet soft drink from the refrigerator, then, looking at the clock, decided on room service. Elizabeth and Tory would have had dinner by now, she thought as she placed her order. Even though she'd been gone only a day, a sudden wave of homesickness hit her. The urge to hear their voices sent her to the telephone and the sound of Tory's voice lifted her spirits.

"Hi, Mom!" Tory said. "How was the plane ride? What's it like in Boston? Have you seen Dad yet?"

"One question at a time!" Hannah said with a laugh. "The plane was fine, Boston's busy and yes, I've seen your Dad."

"When is he coming home?"

Hannah sidestepped. "Don't know yet. We still have some things to talk about."

"Oh."

"Now, don't worry. We'll be home soon." Hannah crossed her fingers behind her back.

When Elizabeth got on the line, Hannah told her everything that had happened.

"Good heavens. Sean must be devastated," Elizabeth said.

"He is, and the last person he wants to see is me. He told me to sign the divorce papers on the way out."

"You didn't do that."

"Absolutely not. All I did was take them with me."

"What are you going to do now?" Elizabeth asked.

Hannah blew out a breath. "I thought maybe you'd have an answer."

"Well," Elizabeth said in a huffy tone, "I'd just barge right in there and tell him what's what. That's what I'd do."

Hannah almost laughed. She could see herself being dragged out of Sean Murphy's office, two huge security guards each holding an arm, her heel marks streaking his carpet. "I'll think of something." She promised to keep in touch, then sat on the bed wondering what that 'something' would be. She unpacked her suitcase and changed into a comfortable robe, her stomach growling all the while. The room service knock came just as she realized how hungry she'd become.

She opened the door, instantly caught off guard. Sean stood there, one arm leaning on the doorframe. He still wore a suit, but the tie was gone, his shirt was open at the neck, and his five o'clock shadow was at least three hours old. He looked wonderful.

Speechless, she stood back as he pushed past her without a greeting. She closed the door and for a minute, he didn't say anything.

"I don't know what I'm doing here," he said finally, his back to her. "I didn't want to see you." He let out a short harsh laugh. "For some reason I couldn't help myself."

"I'm glad you came," Hannah responded. "I'm so sorry about Brian."

Sean rubbed the back of his neck. "Yeah, me, too."

"What will happen to him?"

"He'll go to trial. I'll make sure he gets a good lawyer." After a long second he turned toward her, changed the subject. "Why did you come to Boston? Why did you want to see me?"

"Because we need to talk. You left home rather suddenly."

Her use of the word 'home' seemed to surprise him. She knew she'd never called their living arrangement a home before.

"You want to talk? Let's talk about our divorce."

That shook her but her loss of composure lasted only a second. Pursing her lips, she picked up the file where she'd left it on the desk, leafed through it.

"Did you sign them?"

She shook her head. "No, I won't sign them. And neither will you."

Now he looked totally confused.

"I don't think I ever realized what a very stubborn man you are."

"I'm really not in the mood to discuss my personality." He made a face, shook his head. "This was a mistake. I shouldn't have come here."

Hannah rushed to stand firmly with her back against the door. "You're not going anywhere." She watched him set his jaw, a clear indication of the anger she was ready to deal with.

"What do you want, Hannah?"

"I want you to listen to the truth. Something you clearly don't want to hear."

"The truth according to Hannah?"

She sighed, shook her head, and dismissed his sarcasm. "I'm going to talk now and you're going to listen."

He cocked a brow.

"You left without letting me explain."

When his eyes slid to her stomach, her hands immediately followed. "Actually, the doctor explained everything to me."

"Sean," she said, her voice taking on an edge, "I didn't know I was pregnant."

He laughed for the first time. "Come on, Hannah, can't you think of something more original?"

"It's the truth!"

"You wouldn't know the truth if it jumped up and bit you."

Her eyes flew open. "This coming from a man who's done nothing *but* lie from the day I met him."

"Well, *mea culpa*. How many times do I have to apologize for all the things I've done?"

Hannah hesitated. "Once," she said softly. "Just once."

The import hit him square in the gut. A simple 'I'm sorry.' Two small words he'd never thought to say. God, how stupid could he be. *I never lied about loving you.* "I guess it's too late for that now." He loved her with every ounce of his being, but he had to leave. His heart couldn't take much more. "Sign the papers, Hannah. It's what you want."

"I won't sign. Not today, not tomorrow. Never."

His temper snapped. "Dammit, Hannah. What the hell do you want from me?"

"I want you to listen. Is that too much to ask?"

"I'm done listening."

Hannah jumped away from the door. "Like hell you are."

Sean's eyes widened in amazement as she grabbed him by the lapels and pushed him into a chair with a strength that astounded him.

She trapped him there with her hands on the chair arms, then leaned over, her face inches from his.

"I didn't know I was pregnant because I was told I'd probably never conceive a child."

He could have overpowered her in a second, but the forceful gleam in her eye held him captive. He'd never seen her so... formidable.

"Sean, did you hear what I said?"

He did, but suspicion still reigned. There had to something else going on here.

She rapped her knuckles on his head—hard. "Hello in there!"

"Ow! That hurt," he yelped, rubbing his head.

"You're not listening." She grabbed his chin. "That's why Paul and I adopted Tory. Because I could never get pregnant."

His defenses crumbled fast as he desperately wanted to believe her. Did he dare?

While he struggled with a response, Hannah went to her carry-on and pulled out a large envelope. She dropped it squarely in his lap in front of him. "Being the stubborn man that you are, I knew you wouldn't believe me. So I brought this. Read it. Please."

He opened the envelope, pulled out the paper and began to read the medical report of Hannah Stevens. There in black and white was the truth he'd refused to accept. She hadn't lied to him and the realization lifted the weight from his heart. But would it change anything between them?

"When I didn't have a period," Hannah explained, "I thought it was stress. We certainly had enough of it. Then I thought I had the flu. Why would I think I was pregnant when I was told I never would be?"

"Why are you telling me this?"

"Because I love you, you idiot!"

His world stopped for just a second as the words slowly sunk in.

"I love you," Hannah repeated softly. "And Tory and I—and our baby—want you to come home."

Sean swallowed hard and like a nuclear reactor, his heart began a slow meltdown. He didn't deserve a second chance, yet here she was offering forgiveness for his crimes that should have warranted jail time.

Hannah must have interpreted his dazed expression as hesitation. "I guess I'll just have to show you." She leaned into him and he watched her mouth inch closer to his. Hungrily, he anticipated the feel of her lips and when it came, her kiss was the absolution he thought she'd never grant him.

She teased him with slow, agonizing touches on each side of his mouth, pulling back at his attempts to nip her. "No, let me," she whispered, so he closed his eyes and did a free fall into a black hole of pleasure. Her soft kisses set off small explosions in his head, each one sending a sharp pulse to the place where he was already rock hard.

Finally, unable to stand anymore, Sean pulled her roughly into his lap and crushed his mouth to hers. His tongue found its way to hers, the sweet taste sending his senses into overdrive.

He slid his hand inside her robe, not satisfied until he'd pushed aside her bra and cupped her breast. The feel of her, the taste of her filled him as it always did even as it made him hunger for more. Her breath quickened and caught in her throat then trailed off into a soft moan. It was all he needed.

Featherweight in his arms, he carried her to the bed, all the while his mouth seeking hers.

"Sean..."

He didn't hear her, didn't hear anything but the pounding in his ears. Framing her face in his hands, his thumb parted her lips and he kissed her again, unable to get enough.

"Wait," she said as she pushed away from him.

"Oh, please don't say that," he responded, his voice sounding strangely high. "I don't think I can."

Hannah laughed, pushing the jacket off his shoulders. When he realized her intent, Sean struggled out of his shirt, then undressed her as slowly as his eagerness allowed. He swallowed hard, fighting for control as she stood unflinching before him, small, delicate, exquisite. "You're my life, Hannah Murphy," he whispered, running his fingers lightly down her arms. "I'll never let you go."

Hannah trembled under his touch, then took his hand and placed it over her belly. His child grew there and the wonder of it humbled him.

"Love me, Sean. I need you."

Quickly shedding his pants, he positioned himself over her. They touched, kissed and explored each other like it was their first time. Her mouth sought his in an intimate offering while her hands roamed over the solid length of his back and down his hips. Perhaps she knew he needed this, needed her, the intimacy doing more than words to show what they'd come to mean to each other.

When Hannah arched against him and opened in surrender, he slipped inside her, and it was his own moan he heard when she closed around him. She met his rhythm and urged him on, their bodies finding exquisite harmony with one another.

And when the end came, when the world spun out of control, Sean voiced the words that filled her heart.

"I love you, Hannah."

~ * ~

After what seemed like hours, Sean gathered Hannah in his arms. He didn't believe in happy endings, yet here was his miracle come true. But before he and Hannah went any further, there was one thing he had to do.

"I'm sorry," he whispered into the softness of her hair.

Hannah jerked away from him, her eyes wide in alarm.

"No, no," he assured her quickly, "not for making love to you. Never for that." He paused. "I'm sorry for deceiving you and threatening you and coercing you into a marriage you didn't want."

Her expression softened and she waited for him to continue.

Sean absently brushed at the blond tufts that fell over her forehead. "When you found out the truth about me, I was so scared I would lose you and Tory." The memory still remained vivid and brought on a wave of self-recrimination. "I'd never been so happy, never felt so complete. You changed my life." He closed his eyes, shook his head. "I just panicked."

He thanked God for the understanding he saw in her eyes and pledged again to make up for all the misery he'd caused her.

"I wanted to tell you the truth."

She gave him a teasing, skeptical smile.

"Really, I did," he insisted. "But there never seemed to be a good time." He waited a second, then let out a sigh. "That sounds pretty lame, even to me. Guess I was just a coward." He tilted her chin up. "You have to understand that as misguided as they were, my actions were done out of love, not because I wanted to hurt you in anyway."

"Oh, Sean," Hannah said, hugging him tightly, "we've wasted so much time. We've both made mistakes. I think we looked at each other and saw the people that hurt us the most. I knew you loved me and I should have forgiven you. But after everything that happened with Paul, I couldn't see past my own anger. It was another betrayal I couldn't handle. It took me a long time to put the ghosts to rest."

Sean smiled. "Well, then, I think there's only one thing to do."

"What's that?"

"Let's go home and start over."

Twenty-six

"Do you see my Dad?"

Henry Pipkin opened the heavy oak door of Lovely Lane Chapel and peeked outside. "Nope. Not yet."

Tory stood on tiptoes and looked over his shoulder. "He should be coming soon. I told him to pick me up here at five." She paused. "I hope he's not mad at me."

"Why would your Dad be mad at you?"

"Well, he and Mom just got back from Boston this morning. And because we had so many things to do to get ready, we had to get him out of the way. Mom told him she had to see clients and I told him I was going to Sara's. He had a funny look on his face when we both left him at the same time." Giggling, she added, "Boy, is he going to be surprised." She turned toward the front of the church where Elizabeth added some last minute touches to the multi-colored flowers that rested at each side of the alter. "Gran, what time is it?"

"A quarter of five. Any sign of your father?"

"No."

"I'd better get everyone together so we're ready when he gets here."

Henry followed Tory down the aisle. "Now tell me one more time why your parents are getting married again."

Tory rolled her eyes. "Because they're going to repeat their wedding vows."

"How come? Did they forget them?"

Sometimes guys just didn't get it, she thought. "Henry," she said with a deep sigh, "I'm sure they didn't forget their vows. But they've had some problems lately and Mom wanted to do something special for my Dad. Actually, my grandmother came up with this idea."

Tory was glad Sean and Hannah had spent several days in Boston before coming home because it gave her and Elizabeth time to set their plan in motion. It also gave Tory time to think over the events of the tumultuous past year. She'd lost a father and gained another. She'd learned of a mother she would never meet and became closer to the only mother she'd ever known. She'd been happy, sad, angry, confused, resentful and an all-around pain in the butt. And throughout it all, her Mom and Dad still loved her.

Tory still regretted her mistakes, and her apologies to Hannah and Sean, as heartfelt as they were, couldn't erase her remorse.

I'm really lucky, she thought, *to have parents who will stick by me, even when I act like a brat.*

From now on, she promised herself, I'll do everything right. I'll keep my room clean, help out around the house and I won't argue.

Suddenly, Tory wondered if she'd promised too soon. She still didn't understand why her Mom wouldn't let her go to the annual beach blast at the end of the school year. Absolutely everyone would be there and what was the big deal if it was at night? After all, she was old enough to go to parties without parents being around. Honestly, sometimes her mother treated her like a chi—

She stopped and mentally scolded herself. Well, she wouldn't argue, but maybe Dad could talk to Mom...

"Tory, your Dad's coming!" Henry called out.

"Oh, okay. Gran, Dad's here!"

~ * ~

Sean parked in front of the church, still slightly miffed that Hannah and Tory had deserted him on their first day back. However, he was glad Hannah had talked him into spending a few days in Boston. Although too short, he'd made it into the honeymoon they never had. He took her sightseeing, strolled through Boston Common, shopped at Fanueil Hall and at night, he'd made love to her, slowly, tenderly, and knew there would never be another woman for him.

When they'd returned to St. Simons, the thrill of seeing his daughter had only added to a dream he never fully visualized. Sean Patrick Murphy, a husband and a father. Surely, there had to be a God. Who else could make such a dream come true?

He entered the church and looked around in surprise. "Tory?" Candles flickered at the alter, casting a soft, amber glow against the dark wood of the chapel's interior, and the sweet perfume of freesia and roses floated through the air. The setting felt oddly familiar. "Anybody here?" He could have sworn Tory had told him to pick her up here.

Suddenly, soft organ music filled the room. Obviously, a wedding was about to begin and he didn't want to intrude. He started to leave but looked over his shoulder when a door at the front of the church opened. Sean did a double take when Marsha came in dressed in a gown and holding a bouquet of flowers. Then came Tory and Elizabeth and from the corner of his eye, Sean saw Tory's friend Henry stand discreetly at the end of a pew. Sean felt like he was in the middle of a performance without a part to play.

"Hello, Sean," greeted Reverend Culberth. "Are you ready?"

"Ready?" Sean repeated. *For what?* Did someone forget to tell him something?

Then he saw Hannah. She stood before the minister in her wedding gown, beautiful, radiant, but this time, the smile she wore was genuine, curved with tenderness. He realized then that she'd arranged this wedding, although for what reason he wasn't sure. She held out her hand, a simple gesture that, to him held a huge significance. He felt her commitment in that small movement, to him, to Tory, their baby and their new life together.

At that moment, no one else existed and standing before her, he took her hand in his.

~ * ~

Hannah felt the difference between this wedding and her last one. She felt it the minute Sean looked into her eyes. There was happiness now, a quiet joy that spread a warm glow through her. She sensed the absolute rightness of what was about to happen and welcomed it, longed for it.

Reverend Culberth began the service with the traditional words of the marriage ceremony, each word echoing the love she felt in her heart.

As if on cue, he stopped when Hannah gave him a knowing smile. Then, looking at Sean, she repeated the words that had never left her memory.

"There has never been a lot of love in my life," she began, "and because of that, I don't think I've ever understood it, never knew how to handle it.

"Then you came into my life—not altogether by accident, I'll admit," she said with a chuckle. "And every day with you was a revelation. Was it any wonder I fell in love with you? You filled a void in my heart and opened up a whole new world to me."

His vow became hers as the smile on his face told her he recognized the words he'd said to her not so long ago.

"Sean, as God is my witness, you have my solemn vow that every minute of every day, for the rest of my life, I'll do whatever it takes to make you happy. I love you, Sean. I'll love you 'til the day I die."

The last few words came out on a choked whisper as a wave of emotion swamped her. Her heart melted when she caught the sheen of tears in Sean's eyes just before his lips touched hers.

Reverend Culberth chuckled. "I now pronounce you husband and wife. You may kiss the bride."

Everyone laughed. Tory turned to Elizabeth and gave her a high five. Henry Pipkin walked up behind Tory. He looked at the bride and groom, still locked in a kiss, and whispered in her ear. "Maybe we could try that, huh?"

Tory replied with an elbow to his ribs, but her feigned indignation lasted only a second. She smiled. Maybe they could.

Meet Pat Worley

An avid romance reader, this is Pat's first published novel. She and her husband divide their time between Cumming, GA and St. Simons Island, GA